PRAISE FOR
THE APPLE PIE A

"Do not read *The Apple Pie Alibi* on an empty stomach! It'll leave you hungry for justice as well as for dinner. Amateur sleuth Winnie Kepler is a force that you'll cheer for every step of the way, in romance and in finding her place in the world, as well as fighting to get her grandma off the hook for murder. Each slice of this story is a tasty morsel more complex than the last, slowly revealing rich and unexpected details. Good to the very last bite!"

> **– L.S. Engler**, author and contributor to The Saturday Evening Post

"Lutz cooked up a fun culinary mystery with all the right ingredients—a cast of colorful characters, charming setting and grins along the way!"

> **– Nancy Naigle,** *USA TODAY* Bestselling Author of the *Adams Grove Novels*

"I love reading about food and enjoyed the contest aspect along with the mystery. Anyone who enjoys food, cooking, and reading mysteries will think this book is a lot of fun!"

> **– Sallie Swor**, culinary expert for Nashville's CBS - WTVF, and author of the popular cookbook, *You've Grown, Now You Can Cook."*

"A classic whodunit and feisty sleuth will keep you turning the pages of D.J. Lutz's culinary cozy. Lots of great recipes!"

> **– Maggie King**, author of the Hazel Rose Book Group Mysteries

"*The Apple Pie Alibi* is a masterfully written debut cozy mystery from D.J. Lutz. Protagonist Winnie Kepler is spunky, adorable, and one smart cookie—a delightful character who I thoroughly enjoyed."

> **– Janice Peacock**, best selling author of the Glass Bead Mystery Series

"D.J. Lutz's culinary mystery, *The Apple Pie Alibi*, serves up a sweet and salty recipe for murder!"

> **– Teresa Inge**, prolific mystery writer and President, Sisters In Crime - Mystery by the Sea Chapter

The Apple Pie Alibi
by D.J. Lutz

ISBN 978-1-63393-484-9

Published by

 köehlerbooks™

210 60th Street
Virginia Beach, VA 23451
800-435-4811
www.koehlerbooks.com

DATE DUE

JUN 0 1			
	-SW -	5.4.18 1	102.18

PRINTED IN U.S.A.

the Apple Pie Alibi

A Culinary Mystery

D.J. LUTZ

To my family, especially my lovely wife, Elizabeth. Thank you for indulging a man and his dream. Without you all, this story would have never been written.

1

1:30 *pm: G-ma V! Customer said something happened at the fair. U ok?*
1:34 pm: Fine, Winnie. But Chef P isn't tho. Def dead. Plz clean the coffee pots.

1:34 pm: What???

I waited. No answer. I just *knew* I shouldn't have taught my grandmother how to text. Now someone's dead, and I have to count the hours for her to one-finger type on a tiny keyboard. What was I thinking? Two minutes elapsed. I tried again.

1:36 pm: Who is Chef P? What happened? Sick, accident, murder? Do I need to come?

Still no answer. I could see the text window on my phone blink. Finally, an answer. Not the one I expected, but at least I had proof Grandma Velma was alive.

1:39 pm: Chef P is Pierre St. Pierre. Yes, he's dead. No, don't come. And wrap the silverware. Cafe s/b neat and tidy. Plz and Thnx. Talk L8r.

And that was that. I sent a few more text messages and received no further response. I also tried the old-school method of just calling, but it went straight to voicemail, which was full, of course. My grandmother had left me hanging with several questions. Did she mean no, as in Chef Pierre St. Pierre wasn't sick? Or no, he wasn't murdered? Or no, don't drive over to the fairgrounds and get her?

And the coffee pots looked clean enough. To me, at least. Customers said a clean coffee pot ruins the flavor so I hesitated to scrub much more. I mean, it's not like the time I forgot to add sugar to the lemon meringue pie. I am sure I wasn't the only one who thought it tasted *okay* at the very least. Live and learn.

Without a single customer all day, I had been cleaning since the sun rose above the crepe myrtle trees lining the sidewalk across the street. It was a lot of work, but nothing I couldn't handle. Velma left me, the *college girl* as she was fond of saying, in charge of her Cat and Fiddle Café while she competed at the fair's Saucy Skillet cooking contest.

I felt a furry paw tap my right foot. Tinkers, the local cat about town and everyone's favorite mouse catcher, had snuck in through a back window hoping to abscond with some leftover tuna fish or a bit of butter left unguarded by the sucker behind the counter. Since I was the only person in the café, the role of *sucker* fell squarely upon my shoulders.

I reached into the countertop cooler and found a foil pack of butter. Not the fake stuff; Tinkers was one of my best friends and as such deserved the best. "You should be down at the fair with everyone else," I said. "Stick around here and the only thing you'll get is an extra pat of butter. But Seaview is such a small town, I guess that's *butter* than nothing." It was a bad pun, but I laughed all the same. The fat orange calico ignored me, lapping up the butter and pushing the shiny packaging around like a hockey puck.

"Seaview's not so bad, is it? The waitress at the diner is pretty cute, from what I hear."

I turned my head, almost wrenching my neck. For a split second, I thought Tinkers spoke English. Then I saw the young police officer standing at the front doorway.

"I'm sorry. I didn't hear you come in. For a minute there, it looked like . . . Ah, don't worry about it."

The man chuckled as he made his way to the first stool at the counter. "You thought I was Tinkers? Hardly. Everyone knows she speaks with a British accent. No, wait. That's my phone. Sorry."

I giggled then became a bit flustered, since I had not expected a guy in uniform to appear out of nowhere. Trying to recover my composure, I grabbed a menu and a sparkling white coffee mug. My heart skipped. *Puh-shaw, I'm getting way ahead of myself. Calm down, Winnie. He's just here for food.*

"I've only a few minutes; been on duty down at the fair. Can I have a sandwich? Something simple, something fast?" He glanced first at his watch, and then tapped a few times on his smartphone. Returning his gaze to the laminated menu, the officer asked, "What's a Winnipeg Special?"

I picked up a glass jar of peanut butter and flipped it in the air, deftly catching it with one hand as I took the menu away with the other. "Me. I mean, it's a sandwich. And you'll love it. The sandwich, that is. And it won't take long to make, either." I kept on digging a verbal hole deep enough to hide in.

"I'll just go. Back in a minute." Embarrassed by my poor attempt at flirting, I waltzed over to the sandwich board opposite the front counter and started to assemble the needed ingredients. I faced away from my customer, taking a deep breath and then slowly exhaling, glad I had not broken another jar.

"Pretty fancy footwork. I'd have dropped the peanut butter after the first step."

"Just takes a little practice. And three to four jars plus a good broom. But here you go. This is the Winnipeg Special." As soon as the plate hit the counter, I heard a wistful meow from down below. Tinkers was hoping something would fall from the heavens.

"Tinkers! Stop begging. No one likes a mooch." I nudged the cat away with my foot. "She's great for keeping the mice away, but sometimes she gets a little too friendly with the customers. Thankfully, the health inspector likes her."

"I think she is on her best behavior right now. That cat caused far more trouble down at the fish market. Used up more than a few of her nine lives down there. The old man who runs the place chases her with a butcher knife. Wants to kill her sometimes, I think. Is that a pickle I taste in this peanut butter sandwich? And potato chips?"

Tinkers took the hint and scrambled back to the kitchen, snagging a fallen chip along the way. As I heard the cat escape through an open window, I suddenly remembered my grandmother's plight. "Yes, both pickles and chips. But you said the man wanted to kill Tinkers, which reminded me. I've heard something about a death at the fair. Do you know anything about it? My grandmother is down there at the cook-off. It's probably nothing, but I'm a bit worried about her."

As if on cue, the officer's radio crackled to life. A gravelly voice ordered all officers to report to the fairgrounds immediately. My first and only customer of the day put down the remnants of his sandwich, slugged down one last gulp of coffee, then stood up to pay his tab.

"On the house," I said.

"Oh, no. I can't accept free food. It could be construed a bribe."

I glared at the man with my are-you-serious look. "Not sure why I would need to pay off anyone, but if you want, you can always come back tomorrow and settle up."

He put on his hat, tipping it as if to say *thank you.* The radio's static roared once more.

"Williams—why aren't you here yet, rookie? I've got a troublemaker that needs locking up. She's a real handful."

We both could hear a commotion in the background as the caller ordered people to step back. The events were occurring fast, and backup was needed. My guy responded that he was on his way already. That's when I noticed the name tag on the uniform pocket. In black letters laser-etched against a jet-black background: *P. Williams.*

As he finished, the radio squelched once again, this time just giving us a snapshot of the cacophony in real time:

"Velma Kepler! Put that drumstick down! You're not allowed to—"

The radio went silent. Officer P. Williams stepped toward the door. "I'll be back tomorrow, not to worry. I'll pay cash, and leave you a nice tip."

Then it hit me. "Wait!"

I locked the register, vaulting myself over the counter. The napkin holder went flying and the red ketchup squeeze bottle spun like a top. Once past the row of barstools, I looped my arm around his and dragged him out the door.

"You're not the only one who needs to get to the fair. Let's get moving!"

A flock of seagulls scattered as we left the building. Judging from the white splats on the windshield, a few had been roosting on the telephone line above an old red Ford pickup, the only vehicle in front of the Cat and Fiddle Café.

"This yours?" I asked, as I slid into the passenger side.

My knight in khaki and blue-black cotton armor got behind the wheel. "Yes, fortunately for you. And why the sudden need to get to the fair? I don't even know your name."

I snapped the latch on my seatbelt. "The name's Winnie. Short for Winnipeg. And my last name is Kepler. You can put it all together while you get us to the fairgrounds. Now, Officer P. Williams—hurry!"

2

The cop slammed his foot on the gas pedal. Smoke billowed as he dropped the manual transmission into first gear. We went skidding out onto the road, fishtailing twice before steadying into the right lane. I peered out the back window to see if we had cut any traffic off, but everyone with a car must have already been down at the fair.

"So is that *your* place?"

"My grandmother owns it. When the rare customer gives her a hard time, she offers to sell me everything for a spare twenty. I work there for the money, but I'm a vegetarian. I would make a terrible owner unless I could change the menu entirely. After a cup or two of tea, she calms down and changes the subject, usually to something about my future and a so-called real job. She wants me to work in a big company, one that includes full benefits."

"Is that such a bad thing? I mean, benefits are nice. I get medical, dental, and vision at the police department. Can't complain."

"Works for you, maybe. But after four years of living in a big city, an office job just isn't for me. Too much hype and politics, and that's just in the interview process. No, for me the Cat and Fiddle is perfect. I've been here a year now."

I didn't know why was I telling this stranger my life story. He knew my name, but other than Officer Williams, I didn't know what else to call him. *Tall and handsome?*

"I'm glad the boys at the station told me to stop by sometime. They all love your crab cakes. And they told me your grandmother—well, she's got spunk, they say. I'm partial to your red hair, though. Tall blondes are okay—but when they told me about you. Well, I had to, ah, well, you know, stop by for coffee."

I straightened my shoulder-length hair and tugged on the seat belt in hopes of un-ruffling my shirt. It had crumpled when I jumped in the truck and buckled up. He liked my hair? I needed to find out more about this guy. How long had he been checking me out? Was he checking me out? Did I want him checking me out? My paranoid, self-conscious brain kicked into overdrive. I was a size twelve on a good day. At five foot ten, maybe I needed to hit the gym to lose that freshman fifteen I had carried with me for five years. My mind was racing. This was getting out of control. *Stop, Winnie. Before you buy a package of rice crackers for dinner!*

I took a deep breath. "So it sounds like you are new here. In town, that is. Yes?"

Ignoring my question, he pointed to the orange *Event* sign on the sidewalk; it had an arrow pointing to the left. As we drove off the paved road onto the white, oyster-shell path leading to the fairgrounds, my thoughts went back to my grandmother. The Cat and Fiddle had been my grandmother's diner forever, it seemed. And while it *was* the most popular spot on the Eastern Shore of Virginia to get a crab cake sandwich, the café didn't really qualify as fine dining. You wouldn't find a linen tablecloth anywhere in the place, and the only crystal was on the face of the cuckoo clock on the wall.

This type of diner was typical for the area. And like many towns nestled just off the railroad tracks along the Eastern Shore, the small town of Seaview was quaint, which was local jargon for no stoplight, no chain restaurant, and no social scene for anyone under Social Security age. But there was hope. And he was sitting right next to me.

Velma and I cooked up some decent food, and the reviews were fine enough to get my grandmother invited once again to the fair's annual cooking competition. It didn't hurt she had won the contest before, several times. The row of Saucy Skillet trophies watched over the cash register, almost daring anyone to complain about the food. I aspired to be as good a cook as Velma, but I still had a long way to go.

The best chefs in town were at the contest. The more I thought about it, the more I wanted to go see what was going on; being nosey was in my DNA. My parents were private detectives in Washington, D.C. Some people enjoyed making scrapbooks; my hobby involved solving mysteries. To date, my biggest job had been the case of the missing flounder sandwiches. Tinkers was lucky she didn't get the book thrown at her for that one. Anyhow, if this was a true murder case, it would be my first.

My phone buzzed. I pulled it out of my purse and scanned the number on the screen. It was *not* Velma, rather another call from another corporate recruiter responding to the résumé my grandmother had posted on the Internet on my behalf. Though I wanted to ease into adulthood, Velma had *other* ideas. What could I do? She was my grandmother, after all.

A few days earlier, a huge corporation, Mint Street Bankers, called me to interview with the hiring manager. They were looking for someone with a background in consumer psychology, and with my double major in business marketing and sociology, I matched on most of the keywords in their computer's algorithm. I didn't want the job, but Velma made me interview. I was happy with Seaview, the Cat and Fiddle, and even Tinkers with her daily visits. But once I was inside the plush conference room, something changed.

I felt good about my chances—the competitor coming out in me. Anyway, the manager introduced me to several of the higher-ups, said some nice things about me, and as I was leaving he let me know they would follow up. But no call back, at least not yet. *Maybe I'm not the hotshot I thought.*

"The chief's down at the exposition hall," Officer Williams said, pulling me out of my trance. "Just past the old railroad yard. We should be there soon." He shook his hands at the line of cars waiting to turn off the main road. The fair was popular, drawing crowds from as far away as Maryland. And every car in front of us glared bright red taillights. "Maybe soon was too strong a word," he lamented.

I rummaged through the glove box and found a few slips of paper, the registration and insurance papers. Underneath the documents, I discovered a box of 9-millimeter bullets, presumably for his service weapon. And then I found it. All the volunteer firemen in town had one; I had hoped a new police officer would be no different.

"This'll help," I said. I cranked on the window handle, rolling my side down. I unbuckled my seatbelt and stretched my torso outside. Before Officer Williams could pull me back, I slapped a magnet-mounted, battery-operated, red flashing light on top of the truck's cab. The effect, aided by a few taps on the horn, caused cars to lurch to the side, right and left. An instant path opened just wide enough for our pickup.

"Nice move, lady—I mean, Winnie. But you could have hurt yourself hanging out the window like that. What if you fell out and lost consciousness?"

"I would have been okay. You could have always given me mouth-to-mouth resuscitation, you know."

My college roommate once told me I was the biggest flirt she had ever seen. I would need to write her a letter, telling her I was now much worse. That's what happens when you live in a small town with a limited supply of eligible bachelors, I guess.

He tipped his hat once more. "I suppose I should just say thanks. At least the cars are moving and we can get there before Captain Larson blows another gasket."

"So, Officer P. Williams. If I were to call you by your first name, what would that be?"

The truck came to an abrupt halt; empty soda cans in the back of the truck bed rattled toward the cab. "We're here. If you're coming, you better move a little faster," he said. I loved a man who played hard to get. Two could play at that game, though.

"Ahem!" I waved my hand at the door.

Officer Williams took the hint, quickly walking around the front of his truck and centering himself at my door. He pulled on the handle and ushered me out. "I'd throw a cloak down, but they're not allowed in uniform."

"Thank you, sir." We may have been in a hurry, but I didn't want to waste an opportunity to show him I was a lady. This wasn't Flirting 101; this was graduate–level flirting, if anything.

"This loading dock looks deserted," I said. "Are we in the right spot?"

Officer Williams flipped open his phone. A few seconds later, he was speaking. I worried when he lowered his voice, turned away, and then pointed back at me.

As he ended the call, the thick steel door sealing the loading dock opened, its panels creaking from a lack of lubrication. Pulling down on a massive chain to lift the door was the strongest man in Seaview, probably the entire Shore. It was James Billy Larson, captain, Seaview PD. I had waited on him at the café, and I noticed he never seemed happy. And I never asked him why.

For a guy who could qualify for an old-age pension, with 240 pounds of pure muscle, J. B. Larson saw no need to press a button to lift the door. Brute strength would be faster. Once the lowest door panel cleared his field of vision, the man's face changed to more of a scowl. His eyes were dead set on me, and he was not happy.

"Winnipeg Kepler. Why am I not surprised? Parker Williams, this will go in my report, and it won't look good for you unless you keep your girlfriend here away from my crime scene."

"Yes, sir. I understand, but when you mentioned Velma Kepler was a suspect, perhaps having her granddaughter here might make her more willing to cooperate? And we only just met, sir. No dates, and nothing planned. Just business, sir. Police business."

Parker. Nice name. Nothing planned?

I interjected, not so much as to save Parker, but to better position myself to figure out what was going on—*Velma Kepler* and *suspect* in the same sentence.

I pushed past Officer Williams—ah, Parker, I should say now. "Captain, you are so right. I think I *should* be over by my grandmother, for emotional support. She is a senior citizen, after all." Seeing the man take a step back after my comment about age, I had to do fast damage control. "But, a *young* one, though. Much older than you. Right?"

"We are the same age, so don't press your luck. Everyone is in front of the stage, so go there and sit down by your grandmother. And don't bother asking your parents to come help, either. Just because they grew up here, they thought they could solve every crime faster than we could. I threw myself a party when they moved to D.C. Now? I'd rather call a psychic than deal with them again."

As we walked through the wings behind the stage, the Captain took photos. By the time we stepped into the flood of the stage lights, I saw my Velma over by a row of chairs placed at the front of a makeshift stage. Next to her were three other cooks—other competitors, I assumed.

It was high time to start my investigation.

3

Three rows of five chairs each had been reserved for the competitors. When the contest had started two days earlier, each chair had been filled. Now, after two elimination rounds, only the top four chefs remained. The fifth seat in that final row was now empty.

Sitting in the gallery, perpendicular to the competitor chairs, was a group of ladies, impeccably dressed like they were heading to church. They were the judges, I presumed, and they did not look too comfortable. The heat from the stage lights was intense; each judge had a makeshift fan made from a leftover program.

"Captain Larson, sir, is the victim a chef? I see a vacant chair, but didn't want to make an assumption."

"Yes, Miss Kepler. The deceased is in the break room and his name is Pierre St. Pierre. A simple stabbing like this one does not require your help. Now, if you'll excuse me, we have to get on with our official police business. Officer Williams, remember what I said. Report. Ending. Bad for you. Add it all up and see what you get."

Just the mention of the dead chef's name caused a stir. Competitors and judges alike started murmuring about how the man "got what he deserved." This day was turning ugly fast.

I turned and made my way past Parker to find my own seat. I took the liberty to whisper into Parker's ear. "Hey officer, help a girl out? Add *that* up and we'll see what you get."

He nodded, cracked a slight grin, turned another shade of red, and moved quickly to his Captain's orders.

Velma looked at me as I sat down beside her. She gave me the high eyebrow. I hated that look, and received it often.

Without waiting for her to ask, I explained. "I just wanted to ensure the little details were noticed. Could make a difference when it comes to the courtroom. And I am getting the feeling you are a suspect, so I'm not taking any chances. I told him I would greatly appreciate it if he rose to the occasion, even if it meant a negative report."

"I didn't realize you loved Parker so much, Winnie. That's so sweet. When did you all start dating?"

"Love? Dating? Hardly. I served him coffee and a peanut butter sandwich a few minutes ago. Granted, he's not half-bad looking, I'll admit, but right now I just want him to help, especially since the Captain and his poor attitude won't. I doubt anything will come of it—me and Parker that is. You know what I mean." I was getting myself so confused, I wasn't sure if even I knew what I meant.

"Of course, if you say so, dear. In the meantime, we do need to contend with this situation. It has gotten a little out of hand. Bless his heart, the Captain does seem to be sort of one-sided in all of this, doesn't he? Once the investigators from the VCID get here, I think we'll be okay, though. They are on the way, from what Grimsby tells us."

"Grimsby?"

"Drake Grimsby. The contest organizer this year. If you ask him, he'll tell you he's an expert. In everything. Even if you don't ask, he'll tell you. He even claims to have a contact at the VCID, the Virginia Criminal Investigation Division."

Velma explained that the contest had problems from the start. A chef in the first round had been caught cheating after Grimsby found some extra ingredients in the man's carry bag. The offense resulted in disqualification, since every ingredient was to come from the sponsor. Anything different would be deemed ineligible—even if it tasted better.

Velma pointed to the abandoned cooking station next to her own. "Then Pierre St. Pierre stirred his own pot. He argued with Emperor Grimsby, and screamed out about MegaFood's lack of certified organic vegetables and their use of BPA in their ingredients."

Velma stopped her explanation, shrugged her shoulders, and said she thought BPA was something Roosevelt had created when she was a child. In any event, she concluded by saying Pierre threatened to put down his knives and refused to cook.

"Grandma, was Pierre's complaining the only problem? Doesn't seem enough for a murder. There must be something else."

"Well," she replied, "some people may have heard me threaten to kill him. But, I didn't mean it like that, you know."

"You threatened to kill a man and now he's dead? Grandma, that's the kind of little detail I was talking about. What, exactly, did you say? And *why* did you say it?"

"It was that nasty Grimsby boy's fault. At the start of the third round, we had ten minutes to look at the ingredients in the pantry and the cooler we were allowed to use. Plus, we had to plan our menu. It was to be the final round, a three-course, all-American picnic. I had decided to make fried chicken on a stick, a cold potato salad, and my famous apple pie for dessert."

"And why were you mad at Drake Grimsby? He wasn't even cooking, only announcing."

"See all the cameras? He's making a feature film or something. I think he made sure there were just enough of each popular ingredient so contestants would end up fighting over them."

Velma leaned over and whispered into my ear, saying, "I heard him talking on the phone to one of the network men. Said he would take care of Pierre to increase the program's ratings."

She continued, "All of a sudden, the whistle blew and we were off to the pantry to get what we could carry. I had to find the chicken before anything else. You can't have fried chicken on a stick without chicken, you know."

"Did Pierre fight you for it?"

"Oh, no. We didn't come to blows. In fact, I didn't pay attention to what Pierre was doing. There wasn't any time. I simply picked up enough for my menu plan; he went for the apples, as I recall. I didn't give it a second thought. Once we were back at our cooking stations, Grimsby tried to get me all riled up. He said Pierre took *all* the apples just to spite me. Grimsby was full of that silly talk."

"But you mentioned you *wanted* to kill Pierre?"

"Well, I think Grimsby did some sort of hocus pocus with a microphone to make it sound like I threatened to kill Pierre."

I stood up and walked over to Captain Larson. He scribbled on his legal pad as I asked him about the situation. I took a gander at his notes, but there was no way to read those frontways, backways, or sideways. The ancient Phoenicians would have been proud of his handwriting technique.

"Captain Larson, sir. Is there anything I can do help?"

The man put down his pen, slapping it onto the yellow pages with a sharp *pop*. He took a deep breath; you could hear him counting to ten as he let the air escape his lungs. I had no idea how I had so upset him with my first of many questions.

"You may want to find a lawyer. We haven't arrested your grandmother yet, but after the boys from the VCID get here and confirm my suspicions, she will need some sort of representation. You're a college girl. Did you manage to get a law degree?"

Not another member of the *college girl* club, I sighed. "No, my focus was on business. I specialized in figuring out what makes people tick. What makes *you* tick, Captain Larson? And why do you think there are only boys in the VCID? A big guy like you, are you afraid of women?" I was pushing all of his buttons. The more upset I could get him, the more likely he would divulge his strategy. That is, if he had one.

The legal pad and the accompanying pen went flying across the stage. The poor girl behind the main camera leaped out of the way as the missiles went careening into the production desk sitting off in the wings, stage right. She responded just as I would have— with a salute of sorts. I got the impression she was not happy with any of the goings-on here. How could I blame her?

The Captain took in a huge breath, then exhaled with enough force to blow a pile dust bunnies around the floor. "We have all the proof we need for a jury to convict your grandmother of murder. It's all on tape. Now go sit down before I charge you with interfering with an official investigation. Has anyone seen my notebook?"

The camera lady kicked his legal pad, sliding it back across the wooden floor. She then picked up a remote control device, pressing a few buttons. All of a sudden, every stage light above us focused on the poor Captain. He was temporarily blinded, which frustrated him even more. *Don't mess with girl power.*

I walked back to Velma, who was now sitting comfortably as she knitted a purple something or other. Velma loved to cook, but she was a knitter at heart, through and through. Her yarn bag went with her everywhere, even to a cooking competition. A morbid thought raced through my mind as I watched her click her little stitch counter to keep track of the progress on each row.

"Before you ask," Velma said, "these knitting needles are blood free. I don't know exactly how Pierre died, but I would never ruin a good pair of needles on an old buzzard like him. By the way, I spoke to the sponsor about you needing a job. They didn't have anything open at the moment, but you may want to drop off your résumé before this is all over. You never know, right?"

I clasped Velma's hands, gently thumbing along the gemstones of her bracelet. The last thing I wanted to see was my own grandmother trading in her warm red agates for a pair of cold nickel-plated handcuffs.

"Grandma, you're not the kind of person who loses their cool. I've seen you mediate the weekly tiffs between some of those church lady judges when they come in to eat lunch. I just can't see you falling for a ratings trap sprung by some smarmy contest producer. And Grimsby? Don't I know him, or at least his family? I've heard that name before."

Velma tilted her head toward the show's producer, whose bald head was shimmering from sweat, the result of standing too close to the focused stage lights. As the man pulled a handkerchief out of his desk drawer to clear his brow, he began to argue with his camera technician. If I heard correctly, Drake was blaming her for several poor-quality camera shots. He didn't seem to be a very positive person, at least to me.

Velma answered my question. "You are probably thinking of Janet Grimsby, his mother. She and I took first and second place at every cooking contest the fair could come up with. It was always me first, Janet second. We were unstoppable. Poor woman passed away before she could win one, though. Anyway, her son isn't nearly as civil as Janet. He asked me if I wanted to kill Pierre because of the apples."

"And you said no, right?"

"Well, yes, but not exactly."

The Captain's cell phone started ringing. The entire room became silent as we all heard Larson, now standing over by the producer's desk, explain to the caller how Velma's threat against Pierre was captured on video. I then realized the situation was much worse than I had originally thought. At the first opportunity, I would definitely need to find a lawyer.

Parker, seeing my concern and my frustration about not having access to all the evidence, intervened. "Captain, could I see the other evidence? I was wondering if Velma had been seen holding the murder weapon."

I couldn't believe Parker would side with the enemy so quickly. His chances for a first date were pretty much gone now.

Then, after he winked at me, I realized he was giving me the chance to see the video. Parker must have known there was no way his boss would let me stroll across the stage and cross-examine his theory.

Grimsby's camera technician brought a video monitor over on a cart and, finding the controller's battery now dead, rummaging through the desk's top drawer to find a backup unit. Once she had one in hand, it took only a few clicks for the playback to be queued up and ready to go.

Soon enough, the playback showed Velma confronting Pierre and saying, "I want to *kill* you, Pierre!"

"That's not what I said," Velma protested. "Mr. Grimsby here must have done some sort of trick to make it sound like that. Those were *not* my words—exactly."

Unfortunately, the other contestants, still sitting in their assigned chairs like good little students, had remembered hearing similar words come through the big speakers on each side of the stage. At face value, this was not looking good for Velma.

Larson quietly repeated Velma's words as he transcribed them into his report. "Velma, you and I go a long way back, and we've always, well, mostly always been on good speaking terms, so I am not placing you under arrest—yet—but very shortly I may be advising you of your rights. You may want to do yourself a favor and start now."

"Start what?" she asked.

"Exercising your right to remain silent. And it would be nice if your granddaughter followed the same advice." The man scowled with torment in his eyes as he glared at me. I could not tell if he was upset Velma had murdered someone, that I was there to interfere, or because he really didn't want either of us to be involved.

As for Velma's supposed guilt, I was not yet convinced. While the Captain stepped away to take another phone call, I reviewed the digital drama a few more times, hoping to find some sort of clue that could clearly vindicate my grandmother.

After Parker and I had finished watching the opening few minutes of the competition again, I asked the camera technician, a woman about my size but at least twice my age, if I could see the playback from the break room. "After all," I said, "this is where the murder seems to have taken place. It only makes sense to take a gander, right?"

The technician was very cooperative, I thought, because I acknowledged the skill required of her craft. Everyone likes to be appreciated for their work, and this lady was no different. It was just unfortunate she chose to work for an idiot. *Mental note: talk to her later. Maybe she could film a commercial for the Cat and Fiddle?*

I could see that Drake was taking this poor woman's work for granted. Then again, maybe it wasn't personal. Perhaps he had a character flaw? Did he take *all* women to be second-class humans, or worse? As I saw the man, now using the camera's lens as a mirror, start to comb his thinning hair, I corrected my judgment—he had more than one character flaw.

I glanced over at the Captain, who was looking down, still speaking to parties unknown over his cell phone. I shuffled my feet an inch at a time, rotating my front away from the head officer. Eye contact would have ruined everything. I did not want to draw attention.

Seeing me attempting to hide in plain sight, and his boss about to end the phone call, Parker asked Larsen to help him process the crime scene. As they left the stage and walked over to the break room, I looked at the camera tech, holding my finger up to my lips.

The camerawoman told me she could play back recordings from any camera. Every feed went directly to the processor, a machine connected by a slew of cables to the large television monitor. This was all possible thanks to the handheld remote controller she used, a state-of-the-art model programmed to sync every piece of equipment she had brought. There were even buttons on the controller that assisted with editing. She called it an essential piece of gear that could "do anything." With just a few clicks, she had the break room's video history ready to go.

I asked if I could play with the controller for a minute, just to see how it moved the various cameras. She pointed out everything the controller could do as I watched ceiling-mounted cameras move to the commands of my little fingers. Soon I was recording just like a professional.

Pressing a few more buttons, I changed the monitor's screen back to the old feed from the break area. The screen again showed an empty room. In the lower right corner was a date and time stamp, showing that this particular recording happened at 12:25 p.m.

Several of the judges had wandered from their jury box to see what I was doing. People tend to do that sort of thing when they think they can help. Many were becoming instant experts at murder investigations, offering their advice and opinion. The uninvited gang became louder as each tried to speak over the opinion of the other. This was just the situation I was trying to avoid, but the judges were there to stay.

Soon enough, instead of commenting on the whereabouts of the contestants at the time of the murder, the ladies were more focused on how their hairstyles appeared on screen. *Harmless commentary,* I thought. It could have certainly been worse. At least no one mentioned shoes, the one subject that could have elicited physical violence. Clearly, we had already had enough of that for one day.

While the women chatted, moving from hair to the hats last seen in church on Sunday, I asked the technician if the break room's security camera filmed constantly. She told me the break room's camera was motion-activated. She had opted to use the automatic camera there so she could focus on personally filming the events on the stage. The break room's camera sensor allowed for the entire room to be recorded *only* when someone was taking a break.

I repeated her comment about Grimsby being too cheap to hire a second camera operator. As she gave me a sarcastic expression and a thumbs-up, Drake, who had been standing near enough to watch our little interchange, pointed to his watch. He told *his* technician she was working for him—not anyone else. He then trotted off to find Captain Larson, I assumed only to confirm in his own mind that he was still in charge. Of something.

Unfortunately, I was still at a loss for what had actually had happened at the time of the murder. The break room camera was in good working order, yet there were a few minutes of video showing no one in the room. With the camera set to be activated by motion, what I had seen did not make sense. I wondered if there was a blind spot the lens couldn't see, but the motion detector could.

This called for an on-the-spot inspection. Captain Larson and Parker returned from the break room, the senior officer back on his phone. The judges and fellow cooks sat back down to banter various theories about as I took Parker's arm and pulled him close. I whispered into his ear. "I, ahem, would like permission to visit the powder room, sir. You don't think there would be any harm in me doing that, do you?"

When I was younger, I had watched my grandmother compete in this competition many times. Previous show producers were much nicer than this Drake person, and they had no problem letting a youngster backstage. I knew full well and good the nearest restroom available was just past the break room. The break room with the dead body.

Parker, being a gentleman, waved me through to the curtained passageway leading to the restroom, and coincidentally near the murder scene. What a nice traffic cop he would make once his boss found out how much he had been helping me. It would be an easy job, especially since Seaview had little traffic. Heck, we didn't even have a stoplight.

Before I could take another step, the tension in the room elevated as Captain Larson finished writing notes from his phone call. "Dang pencil-pushers, all of them!" Captain Larson looked at his watch, checking it against the time on the clock suspended from one of the towers of scaffolding mounted with banks of stage lights. "Thank goodness this is just a murder, and not a crime or anything. We have doughnut stores, here, too, you know. What a bunch of idiots!"

Parker tried to remind him that Seaview actually did not have a doughnut store, but the words mattered not to the infuriated chief. Ignoring his young officer, Larson told the crowd he had called the VCID back, asking if and when they would arrive to assist in the investigation. I guessed that the delay was the only reason the chefs, judges, and I had been ordered to sit in front of the stage.

The judges started to mumble, saying Larson had no idea what to do next. I suggested that he call his forensics team to process the evidence. The officer could only muster a benign and embarrassing retort, saying Seaview didn't have a certified forensic technician. At the breaking point of frustration, Captain Larson blew his whistle. With everyone's full attention, he announced the new goal was to "secure and contain" the area and prevent evidence from becoming further contaminated.

I asked if he wanted to lock the doors since the killer was obviously still in the room. The only reply I received was another short blast from the whistle, and a finger wag telling me to stay away.

Captain Larson's conundrum was of no matter to me because I had been given *official* permission to leave the stage by another police officer. So I did. With the Captain back on the phone, he was unable to stop me verbally. As he motioned wildly for Parker to stop me, I wandered to the back side of the cooking stations, past the open-air pantry and found my way to the short, curtained hallway leading to the break room.

The walkway was just wide enough for an average-sized man to ease through without ruffling the dark red velour bordering each side. The heat of banks upon banks of stage lights was a distant memory once I felt the cold breeze blowing from the overhead vents. It was actually kind of chilly. I had a quick thought about Parker, and how he and I could spend a few minutes hidden away here, far from the crowd. That would warm me up!

Entering the break room, I had to step carefully. There were little splatters of blood everywhere. Ironically, the break room was not really built for comfort. No carpet, no mood lighting, no scenic photography by Ansel Adams on the wall. Nothing that would say *relax*. But it did have a coffee table and one overstuffed sofa, a thrift store reject covered with a dark floral pattern that was probably popular back in 1970.

Then there was the body. Chef Pierre St. Pierre was indeed dead. His stiffened body rested in peace on the sofa. The remainder of the area was far from peaceful. The man's long white chef's coat gleamed in the brightness of the lights. In dark, morbid contrast, his stovepipe of a white toque had taken a tumble to the floor and soaked up drips and drabs of the poor man's blood. A white hat rimmed with red blood would appeal to no chef, ever.

Aside from the sofa's tacky slip cover, I took mental note of its position, pacing eleven steps from the doorway to the sofa across the room. I reached my objective, then turned around to face the video camera mounted high on the wall above the door. The little red light on top of the camera blinked. The motion detector had worked, causing the camera to record my every move.

As I walked back to the door, I took out my phone and snapped a few photos of the blood. The red dots on the floor were evenly spaced, perfectly round circles. Had the victim been running away from the killer, there should have been more space between drops, and the circles would have been more like ovals or teardrops. This chef either did not know he had been stabbed, or had resigned himself to his fate. There was no evidence of Chef Pierre running anywhere.

In my care to avoid stepping in a crimson biohazard, I brushed against the coffee table. There were a few hand-drawn maps of the stage setup sitting on top of the table. Pencil lines pointed to certain areas of the pantry, with dotted lines leading back to each of the workstations on the main stage. The chefs had made an action plan in an attempt to not get in each other's way during the prep time.

The sound of clinking glass caused me to stop. I had not seen anything except paper on top of the wooden table, but something somewhere must have made the telltale sound. Sure enough, on the shelf underneath the table were five wine glasses, probably moved to make room for the invasion plans.

Four glasses had the sticky goo of old purple-red wine in the bottom; one glass had fire-engine red lipstick prints gracing the rim. The shade looked very close to the gloss adorning one or two of the competitors, and I didn't mean my grandma. She always used some sort of homemade beeswax concoction. Grandma Velma wasn't old, really, but she was definitely old school.

After taking a few more photos, I continued my short journey to the door. Once again, I was stopped—this time by my own brain telling me something was missing. If there were wine glasses, where was the wine bottle? I had spent my time looking down. Had I missed a key bit of evidence?

There was nothing else in the room. Had the room been cleaned? Grimsby would not have hired a janitor, especially since the money could have been better spent on a second camera technician. Plus, there was no time to clean. I took one more look around, even squatting down and lunging into a poor excuse for an upward-facing dog yoga position, just to see if I had walked by a bottle or two.

Fortunately, the missing bottle mystery was solved when I noticed an overturned, almost empty bottle of wine protruding from under Pierre's stiff leg. Judging from the scant amount left in the bottle, I assumed four contestants had each consumed one glass.

"Well, at least you had one last good meal, chef." I didn't really know the guy, but I felt sorry he had passed away virtually alone, save his liquid lunch companion—a last glass of vino to numb the pain he must have experienced.

It was time to return to the seating area. I had been gone far too long for a normal visit to the ladies' room. I thoroughly anticipated a solid scolding from Captain Larson, who would now have to include my shoe prints in the evidence package, since his own officer had let me *accidentally* wander into the crime scene.

The red velour curtains forming the passageway felt soft and inviting as I walked back. The peacefulness of the cool, lush hallway contrasted with the cold, impersonal feeling I had in the break room. Seeing the corpse made me want to do more than prove my grandmother's innocence. Now I had to find the killer. Indeed, I was an acorn falling from my parents' tree.

I returned to the stage; there was work to do.

4

Captain Larson loudly cleared his throat and announced that the boys from the VCID would be delayed for a few more hours. "Apparently there is a higher-priority case in a rather well-to-do neighborhood in Norfolk," he said. "They told us to take a few photos and then lock the place up once the funeral home takes the body away. Well, in my opinion, no one leaves until I give the authorization. This is *my* crime scene!"

My grandmother started to interject, but Grimsby beat her to the punch when he stood up and asked, "What about the contest? Can't the judges at least *taste* the food? We need to declare a winner. There's a lot of prize money at stake here."

"Everything here is evidence, sir. For all we know, the killer poisoned every fruit and vegetable. We may have a single victim now, but we can't assume Pierre St. Pierre was destined to be the only corpse." The Captain looked over at the adjudicators sitting back in their seats. After hearing the police chief's theory, none wanted to take the chance.

I knew Velma would always be a competitor, even under such unusual and risky circumstances. I had to say something before she challenged police authority, an unwise move for someone considered a murder suspect.

"You know what you *could* do?" I said. "Why not have everyone prepare their picnic meal again, at their own place of business? The judges would visit each restaurant, maybe one place per day. You'd have your winner by Friday. Plus, think of all the extra video your camera will get. It could end up being a weeklong miniseries on television. And you, Mr. Grimsby, you would be the host for the entire thing. This *could* get picked up by a major food network. Plus, if someone doesn't show up, you will know who the killer is. You will be the town hero!"

Playing to the man's ego, my impromptu plan worked better than I expected. In no time, Drake had his clipboard out and was scribbling down production orders and tearing the pages off, throwing them at the frazzled girl behind the camera. I began to think she was his personal assistant, too. *Poor woman.*

Grimsby finished a skeletal first draft as the judge's grumbling increasing in frequency and volume. The ladies demanded to know when and where each meal would be, and a few rattled off the order of restaurants they wanted to visit. Grimsby was being usurped.

This boldness frustrated the producer. After a while, the scratch-outs covered more of the paper than the original bullet points. He put the clipboard down on the desk, where upon closer inspection I decided free-range chickens made more legible scratches.

Regardless of the hubbub, all I really wanted to do was get my grandmother back to the Cat and Fiddle. The scene was madness. Drake Grimsby was about to explode. Then there was Parker Williams. His *rookie-ness* prevented him from taking any sort of initiative to steer the investigation toward another suspect. *Any* other suspect.

I would have to channel both Nancy Drew and Sherlock Holmes to solve this case on my own. *Will Parker be my Watson or my Ned? Could he be both?*

Velma and I stood and started toward the exit. Captain Larson, tired of raising his voice, blew his whistle like a traffic cop during rush hour. We stopped, but did not turn around.

"And where do you think you two are going?"

"Well, we aren't leaving town. You already put the kibosh on that plan," I said, my words interspersed with giggles. "We figured we would go back to the Cat and Fiddle and wait for the judges to arrive. Our food is good *every* day." Nothing like throwing a little smack talk around.

The Captain pointed his finger for us to take our seats again. I had seen my grandmother use the same unspoken commands. I had pushed about as far as I could, so in an effort to keep myself, Velma, and Parker out of more trouble, I slipped back onto the cold metal folding chair. Velma adjusted her chef's jacket, and then joined me. At least he didn't have a wooden spoon to shake at me. *That* would have brought on flashbacks to my childhood.

Suspects. All murders had them, and this would be no exception. The people who were physically closest to the deceased during the competition were still sitting with us. On one side, a well-dressed gentleman sat mumbling about how he needed to get back to work. His Southern drawl made him sound like he walked right in from the set of *Gone With the Wind*.

Next to him was a young chef attired in black leather, silver chains, and tattoos. He kept quiet, instead glancing at a younger woman sitting at the opposite end of the row. She reciprocated, mouthing *"I love you,"* and flashing the same in sign language. This bunch, while appearing to be a strange lot, hardly looked like a lineup of hardened felons.

But unlike the leader of the Seaview police force, I considered them *all* suspect, every single one of them. Except my grandmother, of course. My new goal was to see how these other people acted in their own environment, a place where they would be more relaxed, less defensive, and with luck, might let a clue or two slip out.

Drake Grimsby walked the line of chefs like a general inspecting his troops. He stroked an imaginary goatee as he confirmed how the contest would now conclude. As he reached each contestant, he presented them with the news. Then Drake Grimsby walked to the center of the stage, conveniently under the main spotlight, and after ensuring the camera was focused on him alone, he announced that everyone associated with the contest would be given Sunday off as a day of rest. The church ladies gave him a polite clap, saying the Lord must have heard their prayers. On Monday, he continued, the judging would move to the individual restaurants of the contestants.

The Seagull's Nest Bed and Breakfast would be first location, since two of the contestants worked there. George Harrison Windsor, our Southern gentleman, was the B and B's executive chef. He addressed everyone as sir or ma'am, except for the early-twenties couple, whom he referred to as son and young lady.

I found his idioms charming at first, and condescending soon after. However, many people considered George the contest favorite to beat Velma this year, especially since his skill in the kitchen was supposedly superior to the late Pierre's.

Velma whispered in my ear, "He has formal training as a chef. None of the rest of us do. I still think I can take him, though."

I slid my finger across my phone's glass screen, tapped on the little gallery icon, and scrolled through a variety of photos. I found a shot of our café with shiny statuettes lining the shelf behind the cash register and held it up for Velma to see.

"Grandma, how many of these Saucy Skillet trophies have you won? More than any trained chef, that's for sure."

Velma, a perennial winner, had no such formal culinary school education. Yet, the long line of awards testified to her ability to produce quality food. I had been working in the café for over a year and had not heard a single negative comment about Velma from a customer.

My skill? Hit or miss. Apparently you have to stab potatoes with a fork *before* you bake them in the oven. That was a definite miss.

A few judges commented on how they loved Velma's apple pie, but she could not overcome the fancy blue-plate specials a handsome man like that Mr. Windsor could produce. And when the judges, church ladies all, discovered he was an eligible bachelor, many asked if George had met their daughters. If not, they would be happy to bring them over sometime.

Ego and greed. Two main ingredients for any dish served up as murder. George, thankfully, was ever the gentleman, politely conversing but never committing. Now, with the contest moving in a new direction, he would have to concentrate on the food more so than the guests. He would be competing first, serving lunch.

The second chef from the Seagull's Nest was considered a dark horse. Grimsby had invited the lad in hopes of adding a bit of shock value to boost ratings. The boy, who also happened to be George's dishwasher, was one Cosmo Finnegan. And though he was just twenty-two years of age and lacked formal culinary training, the judges commented that "the kid" had shown flashes of brilliance during the first two rounds. Every time his name was mentioned, the judges recalled something he had cooked.

Cosmo's culinary specialty was Euro-Asian cuisine. I didn't know what the term meant, but as I found out later, Grimsby was correct in that Cosmo had a flair for the dramatic, and his food went right along with it. Cosmo's face had two basic expressions: one of happiness as he silently communicated with the girl sitting on the opposite end of the row, and contempt for his boss, the self-appointed king of Southern cooking. I assumed it was an us-against-them animosity—class warfare behind the steam tables.

Velma motioned toward the leather-clad cook. A lifted eyebrow told me there was more to the story. Her shaking head spelled out that it was a sordid tale. I asked Velma about the history between the two chefs, and she said the problem stemmed from working together at the B and B. The men had been at odds ever since George refused to let Cosmo try any of his exotic dishes at work.

I gave them the old up-and-down inspection, hoping to gain some insight as to why and/or how one of them could have killed Pierre. At face value, the senior had on a pristine white chef's jacket. Very professional, clearly at the top of his culinary game. On the other hand, the junior's attire was sloppy, a mash-up of black leather clothing streaked with visible food stains, the residue of . . . well, I had no idea what they were from. Best not to know.

Cosmo's disheveled look reminded me of this one evening when Velma and I were walking to the ice cream store. As we passed by the B and B, I saw bright flashes of light coming from somewhere behind the house. Poking my head around the corner, I discovered Cosmo working on something in a tool shed. The flashes had come from his welding torch.

The welding smelled terrible, the same bad smell you get when your toaster catches on fire. And that wasn't my fault; I wasn't aware it was safer to butter the bread *after* you toast. I was just trying to save time. But Cosmo? He was a strange one. Many of the judges were complimentary of his cooking. He must have had some skills. *But did he have the skill to kill?*

With two of the suspects cooking at the Seagull's Nest Bed and Breakfast, I couldn't let the opportunity to investigate go by. I told Velma I would tag along with the judges to help out; help my grandmother out of a murder conviction, that is.

There was, however, the logistical dilemma of two contestants working at the same establishment. It wasn't my problem, really; it was more of a problem for Grimsby. He was the one who realized that he could save money by scheduling two events in one day. After a bit of scoffing by Windsor, and an immature but snarky retort of *nanny-nanny-boo-boo* from Cosmo, the show's producer mediated a solution. It was agreed that the latter would cook for the judges at lunchtime so the former could use the afternoon to prepare for the dinner service. Each chef would allow the other to work without interference.

George snapped his head to the side, saying he could out - cook Cosmo any time of day, any day of the week, and with the Mormon Tabernacle Choir watching him from behind the sandwich board. I almost asked him how they would all fit, but Velma nudged me in the ribs before my sarcasm went public.

You could tell from George's contorted face that he was not happy. On the other end of life's bell curve, Cosmo could barely keep his huge smile from reaching his ears. So much for lessening the tension. *Good job, Grimsby.*

Tuesday's visit would be to the kitchen of the third contestant, an unusual establishment found at the old Shoreway Railroad, just south of the fairgrounds and within easy walking distance for the tourists meandering down Front Street. The rail yard, overgrown with tall grass and a daily resting point for flocks of seagulls and pelicans, was a relic of a much more prosperous time, decades ago. Now, only a few flatbed rail cars stood at the ready, poised to take on huge caissons made by Seaview's one remaining industrial factory, a cement production facility built on the far side of the lot. On a side track sat an old steam engine with its accompanying coal carrier. Coupled to those two were a blue Pullman dining car and a classic red caboose.

The Pullman car had been converted into a coal-fired, mobile kitchen and was also the home of the next suspect, Miss Bailey Babbitt. I suppose I should have considered her a competitor first, suspect second, but at that point in the game, everyone was a suspect in my eyes.

Bailey stood up at the announcement of her day. I thought it was an innocent gesture-of respect to the producer, but soon learned otherwise. She waltzed over to her companion Cosmo and, bending over at the waist, whispered something into his ear. Bailey gave him a light kiss on the cheek, and then returned to her chair. Cosmo took out a handkerchief and wiped away the red lipstick. From the looks of the white cotton cloth, this had not been the first time he had done this.

Bailey was young, not quite my age, and like me, she was of restaurateur stock. At one time, her parents operated a popular family-style restaurant in town. But with the economic downturn a few years earlier, their business withered. When the nearby tractor company closed down, the assembly line workers left the area in search of other work. The tens and twenties in their wallets went with them, forcing the doors to close for good.

After a short foreclosure hearing, the Babbitts' restaurant was sold plate, glass, and dishrag to an out-of-town investment group that gutted the place. From what everyone had told me at the café, it was a sad day in Seaview. No one liked seeing any local business go under.

The new owners packed up everything from the stoves to the saucers. The boxed contents were put in a rental truck and driven less than a mile away, to a building at the farthest end of Front Street. Then the building sat vacant.

According to newspaper reports, the investment group's new building involved a business plan requiring an unobstructed view of the Chesapeake Bay. The amount of money needed was immense, but the investment group seemed to have enough cash. The whole idea was a gamble, but if it worked as planned, Seaview would have a new tourist attraction—a tiki bar on a fishing pier attached to the beachside restaurant. This was not in our little town's character at all. It was all about a stampede for the tourist's dollar.

While the buildings were constructed, the investment group looked for a new chef to help sell the sizzle. They knew publicity was needed, and it would be a challenge competing with the popular restaurants in the resort city of Virginia Beach just a half-hour away. The question became, Who could pull this off?

5

Pierre St. Pierre made a name for himself in Paris and left the City of Light to become Seaview's first resident celebrity chef. The advertising flyers claimed Pierre would bring intercontinental cuisine to Seaview, though no one knew what that was. I asked Velma about it and she guessed Belgian waffles.

Regardless, Seaview's first white tablecloth, fine dining restaurant opened under the name "P-Squared." Who said chefs have no ego?

My family knew some of the Babbitts' financial problems and could only watch as the Babbitts lost their house in the bankruptcy, forcing a move into an abandoned train caboose. A short time later, Bailey watched as her parents died of broken hearts—her mom passing first, her father the next week.

She moved on with her life as best she possibly could. She used her parents' life insurance money to buy the three rail cars attached to the caboose, hoping to rehab them into a nicer home and a rolling diner. She dreamed of turning the short train into a different kind of tourist destination—Seaview's first modern-day railway dining experience.

The judges tapped the new schedule into their smartphones as Grimsby and Larson conferred. Every time Grimsby asked to use something onstage, the Captain told him, "Nothing should be moved—and by nothing, I mean abso-frikkin-lutely nothing."

Grimsby saved Wednesday for a visit to the Cat and Fiddle. In an offhanded comment, Larson announced, "Mark my words, Miss Kepler, I'll have no problem enjoying your grandmother's fried chicken on a stick in one side of my mouth while reading her Miranda rights from the other."

Decades earlier, the Captain and Velma had grown up together as classmates in school; despite their long history, Larson repeated the motive, opportunity, and verbal threat that made his case against her all the stronger. The proof was evident, in all its digital, hi-def, and surround-sound glory. The video playback would not go well for Velma in a courtroom, he claimed.

In spite of his personal conviction, Grimsby's schedule was completed, and Larson followed the advice of the VCID to send everyone home. As the entire entourage was leaving, I turned to Captain Larson. "Excuse me, sir, but have you found the murder weapon?"

Larson said his so-called forensic technician, just a skilled patrolman wielding something akin to a high school science fair kit, had done a cursory test on all the competitors' knives and found that the only one with human blood on it was from Cosmo's workstation. However, seeing a fresh knife cut on Cosmo's hand, Larson thought the blood might prove to be Cosmo's. A quick check of the video showed Cosmo cutting his hand while cooking, so the benchmark for probable cause had not been met—at least, not yet. The Captain acknowledged that the VCID would need to decide, since the state forensic lab was certified and used much better equipment.

I reminded Larson that the security video showed no one walking into the break room, with or without a knife in their hand. I tried to put the man on the defensive, and I could tell by his bark that he now felt the need to prove me wrong. That was just how I wanted him to react.

To be extra certain he had not missed something, Larson did a recount of all the knives collected as evidence. None were missing.

"Amazing," I said. "How does a corpse end up so *dead* if there's no murder weapon?"

Puh-shaw—this case is mine to solve.

I gave Parker a quick wink. He responded by blushing a nice shade of red.

* * *

The next day, a pleasant Sunday afternoon, Seaview's pseudo-upper-crust social elites crowded into the Cat and Fiddle for high tea. These housewives dressed in their finest, in direct opposition to their bait-stained-denim-and ripped-T-shirt-wearing husbands, who were out fishing. Although the ladies said they came for the little crustless sandwiches and dessert treats, the opportunity to hear juicy gossip was what kept them there.

Cups clinked and pinkies pointed as the smell of lightly warmed cinnamon pastries came fresh from the oven. Both sight and sound made for a most memorable ambiance. As much as the men loved to be out on their boats, the women of Seaview enjoyed their time away from them.

Grandma ran the register and greeted customers as I slapped tuna salad on bread and delivered the goods. I was still a novice cook and had plenty of culinary gaffes to my credit, but my grandmother had taught me the basics of sandwich-making. So far, I had yet to repeat another round of food poisoning. No one questioned why Velma was a perennial invitee to the Saucy Skillet competition. Me? If I entered, there would be questions—a plethora.

There was a low hum of muted conversation, muffled somewhat by the customers politely sampling the vegetable crudité. My grandmother pointed at me, gesturing for me to take over the cash register. High tea in Seaview was about to rise to a new level.

Velma left for the kitchen, and people noticed. My tuna fish sandwiches were good, but the ladies immediately stopped eating to clear away a space for the final course. They all knew about the hot hors d'oeuvres to be served next. The Cat and Fiddle Café become as silent as a church on Stewardship Sunday. Napkins were in hand, ready to go. Forks would not be needed.

The signature dish, a spicy crab popper, tasted great, and we sold out each week. Velma assumed her post in the kitchen, sauté pan in hand. She pan-steamed the vegetables used for the stuffing; the hiss of sizzling water was audible throughout the café. Velma added the crab meat to the vegetables and combined everything with a sauce. After wrapping the mixture up in puff pastry, she brushed it with egg wash. A few minutes in the 375-degree oven, and the light brown savory pastry burst with flavor.

Velma slid the spatula under each popper, removing them from the baking sheet. She arranged them in military formation on a silver serving platter garnished with brilliant turnip greens for an elegant presentation. As she prepared more poppers, I walked the still-steaming tidbits around the café, offering them to whoever wished to enjoy one. There were never any leftovers.

That day, however, I had the surprise of my life. Well, maybe not as surprising as Velma being charged with murder, but still, a surprise. I had finished taking the last of the crab poppers on their tour of the Cat and Fiddle when I felt someone tug at my apron.

I almost dropped the platter when I looked down and saw my old roommate, Francine, sitting at a two-top table with another woman. Both women were dressed smartly in matching business casual attire. I loved their shoes, but three-inch heels just wouldn't work for me; at least, not for working in the café.

Francine grabbed my hand and pulled me over.

"Winnie? Winnie Kepler? What are you doing here? I didn't know you worked here. Weren't you getting a job at some bank? Wow, it's so great to see you. What a coincidence!"

I tried not to show my embarrassment. How would I tell one of my best friends from college that my only goal in life—now, at least—was not letting the coffeepot boil down to a tar pit of sludge? This was going to be awkward.

"Francine, hi . . . um . . . hello. I didn't expect to see you here, either. Bank? You must have been talking to my grandmother. She is dead set on getting me to leave this place to work in some stuffy old office full of sticky notes and broken red staplers. But look at you, all dressed up and ready for a board meeting. What brings you to our little town of Seaview?"

"Winnie, let me introduce you to my boss, Patricia Vandellan. She graduated from State a few years before us. Isn't that awesome? And bonus, she's Phi Delta Sigma, too! Tricia has her own consulting business specializing in corporate talent acquisition. It's so awesome, and with lots of travel. The two of us work job fairs all over the country. I bet we can help you, too! That is, if you want our help. I mean, I am sure you have your situation here under control, but we might be able to move things along a little faster. Unless you like it here. And please excuse me, I am not saying this isn't a nice place—love the kitsch?—but I envisioned you as an executive, not a server in a roadside diner. Uh, no offense. Sorry."

Francine had a habit of babbling on and on, hardly taking a breath. People said she was worse than me, which I found hard to believe. Then we roomed together our sophomore year and my opinion changed. Still, I could hear my grandmother's voice in Fran's. My parents just wanted me to be happy. Was there anything wrong with that?

I could feel the tension throughout my body ratchet up as she kept on talking, mostly about their recent job fair in Richmond. I saw that her friend was trying, without success, to enter the conversation, so I decided to help out.

"Patricia, I did interview with a company called Mint Street Bankers. I received a letter back from human resources, saying I was short-listed for a nice position in marketing. Right up my alley, if you consider my studies in college, but honestly I prefer the family business here. What do you think? Should I give them another chance?"

Tricia seized the moment, putting down her drink and fluffing her hair back as if to say she was taking charge of the conversation.

"Let me guess. They'll send you an email once they have a decision, right?"

"Yes. How'd you know? That's what they said in their letter, at least. I did, in fact, like their building. Nice offices with a cafeteria on site. I suppose if the offer was good enough, I could hang up my apron here and give it a shot. And the interview went well . . ."

My confidence waned as they faced each other. They didn't have to say anything—the frown, the rolling eyes, the exasperated deep breath, stalling for time as they tried to figure out how to let me down gently. I felt like a kid caught sneaking a cookie from Santa's plate on Christmas Eve. *What* did they know?

The silence was too much for me to handle. I broke the tension, saying, "At least, I think it went well." The hesitation in my voice was unmistakable.

"Winnie, we've heard this song before. Plenty of times, in fact. If you were shuttled around from office to office in the C-suite, you were being played," Francine said.

Tricia added, "That's the problem with pretty college girls and new jobs. The old men in charge don't need you for a meaningful job in their company; they just want something nice and young to flirt with before they go home to their old, trust-fund trophy wives. And by flirt, I mean sexually harass."

As if they had practiced it, Tricia and Francine sang out, "Bless their pacemaker-powered hearts." We all giggled, knowing what the bless-your-heart idiom really meant.

"And don't forget, they also give extra points if the girl is someone who wouldn't mind being hit on at the company Christmas party," Tricia continued. "Sometimes we do ourselves no favors."

"So, you *do* know someone at Mint Street?" I had to find out if the whole interview had been a mistake. Working at the Cat and Fiddle was nice, and I could see myself doing it for a lifetime. But the siren's call of a high-paying gig in corporate circles had started to crescendo.

"Winnie, and I mean no disrespect to you or anyone, but I know some of the board members at Mint Street. If they make you an offer, take the highest salary you can negotiate and then network like crazy to get a better job somewhere else a year or two down the road. Just watch your backside. Trust me, the CEO will be watching."

This was not the news I had been hoping to hear. Learning how to cook a spicy crab popper was starting to sound appealing again.

"Francine, you said something about being able to help.

What did you have in mind?" The girls had some connections, obviously, so I decided I might as well take advantage. Networking. That's how it went in business, or so I'd been told. There could be no harm in that.

Francine took a deep breath and then smiled, knowing she had finally convinced me.

"Well, on our way back from Richmond to D.C.—that's where we have our main office—Tricia gets a phone call from a big— and I mean *really big*—client. They are looking at relocating their headquarters to southeastern Virginia, somewhere in the Hampton Roads area. They are leaning toward building right here in Seaview, to be specific, and they need people. *You* could get in on the ground floor of this new office. It's an awesome opportunity!"

"And," Tricia added, "since not everyone in this company wants to relocate, we have been asked to help fill the gaps in their personnel. So naturally, we were thinking of places we could hold a mini job fair. As we drove by, I saw this little place of yours and thought it would be the perfect location, right in the center of the town's business district. We wanted to ask if we could reserve the entire café on Thursday. And here we've discovered a connection of our own!" Tricia smiled, and I smiled back. "We'll pay you a finder's fee, of course, and compensation equal to your average Thursday revenue, plus you get the first and last conversation with the employer over coffee and biscuits."

"That is a great deal, but also a lot of work. And as much as I appreciate the inside track, it would be very difficult to pull off something of this magnitude this week. We are having some family drama you don't even want to know about. Could we make it next week?"

"I understand, dear," Tricia said. "Executive positions aren't for everyone. We can rent an empty storefront down the street." She gestured at the vacant Bailey's Family Bistro. "Fran, contact the realtor and have him open it. And hire a temp crew; we'll have ourselves a job fair in no time. Maybe your friend here could serve drinks?"

I didn't like what Fran's boss implied. After all, she didn't know me at all. Yet, I felt I had to defend myself.

"No, that's not it. I really do enjoy the work here. But if I had to take a management position, my goal would a job in marketing, in a building where I have an office with a window, maybe a plant or two. I'm a contributor and feel I bring some good stuff to the table for any company." I went for gold, hoping not to get it.

Tricia, proving she was a true professional, moved in to close the sale. "So you'll host the job fair on Thursday?" Not giving me time to answer, she continued, "Outstanding. We'll have a few meetings before then, of course. And I'm afraid it will take up a bit of your time, and you seem busy with, what did you call it? Oh, yes, family drama. But, I'll take you at your word you can do it."

Tricia refused to make eye contact again, instead opting to pour a little salt onto her square, white paper napkin. She placed her tea glass on top, lifting it a few times to ensure that the napkin did not stick to the condensation on the bottom of the glass. A delaying tactic. I could tell she was very good at the soft sell: finding what motivated people and then using urgency as a way of putting the screws on someone to get approval. Before I could answer, Tricia looked at me defiantly, flipping her hair again, and daring me to say something other than *thank you.*

I snapped my little black order binder closed and held it about a foot above the table top. The corners of my mouth pulled back into a smile as I simply let go. The pop of the binder hitting the tabletop caused more than a few heads to turn. One nearby woman gasped, thinking I was about to give a rude customer *what she deserved.* Two men at the counter gambled a ten dollar bill each, eagerly awaiting my move.

It was past time to take control of the negotiation. Looking Patricia square in the eye, I announced, "Tell you what we'll do. You get the Cat and Fiddle on Thursday for the average revenue determined by the receipts from the previous ten Thursdays. My grandmother and I will work the room so you and Francine can run herd on the big dogs from your sponsor. I'll take thirty minutes up front with the hiring manager and an hour after the event. As for prep meetings, I'll also give you sixty, no, make that thirty minutes. Each day, Monday, Tuesday, and Wednesday, to review the status of the event. This is a take-it-or-leave-it deal."

I wasn't sure if I could exhale. Or if I should.

Tricia smiled. "Frannie, we found our girl. The company wanted someone who wouldn't take any crap, and it seems your friend Winnie here fits the bill." She extended her hand as a sort of peace offering. "I'll shake on your offer, Miss Kepler. And maybe you will end up with that office with a window, *and* a plant in the corner by the time this is all done."

I liked how she called me *Miss Kepler.*

A firm hand grasp sealed the agreement. After a few subsequent hugs, Fran and Tricia left to find suitable accommodations for the week. While they may have been satisfied with the outcome of our negotiations, I was still skeptical. Had I just played into my grandmother's plan to move me from the cash register to the corporate board room?

6

Velma came out of the kitchen, holding a tray of nasty-looking, burned hockey pucks. "This your work, Winnie? I taught you how to bake cookies better than that, yes?"

"Grandma, that is my first try at black bean burgers. It looks like I need to work on more elevation. Next time I'll add more flour, maybe an extra egg, and then I think I'll top it with some fried red seaweed. Tastes like bacon, you know."

Everyone at the service counter laughed at my bacon comment. The man nearest me snatched his five-dollar tip from the counter saying, "You make a veggie burger with fake bacon, one that tastes like real bacon, and I'll triple this tip. Can't be done."

"You're on!" I might have been a novice cook, but I could figure anything out if someone was foolish enough to tell me I could *not* do it. I plucked the greenback from his paw. "Thanks for the down payment on my winnings."

After the majority of the customers had finished, I took a break long enough to speak to Velma about the upcoming job fair. As we were putting the clean dishes away, I found to my surprise that she was in favor of the idea.

"Thursdays were always slow, business-wise," she said. "And I think a college graduate like you *shouldn't* be satisfied just running a small-town diner for the rest of her life."

"I like it here, Grandma. You know that, right?" I tried putting up a good front. "But if you think I should take the best offer at this job fair, I'll give it serious consideration." I was a terrible liar.

We walked to the scullery, a traditional name for what the casual observer would call the dishwashing room. Velma always cleaned as she cooked, a skill and dedication I had yet to master. A few pots and pans were the only items left to clean and stow away.

I noticed that my grandmother moved slower than her normal fast shuffle. She meandered on purpose, pausing to speak, and then stopping, as if unable to find the right words. She picked up a wooden spoon as she faced me. Velma flicked the utensil at me twice. If she wanted my attention, she had it.

"Winnie, you are destined for great things. Not sure what they are, but they will be so much better than the choices presented to me when I was your age. Who knows? You may just like what you find. And if it doesn't work out, the room upstairs will always be there."

Surprise! No wooden spoon beat-down or looks of disappointment. Not even a guilt trip. What could I say? I gave her a hug. "Grandma, you always say the nicest things." I didn't normally get sentimental, but I think a tear formed.

Then Velma got all philosophical. She took my hand with both of hers and whispered. "Sometimes, what we *want* is not what we *need*." Was she referring to what I thought I wanted? Or what she knew I needed?

Velma hung up her apron on a plastic hook on the wall. She finished her grandmotherly advice with a cryptic, "It helps if our eyes are open wide enough to see it. Whatever *it* is."

Thanks, Grandma. What the heck is that supposed to mean?

A few minutes later, the last customers of the day had left. Before we locked the café for the night, the front door opened. It was Parker, still in uniform. I noticed right away the handcuffs were out of their pouch.

Stepping between my grandmother and the man with a

badge, I asked, "What are you doing here? Has the VCID finished their work at the fairgrounds?" I couldn't help but continue staring at the shiny shackles dangling from his hand. Velma excused herself to the kitchen so we could speak in private.

Parker straightened his tie. I didn't know if he was using the accessory as a way to look more official, or if he couldn't fathom how to tie a decent Windsor knot. But once he determined his ensemble was in good order, he resumed his task.

He reached into his back pocket, producing a small notebook, and then pulled a pen out of his front shirt pocket. Parker's hands trembled. His attempt to balance everything in his hands while writing failed as he dropped the handcuffs.

The clang brought about another noise, this one from something scurrying from underneath the beverage station, out into the dining room, between my legs, up *and* down Parker's uniform, with a short interlude swinging around Parker's belt, and finally out the door. Parker was now as stiff as an Egyptian mummy.

I laughed, saying, "Tinkers! It's okay."

Parker exhaled. "Winnie, the cat can wait. I have to tell you, this wasn't my idea. I argued against it, but the Captain gave me an order. In fact, he will call me back any minute now."

"An order? And what order would that be?" I refocused on the situation, this time with a gut feeling that I already knew the answer.

"Once Captain Larson gets the paperwork in order, I'll be forced to take your grandmother into custody for the murder of Pierre St. Pierre."

"Are you kidding me? There's no *real* evidence, just one statement. I think the video is misleading."

My frustration meter surged into the red zone, but I didn't want to let Parker see me upset. "Let's think about this, shall we?" I gave him a smile and a wink, hoping to lower his defenses.

I sauntered up to the man, my chest almost touching his. My fingers crept up his shirt like a gentle spider, then latched onto the man's shirt collar. I looked up, forcing Parker to maintain eye contact. So far, so good.

"Officer Williams, are you saying that based on a flimsy premise thrown around by a creepy television producer, you are here to arrest my grandmother? She's as honest as they come; a regular church-goer. And above all, she's innocent. That should count for something, right?"

Velma was walking back in from the kitchen carrying a tray covered by a kitchen towel. She had caught the tail end of the conversation.

"Don't worry, Winnie. I expected this turn of events. This is the standard procedure. Do I need to pack an overnight bag? Oh, and anyone seen Tinkers? I have a treat for her."

"Ma'am," he said, "I have to inform you that once I place you under arrest, you will have the right to remain silent." Parker droned on, reciting the Miranda rights from a small card he carried in his shirt pocket. "Do you understand your rights, as I have stated them this evening?"

Velma smiled. She was always smiling as if she knew what people would say and do. She never once looked worried. Her head remained high, her hands calm, steady as a surgeon's. Velma's feet were shoulder-width apart and her toes were pointing inward, giving the woman a commanding stance.

Parker's body language spoke volumes, too. He wasn't standing up straight. His eyes kept looking up and down, left, right, never finding that comfort zone of a point of focus needed to communicate well. Parker's shifting body steamed of *conflict* on two feet. He was not being very successful in his attempt to satisfy both an intimidating police captain and me.

Velma surprised us all when she uncovered the tray, producing a baker's dozen of fresh cookies right out of the oven, little wisps of steam rising from each. My stomach rumbled as Velma said, "Well, if I'm not under arrest at this moment, you can have cookies and I can still say what I want, right?"

Parker hunched his shoulders. "I guess so. It's a free country, as they say."

"Yes it is, so I say that I would like to be excused to visit the powder room. It's right over there." Velma motioned to a set of two doors in the back of the room. "You can stand guard at the door if you would like, officer. Oh, and please, help yourself to the cookies. They aren't poisoned."

Velma and I both laughed, leaving poor Parker wondering whether my grandmother was kidding. I gave him the same shrugged-shoulder routine, not helping him at all.

After Velma and I chuckled, I looked at Parker and said, "Oh, have a cookie, for goodness sake." I found my cell phone and pressed button after button, trying to web-search an attorney. The Seaview criminal justice system was a new subject for me, and this problem was not like cramming for an exam in home economics. No, this was life or death, and I needed help.

It was late and I couldn't find any law offices open for business. I was certain the nearest bail bondsman was across the water in Virginia Beach, a long drive to make under such circumstances. But I'd go, if it meant I could get the help.

I noticed Parker opening the clasp of one handcuff. That set me off. I had tolerated the charade long enough. I slammed down my phone and demanded an explanation.

"Parker, how *could* you?"

"Winnie, I don't want to. I *have* to. Captain Larson got a call from the magistrate. The Commonwealth's Attorney received enough information from his preliminary report to force an arrest warrant. But I understand the judge will let her come back home after processing. Believe me, we don't want your grandmother in jail, either. At least, I don't."

On her way to the restroom, my grandmother had heard me tell off Parker. She stopped short of the door to pass on one more bit of wisdom.

"It will be all right, Winnie. The truth always prevails. But if you want to call someone, try to call Doc Jones. You remember him from when you came to visit as a kid, right? He and your grandfather took you and the other kids to the park to pick blackberries? He'll know just what to do. Tell him it's just like old times."

"Doc Jones? The man's almost ninety, Grandma. What can he do for you?"

"He'll know. Trust me. And no matter what happens tonight, don't lose sight of your young man there. He's going places. Knows what's right and stands his ground to protect it. Not half bad-looking, either. A keeper, I think."

Parker blushed, the only thing saving him from total embarrassment being the cell phone—his, not mine—buzzing. It was the Captain, asking if he had taken Velma into custody yet. Parker stumbled, trying to explain the delay.

"No, sir. Not yet. You told me to wait until you got the official warrant. Remember?" A few moments of silence followed. "I understand, sir, but I don't think that's legal, is it?"

Now I could hear the voice on the other end of the conversation. Yelling. Definite yelling. Parker had the look of a dog with its tail between its legs.

"Yes, sir," Parker said. "I understand, sir. No, sir. No problem at all, sir. Yes, sir." Before he could say another word, he cupped his hand over the phone to keep the conversation private. However, it was too late, and we both knew it.

There was no mistaking the Captain's intent. We had all heard the direct orders being repeated over and over from the phone's tiny speaker. Parker stood up straight, clicking the back of his heels together and locked his free hand down at the seam of his trousers. "Right away. Yes, sir. No, sir. Yes, sir. Five minutes. Yes, sir."

I could tell the answer was hollow just by looking at Parker's eyes. That and the insubordinate smirk that graced his countenance. Perhaps my grandmother had been right?

Not wanting to take any chances, I grasped his arm with just enough force to draw Parker back to reality. "Parker, you can't mean he gave you five minutes to arrest my grandmother? I need more time. I have to find Doc Jones *and* a lawyer. Can't you wait for a few more minutes, Parker? Please?" I did not like to beg. It wasn't in my DNA.

Parker held his palms out showing he had nothing to offer. "Winnie, you heard the man. He'll call back in a few minutes once he has the warrant in hand. Then I *will* have to arrest your grandmother. But like I said, she'll be processed and then released to await arraignment. I think this will end up going to a grand jury anyway, and they will drop the charges based on a lack of solid evidence. Your grandmother was right, this is more of a procedural thing. Nothing personal. At least, I hope you don't hold me responsible for all of this. You don't, do you?"

I needed Parker's help, so it was not time to tell him how wrong he was acting. I ignored his somewhat rhetorical question. Velma was a smart cookie, and she always chose her words carefully. I could not help but think she was trying to give me a clue. To what, I did not know, but why mention an old physician who had nothing to do with any of the events of the day?

And Parker was a keeper?

If I could get Velma out of this immediate trouble, I would not have much time before I would need to face the next big problem, that being the job fair at the Cat and Fiddle on Thursday. What if the judge decided Velma needed to stay locked up until bail could be posted? I had a few dollars saved up, but not enough to get someone out of a murder charge. And I had turned into a decent server, but I wasn't certain I could handle a full rush at the café by myself.

The clock on the wall struck half past seven. It had been about five minutes since Velma went into the restroom and I got worried. Parker wanted to make sure everything was okay, too. He asked me to check on her.

When I returned, my exuberant happiness told rookie officer Parker Williams a story he did not want to hear. Before he could check the restroom for windows and back doors, his omniscient cell phone buzzed again. He took a deep breath, knowing this would not be pleasant.

"No, sir. Not yet. No, that's not it. Um, well, no. It's just that I think she may have escaped. Um, yes, that's right. I said *escaped.*"

Our victory may have been small, but it was sweet. If there were ever a time to have cupcakes for a late-night snack, this would have been it.

Poor Parker.

I giggled. Velma had done it again! Now I needed to figure out where she went.

7

Velma's request to find Doc Jones had me lost and confused. More than normal, some might say. My grandmother, an old woman who loved to go to the big city of Virginia Beach and walk the shopping malls with a cane, had somehow escaped police apprehension by excusing herself to use the ladies' room.

Parker did a systematic, by-the-book investigation, looking for avenues of escape from within the restroom. There were no side or back doors, just the front one, and there were no windows, either. It was like the woman had vanished into thin air. What concerned me more, however, was the fact she had gone on the lam instead of letting the evidence, or lack thereof, speak for itself in a court of law. Maybe I was naïve? And how did she do it? Even I could not figure this one out.

I had it in my mind to ask her, once I found her, if her behavior was a good example for the rest of us. If I had done something similar when I was a kid, I would have been grounded for a year. Then again, Grandma always seemed to have a plan. I hoped it didn't involve stowing away on a banana freighter heading to Honduras.

Parker had just received an earful. After his phone call, my knight in khaki cotton armor asked me if the café was hiring. Given the sarcastic and threatening tone of Captain Larson, he must have thought his job was no longer on the line; instead, his employment status was so far past the line, he couldn't even *see* the stupid line anymore. With Velma missing and his boss fuming down at the station, my Parker was left with no one else to talk to except yours truly. That's when I brought up the job fair on Thursday.

Did I really just think of him as *my* Parker?

"First, let me tell you, I don't know where my grandmother has gone. But, I am sure she has a superb reason for leaving. Remember, she's well over sixty so when you find her, excessive force will not—I say again, will not—be needed. Do we have an understanding? She's a kind, sweet granny, so be careful. No rough stuff. Got it?"

He nodded in agreement before I had finished speaking. I loved his concerned look, but I still put up the tough-girl front.

Parker felt the heat, taking out a handkerchief from his pocket to wipe his forehead. "I'll let the other guys know. I wish she hadn't run, though. Now she can be charged with evading, too."

I told him the evasion charge wouldn't withstand the scrutiny of a judge. Captain Larson would have to explain how a feeble woman evaded his mighty force using their formidable dragnet.

Parker missed the point. "It'll only get worse the longer she stays out. Do you have any idea who she may visit? That cold wind coming off the Chesapeake can seep right into your bones. I'd hate to see your grandmother hiding outside in the elements."

"Well, why don't you tell your fellow officers to turn off the new über-high-def flat-screen television in the Captain's office and go find her? She drives nothing faster than a golf cart these days. Just how far do you think she could have gone?"

"Captain Larson has a new flat-screen? HD, too? I didn't know that. How'd you know that?"

"I know a lot of things, Parker, from hearing customers at the restaurant. The delivery men who brought the television to the station house came in for a bite to eat the other day. They complained all the way through dessert about remounting it because someone, your Captain Larson, couldn't decide where to put it. They said something about his badge being stuck up his butt. I could have heard it wrong?"

Parker laughed. "That's funny. But J.B. is a good boss. I'm not sure why he acted the way he did, though."

I couldn't let him off the hook. Now was the time to set him on his best course of action.

"Parker, I'm not trying to tell you how to do your job, but find Velma. A vicious, calculating fried chicken killer or not, she's my grandmother. That should count for something. Now, about that call?"

"Good idea, Winnie. I'll ask everyone at the station to look for her. If J.B. asks, I'll tell him your grandmother is out there somewhere. Not sure where, yet, but at least we know she's not here. But please, let me know if she comes back. Promise?"

Parker didn't wait for an answer, instead turning to leave. He had to come back twice—first to retrieve his hat, second to pick up his keys. I did my best to keep a stern face. He was so cute trying to impress me.

With Parker away, I grabbed a broom and tapped on the ceiling. It had taken me a while, but I had figured out what Velma had been trying to tell me as she made her getaway.

"Grandma, it's safe to come down. He's gone."

A shuffling of footsteps could be heard upstairs. A few seconds later, Velma reemerged from the restroom. "I was hoping you had remembered the escape route."

"At first I had forgotten, but when you said picking blackberries, the memories came back. I loved the stories about the café's secret history during the Prohibition days."

"Yes, old Doc Jones, who wasn't so old back then, would gather us younger kids and take us down to the park to pick berries," Velma recalled. "He was only a teenager, but he did not want us to see the bathtub gin your great-grandparents had flowing through the joint. By the time we came back, there was not a stitch of evidence the place had ever been a temporary speakeasy. When I was old enough to keep a secret, my mother showed me the bootleggers' escape hatch in the ladies' room."

My memory of the whole story was missing a few details, and my curiosity was spilling over the brim. "It's the mirror, yes?"

Velma just winked at me and walked back into the restroom. I had to follow. This cloak-and-dagger stuff was so much better than the Porter's Five Forces model of corporate competition. My business marketing advisor was correct when he said *college isn't for everyone.*

Velma lifted the octagonal lid off an old canister of face powder sitting on the vanity. Using her free hand, she traced the ornate frame surrounding the wall mirror, stopping at a section where some of the wood had fallen away with age. The carved top fit the missing intarsia like a key in a lock.

Giving it a counterclockwise twist, I could hear a set of springs and gears turning within the wall. With a subtle *ping*, a wall panel next to the mirror slid open, revealing a hidden staircase descending into darkness. I could feel a rush of cool air.

Looking inside, I noticed there were different shades of dark. "Are there two passageways? How did I not know we had a basement?"

Pointing downward, she said, "Not a basement, Winnie, but one route leading back upstairs, and another connected to an old labyrinth built when Prohibition started. If the revenuers raided one place, the booze shifted to another establishment. The agents just gave up after a while; some of them even joined the clubs. They were human, too, you know."

My grandmother had a good point. "I guess not every police officer is a jerk," I said, making a mental note to apologize to Parker later for ordering him around. Velma and I tiptoed up to our rooms via the way-cool secret passage. I had lived above the café for about a year, but finally felt at home, knowing Velma was safe and in the next room.

8

The morning sun poured into the upstairs windows above the Cat and Fiddle, the brightness hitting me in the eyes and forcing me out of bed. There was a lot of work to get done. I walked down the creaky wooden stairs and entered the kitchen, trying to be quiet so as not to wake Velma. But as I passed by her room, I noticed she wasn't there. I finally found her just inside the hidden passageway, sleeping soundly wrapped inside a warm quilt on a camping cot. Probably a precaution in case J.B. decided to raid the place.

With some potatoes and onions now frying on the flat-top grill, I checked the prep work for the lunch run. Customers came first, but Velma's murder charge, however, still worried me. I had to get into each event; there was a murderer in the bunch somewhere. I had to find him. Or her. Or them.

I added a touch of diced garlic, and rough-chopped red and green bell peppers. It smelled superb in the Cat and Fiddle. A reheated pan of yesterday's dinner special, a black bean, jalapeno, and olive tapenade, completed the meal. My breakfast bowl special was a favorite among truckers, fishermen, and unsuspecting tourists.

While I waited for the spattering oil to subside, I considered the other suspects. Even if George Harrison Windsor *and* Cosmo

Finnegan had stabbed Pierre St. Pierre in the back, it was wrong. It didn't matter that everyone else seemed happy the arrogant chef was dead; a side dish of murder was still a crime.

I ladled a heap of taters and tapenade into a bowl. A soft *pit-pat* of slippers caressed the wooden floor behind me. It was Velma, dressed for the day except for her bunny slippers. I wasn't sure, but the informal footwear may have violated the state health code. But I would have felt ridiculous reporting it.

Excuse me, I would like to report unauthorized cute, fuzzy bunny slippers. No, they don't come with carrots!

Nope. That would not happen. Ever.

"Would you like a breakfast feast, Grandma? Gets the ol' blood pumping in the morning. Better than coffee, I'd say."

"That sounds delightful, dear, but you will have to deliver. I can't step out much further without coming into view. The police think I escaped, but if I know J.B., he'll have an officer in an unmarked car watching the house to see if I doubled back."

I walked over to the deep sink and washed a juice glass. Through the window, I could see an off-white sedan, exhaust drifting up from the tail pipe.

"It looks like you have an admirer, Grandma. Should we send him some breakfast? I bet he's cold. Where's that hot sauce?" I relished blowing the undercover cop's stakeout. It would serve him right. I reached for an extra spoonful of chili powder for good measure.

Velma sat at the foot of the stairs. "You feed the poor man and distract him for a few minutes. I'll head over to the pantry and finish the prep work so you can have more time to investigate. Once the coast is clear, let me know and I'll retreat upstairs. Later on I'll call my friend Mr. Larson and say I'm lost in Maryland. That'll keep him busy for the rest of the day. We should be back in business together by dinner."

Awkward?

Yes.

"Job offer to Miss Kepler postponed until her appeal."

Oh, yeah. That'll make a great first entry in my employment file.

Right.

Not.

Velma gave me a half-hug and two air kisses, one on each cheek. "Listen, this will all work out. There's nothing to worry about." She turned away from me, hoping I would not see her scribble down instructions for watering the plants.

I snatched up the paper. "Nothing to worry about? Then why do I need to spritz the orchids at sunrise and prune the roses if they get too bushy? Is that even a word? Bushy? Methinks you are more concerned than you let on, Grandma. What gives?"

Velma put down the pen. Hands on her hips, she let it all out.

"I am sorry you have gotten mixed up in all of this mess. All I wanted to do was cook my fried chicken on a stick and bake my apple pie. And, I didn't even need all those silly apples that Pierre took. He was just being an idiot. But still, even being an idiot was nothing to get upset over; no reason to kill him."

We hugged again, this time a full-on embrace. I had a definite tear in one eye, mist in the other.

"Grandma, you *know* I've never thought you killed the guy. But let me ask you, who among the other chefs would have a reason to kill Pierre?" *Someone* killed that poor guy. The only way to prove my grandmother innocent was to prove someone else guilty.

Grandma raised her hand like the kid in the front row of class, the one who always knew the answer. "I've got it! You are visiting the Seagull's Nest today, right? Two of my fellow competitors work there and both have their reasons to want to see Pierre St. Pierre dead." Velma paused, and then whispered, "They have very, very good reasons."

I knew that George Harrison Windsor and Pierre had gone to the same local culinary school, and how Pierre finished at the top of the class. As I searched the shelf for the cayenne pepper bottle, I asked, "Do you suppose George is still harboring a grudge because he finished second in culinary school to Pierre?"

"Oh, there's a lot more to that story, Winnie. And yes, the grudge is still there. In fact, it has grown over the past several years. They wouldn't even walk on the same side of the street if they saw each other. Comical, in a sad sort of way."

I fried up another skillet of potatoes, this time sprinkling a heavy dose of cayenne on top and adding a few pieces of crispy bacon. No officer in his right mind would turn down bacon. After tossing on a handful of shredded cheddar cheese and spooning a few glops of salsa on the side, I deemed the dish tasty and fit for the unwelcome observer.

"This ought to warm up the squad car, in more ways than one," I said.

Food in hand, I approached the car. Though the windows were fogged with condensation, I saw the driver scrunch down in the front seat.

I tapped on the driver's-side window glass. "Excuse me, you looked cold out here so I brought you something warm for breakfast."

No response. The driver slumped over to feign sleeping.

"Hey! Guy! I have food for you. Just take it. I won't tell your captain."

The man raised his head, yawned, and then lifted himself back into a full upright position. The window, still opaque with moisture, rolled downward. My jaw almost hit the ground.

"Parker! What are you doing here? Were you stalking me?"

"Winnie, it's not what you think. Well, it sort of is, but not the stalking part. The Captain thought your grandmother may have come back during the night and he wanted an officer here to arrest her on the spot. So I volunteered."

I thought about dropping the food in his lap. "I don't know why the Captain is so stinking hard-headed and set to put my grandmother behind bars, but he is wrong. Just plain wrong. And what's more, I think you know it. Look, I know we really just met, but I'd appreciate a little help before our first date."

Speechless, Parker looked at his radio, then back at me. The smell of the food finally grabbed his attention.

"Here," I said. "I brought you some hot breakfast. I'll get you some water in a few minutes, if you like. You'll need it." I took a few deep breaths to regain a sense of calm.

Parker looked up at me, and with a deep voice resonating with clarity, he stated, "I chose a side, Winnie. Last night. That's why I am here, instead of one of the other guys. They're all good officers, but the last thing I wanted was—well, here I am."

"So you never intended on arresting my grandmother this morning?"

"I didn't even bring the paperwork."

"But what about Captain Larson? Won't he get suspicious if

he finds the arrest warrant back at the station?"

"He won't find it. Winnie, there is something I need to tell you about Captain Larson. I found out why he has been so intent on putting your grandmother in jail."

"Don't tell me he had an affair with Velma at one point. I don't think I could handle news like that this early in the morning."

"No, but this issue goes all the way back to when they were in high school."

"Parker, they were in high school a lifetime ago. Who keeps a chip on their shoulder for almost half a century?"

"You'd be surprised. It gets worse. The problem began during their senior year in high school. There was a small confrontation between the Captain and your grandmother during the senior prom. Since then, while the two have lived in the same town, they have been very far apart from each other."

"Are you sure about all of this? I mean, the Captain stops by the Cat and Fiddle for a meal almost every evening. That doesn't sound like the act of a man with a skeleton in his closet. And my grandfather proposed to Velma during that dance. I've heard the story a million times. Funny, no one mentioned anything about a fight, though."

"I think he stops by just to let her know that he remembers and is still keeping tabs on her, waiting for her to slip up. The Captain is obsessed with keeping the secret."

Parker shoved in spoonful after spoonful of the tasty breakfast between quips about the history between his boss and my grandmother. "I've said too much already. Your grandmother can tell you the rest of the story. It's really her place to explain, not mine."

"Why are you telling me this now, Parker? What changed?"

"Last night, at the station, Captain Larson argued with his current girlfriend over the phone. He's not one to embrace technology, and he accidentally left the phone on speaker. Everyone in the station heard more than we should have. She accused him of holding a torch for Velma. That's when he came clean about how he felt about your grandmother. It wasn't a pretty picture after that. I'm confident his girlfriend is history now, but the important thing was this: once I heard the facts, I knew Captain Larson had pencil-whipped the arrest warrant."

"So the truth of the matter is, if I understand you correctly, the arrest warrant for my grandmother is not a legal document?"

"You would be *almost* correct, Winnie. It is a legal document, but one based on the Captain's version of the truth. The city is now in a losing situation. If I arrest your grandmother based on that warrant, the truth will come out in court and not only will she be freed, but any decent lawyer could get her to sue the city for wrongful arrest, denial of civil rights, abuse of power, and possibly even elder abuse."

"And if you don't arrest her? What then?"

"I will be fired. And if that happens, I'll get the same attorney and sue for wrongful termination. So as you can see, at face value there doesn't seem to be a way out of this that won't involve a nasty trial, bad publicity, and result in at least one reputation ruined . . . Thanks for the taters. Love the salsa. What's in it?"

"I'll tell you after all of this is over. I guess I owe you one, Parker. Sorry for the attitude. But what happened to the warrant? You mentioned the Captain wouldn't find it. Did you destroy it?"

"No, it's still a legal document. But, I did what any self-respecting police officer would do when confronted with an illegal situation within the department."

"You gave it to Internal Affairs?"

"You have been watching too much television, Winnie. We have one Captain, five officers, and three patrol cars, two of which work sporadically. So no, involving IA does not exist for us here. There is no IA in Seaview."

"Which means what? What did you do with the arrest warrant? Eat it?"

"No, silly. I typed up a statement regarding what I heard the Captain say inside the confines of the station. Sent everything to the VCID in Richmond. They can weigh the evidence and decide if an abuse of power has occurred."

"Oh, Parker. Are you sure that was the right move? You could have opened a big can of worms."

Parker looked away, embarrassed.

"Parker, that's wonderful. I am so proud of you. This puts a whole new spin on things."

Grandma was right. Parker Williams was a keeper. I didn't know how long I'd keep him, but I would hold on to him at least until my grandmother was safe. After that? We'd have to see what developed. I had hope and was all smiles.

He was still shy about regaining eye contact. I tried to boost his spirits, saying, "And it's no reason to hang your head so low. We'll get through this just fine." I decided it was time to shake things up. I leaned in through the window and gave him a quick peck on the cheek.

I thought Parker would have been happy to receive the kiss, but his eyes rolled back in disbelief. He lurched his head downward. *Gads, was I that repulsive?* Then I understood his response. He pointed at my midsection, saying, "Winnie, I think your cell phone is buzzing."

In all the excitement, I had forgotten about the phone clipped to my belt. Now standing still, I could feel the vibration. The caller ID mocked me by showing I had once again missed an annoying call from the fine people at Mint Street Bankers.

"I never expected a call *this* early in the day. I should just call them back and explain everything was a mistake caused by my well-intentioned grandmother. Surely they have grandmothers. They'd understand, right?"

He gave me the old hunched-up shoulders routine.

"I'm staying out of it, Winnie. Once this legal mess is over, I'd like to ask you out on a date, so the last thing I want to do is get in between you and your closest living relative."

"Says the man who came to arrest her."

"Ahem, fraudulent warrant? Ring a bell?"

After a resounding *hmmpft*, I tried to return the call but it went to a generic voice mail system. And since I didn't know *the extension of your party*, I could not *press the number now*. I put the phone away.

With a straight face, I looked at Parker. "I'll just have to be ready next time. Not a big deal. Hopefully they'll stop calling. Regardless, I'm not taking any job where the men in charge expect my heels to be higher than my IQ."

He thanked me again for the food and said that if Velma returned, she should stay out of sight for a while. The engine throttled down as Parker shifted into drive.

I blew him another kiss as he drove off. I turned around to return to the diner only to see my grandmother at the front window. She was laughing and making childish faces at me. I could feel the love.

Some decisions, like whether to keep my diet or give in and get a scoop of ice cream with a fresh-baked brownie, were easy. But what to do about the potential new job, the current job at the café, and now Parker? There were no simple solutions.

Yes, there were, actually. My business career could wait. I needed to concentrate on helping my grandmother and building my relationship with Parker. Nothing else mattered at the moment.

The first test of my resolve didn't take long in coming. As I walked back across the street, my phone buzzed again. I stopped. The caller ID *Lonely Kitty* glared back at me from the glass screen. Francine, my old roommate, had acquired the unusual nickname when she applied for a job at a lounge of the same name, thinking it was an animal spa and boarding house. That wasn't the case.

"Winnie, is nine still a good time for a meeting?"

"Um, I'm sorry. What were you saying? I mean, I couldn't hear you. I, well, I was expecting someone different."

"Thanks for the ego lift, girl. I love you, too. Tricia has been on the phone all morning. She keeps mentioning big dollar figures. So, is nine good?"

I had no answer.

"Winnie? Are you there?"

I felt like crying. On the one hand, I had just learned that my almost-boyfriend liked me enough to put his career on the line for my family. I also just missed a call that could have led to a well-financed albeit unintended career in business. The last thing I needed was the time-consuming distraction of an old friend coming into town, taking over my restaurant, and forcing me to suck up to a total stranger.

I didn't know how I would get out of this one. Anyone want a grilled cheese? That I could handle. Not much else at the moment. *Where's Tinkers when you need her?*

Grandmothers are good for a lot of little things—hugs, rhubarb pie, sage advice—that get you through life. I remembered mine saying, "You don't always have to agree with your friends. You just need to remember there was a good reason they became your friends in the first place." She was right. Francine was one of those good friends.

"I'm sorry, Fran. When was the meeting time again?"

"Nine, if you can swing it."

"No worries, Fran. Nine it is. But I still have to limit you to a half-hour. I need to finish setting up everything for lunch, and I plan on being over at the Seagull's Nest by eleven."

I hated the fact I couldn't spend more time catching up with the old roomie, but with my belief in my grandmother's innocence came knowing that the real killer was still out there. Somewhere.

9

I walked to the office and set the agenda for the planning meeting. Maybe start with a serving of sweet potato biscuits? Add tea? No. Coffee? Tea was more for the afternoon. I could cook up a frittata, perhaps? Or something off the regular menu? Whatever I did, time was running short, and I needed to do something. I could always get a box of donuts from the gas station down the road.

But, it would be poor form to have any meeting without at least a tidbit of Cat and Fiddle goodness to share. And nothing against the gas station, but I would not serve their donuts. Who knew how long those babies had been sitting inside a hot truck? Could have been days.

My indecision cost me. Now there wasn't even enough time for a simple French toast casserole, even though I had yet to meet a person who did not like mine. The point was moot since the muffin pans were calling my name. A-ha! French Toast Casserole Muffins! Perfect!

These muffin pans weren't the typical ones one would find at home. These were brushed steel, commercial kitchen pans yielding three dozen muffins at a time. Every time I lifted one, I made a mental note to spend more time at the gym. I needed something a little more wieldy.

The mini-muffin pans had been staying silent, hoping not to be noticed one shelf down. But once I saw them sitting there, I knew smaller muffins would be just as tasty as the big ones. With the clock ticking, I could crank out a few pans, more than enough for the three of us. Mini-muffins for everyone, I thought, and with luck, we would have leftovers for a late-morning snack. Bonus!

Off the pantry shelves I picked the needed ingredients: potato bread, white and light brown sugar, cinnamon, nutmeg, and vanilla. It all went into the basket. Then, after a bit of searching, I found the butter and fresh eggs hiding in the cooler, behind the heavy cream I took out. I wanted to add one more ingredient, cayenne pepper. But when I pulled the spice jar out of the rack, it was empty. I had already used all of it for the new police-officer-stalking-me breakfast special. *How could we be out of such a common ingredient? Who stocks this pantry? Oh. Never mind. I plead the fifth!*

Crushed red peppers? No, too much. I reached for the coriander. A different effect, but still powerful enough to put some *umami* into the muffins. But then I found a can of minced jalapeño peppers. I tasted one and decided enough was enough. Fran was a friend. Why pack too much extra heat into a sweet muffin like these?

With regular muffins safely rising inside the oven, I arranged three settings at the larger round table in the front corner—our most popular table, since it faced the picture window.

The smell of warm muffins had wafted through the air just as Francine and Tricia walked up. I didn't know how the day would unfold, but I had a positive feeling things would go our way now. Muffins right out of the oven, slathered with a spoonful or two of warm maple syrup, can elicit such feelings. You can't argue with maple syrup. I wouldn't even try.

Without realizing it, however, as Fran and her friend Tricia walked in the door, my left hand brushed up against that dang cell phone. I couldn't seem to get away from the device. The only solution was to turn it off. There would be time later to check for calls from Mint Street.

"Good morning, Fran *and* Tricia. How was the stay at the hotel?"

"No hotel this time," Francine said. "We ended up at a bed-and-breakfast down the road, the Seagull's Nest. The décor was *very* nice; and our room was to die for."

Would they have chosen the Seagull's Nest if they had known the chef was a killer? And if not him, his pot-scrubbing assistant? My cynical side was resurfacing and about to get the best of me. *Crap. Maybe it was a team effort?* I filed the new suspicion away back into the inner reaches of my brain.

"It's a wonderful place, from what I hear," I said. "Have you had breakfast yet? I've made muffins for us, if you would like some."

Tricia took in a deep breath. The smile on her face told me to bring out the platter of French toast muffins. Both visitors couldn't help but salivate at the fresh-out-of-the-oven treats.

"Winnie, I hope you didn't go to too much trouble in making these, but they smell awesome," Francine said. "The Seagull's Nest had breakfast, too, but to be honest, it wasn't all that good. The cook there puts too much salt in everything, especially the pancakes. Even the tea tasted salty."

I had never eaten George's cooking. He placed so well in the culinary school, I assumed he must have had at least a semi-decent set of cooking chops. And salt was one of my favorite seasonings, too, but I used it only to enhance the flavors, not overtake them.

"I'm sorry your breakfast experience wasn't the best, Fran." To restart her day on a better note, I tempted her with the fresh muffins and tea diffusers loaded with an assortment of imported flavors. "These should help. And how about some fresh tea?"

Francine chose a nice cinnamon tea and lifted her cup so I could pour the hot water from the kettle. Tricia declined, saying "Thank you very much, but I'm not a tea drinker."

"I should have known better," I replied. "You must be a coffee drinker, a Starbucks regular I imagine. I can make a pot if you'd like some. Not as pungent as their dark roast, but still packing a nice aroma. Unless you have already had some?"

I stopped my speech for a moment, looking at Tricia. "Of course, you've had some already. This morning, yes? Within the past half-hour. Glass of water, then?"

"No thanks on the water, Miss Kepler. But to affirm your statement, yes, I have already had my usual cup this morning. We had to drive across the bridge to Virginia Beach just to get it, though. Well worth it, in my humble opinion. I can't get going without my grande double shot soy light mocha cappuccino with extra whipped cream." She then asked me if it had been a lucky guess or was there an unexpected chocolate stain on her blouse somewhere.

I giggled, since it was obvious with the matching slacks, top, and scarf that Tricia was a person who took much pride in her appearance and her wardrobe. Her dry cleaner hadn't dealt with a stain on her clothing in years. I looked at the raw egg splatter on my black work shoes. *Maybe she wouldn't notice; hopefully she wouldn't judge.*

"Oh, no. Your blouse is fine," I said with all sincerity. "And it looks like you coordinated your outfits. That's awesome. Or is that a company uniform or something?"

The two women looked at each other. I knew there must be an inside joke going on here, but alas, I was still on the outside.

"Winnie, you certainly are perceptive. How'd you know we went over to the Starbucks? Do you have spies everywhere?" Francine used a tone of voice that made light of our conversation, until she realized her friend Tricia was genuinely interested in how perceptive I was.

I gave Tricia a wink. "To-go nose."

"What?" Tricia pulled her compact out of her purse and opened the mirror. She turned it several angles, trying to discern what I had observed. The vanity switch was always a good one to flip.

"It's nothing. Most people would never notice, so there's no need to put on a whole new face," I said. "It's just a tiny little red skin prick on the tip of your nose. Gives it away."

To illustrate my point, I walked over to the counter and picked up a paper coffee cup and its white plastic lid.

"People who order their coffee in a to-go cup never think about it, but the lids that come with it have tiny punctures on the opposite side from the opening you drink from. It allows air to flow into the cup as you drink; no vacuum problems this way. Helps the coffee go down smoother."

As the two women looked at the plastic lid from each angle, I continued my class on the structural engineering of coffee cups, saying, "The downside of using the lid is a miniscule flap called a chad. This flap is created when the hole is punctured through the lid."

I lifted the cup up to my mouth and pretended to drink.

"Hold the cup up like this to get the last dregs of caffeine and *viola*, the skin on your nose comes in contact with the flap. Next time you have a cup, see if you notice the plastic nib rubbing your nose the wrong way."

Tricia's fingers rapped the tabletop in a frenetic rhythm, and caused the silverware to quiver. Worry had set in. "I don't know if I should be concerned more about a tiny red scar on my nose or the fact that a total stranger was just able to nail me on one of my daily habits. You should be a detective, Winnie."

"The thought had occurred," I said. Like parents, like daughter? If flipping burgers at the Cat and Fiddle didn't pan out, and if Mint Street never ever called back, at least I had a backup plan now. *Winnie Kepler, private eye?*

As the girls continued chatting about the job fair, my mind focused elsewhere. If only I could recall any stray remark they may have already said, giving me a clue about the attitude or actions of George or Cosmo. I would soon enough be in enemy territory, that being the Seagull's Nest, but I couldn't pass up first-hand intel from two non-combatants who had just spent fourteen hours across enemy lines.

The conversation focused on the space requirements for the job fair. Tricia walked around the room, measuring for space. She looked like a film director, trying to set up the best camera shot.

"I'm afraid it may take you some time to set things up, Winnie. The layout of your tables and chairs just won't do. We'll need a steam table off to the side, and can you hire about four or five temps? We'll need them to serve the food and keep the wine flowing."

I raised my palm up as if to stop a car speeding through the intersection. "Hold on a minute. Isn't this supposed to be a job fair? What you're describing sounds more like a catered wedding reception or speed dating. We don't even have a license to serve wine, you know."

"I thought you wanted to impress people with your managerial skill, Winnie. If you can't make it happen, just let me know. We can still hold the job fair down the street."

"You know," I replied, "I'll take the moral high road here and say I think we can make this work. Just not the wine; it's a Commonwealth of Virginia thing, you understand. Permits, licenses. Those take time to move through the bureaucracy. Thursday is just too soon. Anyway, how many people are you expecting?"

"I've had just the one company call about holding the job fair. They have a team of about ten people. So we'll make this a closed event, meaning no other company will be here."

"And job seekers? How many do you think?" The café was big, but not that big.

"Could be hundreds. You know the community better than we do, my dear. If you were looking for a nice job here in Seaview, would *you* come?"

I calculated the number of unemployed people I had seen wandering around town. One hundred would be a stretch, even on a bad day. Then the calculus of the event made good sense. Occam's Razor, meaning the easiest solution is most often the best solution, could be applied here.

Pointing to a framed certificate on the wall, I said, "The fact of the matter is the fire marshal will be the first person in the door. And since we are certified for fifty people, if we have ten people working the event, then we will only have forty people here looking for work at any one time. The more staff we have, the fewer people we can let in. But I can still make this work for everyone."

Fran smiled, an expression not seen often since she and her partner arrived in town. "What's your plan, Winnie? Even in college, whenever something needed to get done, you had a plan. And not just any plan. Everyone loved to say the one and only Winnie Kepler always had the *best* plan."

With such a glowing introduction, true or not, I had to produce something of a plan. I had been bluffing, just to see what Tricia would say. She had remained silent, trying to out-bluff the bluffer.

Letting the words fly like a general ordering her lieutenants, I said, "Five staff, five interviewers, forty job seekers. The interviewers are stationed at small two-top tables, set up alongside the walls. In the center of the room, I'll put two long tables for the finger foods and beverages. People come in, they take a number. When their number is called, they go to a small table. In the meantime, they can network to their heart's content by the food and drink."

"What if this goes on all day?" Tricia asked. "If you had other plans, cancel them now, Miss Kepler."

"Oh, I know we'll have plenty of business. Once forty job seekers are in, the forty-first person will have to wait outside until someone leaves. I can put an ice chest outside with soft drinks for those waiting. No reason for them to suffer in the heat of this summer."

"You seem to have a grand idea here. Can you pull this off, Miss Kepler?" Tricia was offering one more chance to decline, her snarky tone evident with her continued use of my formal name.

"This won't take too much work at all," I said. At last, I felt I was in command of this operation. Remembering the plight of my grandmother, I was thankful I was in command of *something*.

Tricia added the caveats to her contract, but was still hesitant to slide the agreement across the table for me to sign. After a tense few seconds of indecision, she agreed to go ahead with the arrangement.

I eyed Fran as Tricia signed the contract. I wanted to get a word with Fran in private. I didn't know Tricia at all, and although Fran could vouch for her, something told me to be a little more careful around her friend. My instinct told me she had secrets.

What was her motivation? Help the unemployed? Get a big fat finder's fee from some corporate giant? Waste all of my time?

Before the two could steal away, Tricia's phone rang. It was her client, so I strained my ears trying to listen without being too obvious. The conversation wasn't sounding too positive.

After a few muffled words spoken into the phone, and more listening than speaking, Tricia pocketed her phone. "Francine, I'm afraid we may have to cancel the job fair. Winnie, my apologies. The client is thinking of backing away from hiring at this point. Apparently, there is local controversy hitting the press and the company wants to keep their distance for now."

Tricia turned towards me. "Miss Kepler, I am truly sorry. I was certain you could pull it off, without help. At least, I assumed you were alone here."

"Well," I said, trying not to lie outright, again. "You have another thirty minutes of my time tomorrow, if you need it. Give me a firm answer then. I can pull off miracles as good as the next girl, but sometimes it takes a little time." Holding up my copy of the signed contract, I pointed to the signatures. "And I'll expect certified funds for the guaranteed revenue."

I offered to shake Tricia's hand, giving her a look that said *in your face, sneaky one.* Our eyes met. I knew she understood my power position. When you are talking about Type-A personalities, it takes one to know one, and this time, we both knew. Tricia had not put a cancellation clause in her own contract. She was on the hook for a day's revenue whether her job fair occurred or not. There was no handshake.

As Fran and Tricia walked to the front door, I tried one more time to reach out to Francine.

"Fran, don't be a stranger, now. You can call anytime; the door's always open. Who knows, maybe we can find enough time to stay up all night and catch up on girl talk. You know, like we used to do every Friday night in college."

Fran gave a slight wave. Not smiling, she moved around to the passenger side of the car, dragging her finger along the vehicle's pin-striping. Her feet were moving toward the door, but her mind was nowhere near it. I hoped my offer to chat would be accepted.

I also prayed Fran would understand I knew something wasn't right between her and this Tricia person. In college, Fran and I were bookworms, preferring to haunt the stacks at the library, trying to educate ourselves into better lives. Staying up all night to catch up on girl talk? Hardly. We'd rather improvise a compare-and-contrast analysis of Jane Austen versus Isak Dinesen. Often our almost nonexistent love lives matched one or the other author's characters. Book nerds we were. Probably still.

Besides, we had early classes every semester, and we *never* skipped class. The library closed at ten and rare was the occasion we were not both asleep within an hour of returning to our little rectangular prison cell of a dorm room.

As the car took its two occupants down the road and out of sight I wondered what was motivating Tricia; it could have been greed, or maybe it was just that she, too, had to prove herself. The corporate world could be unforgiving to someone with three strikes against them from the start. The first was that becoming an entrepreneur was a challenge, and a very difficult one for women in particular, considering that business had traditionally been a *man's* domain. Another strike against her would be the fact she was a *young* woman. Old men smoking cigars while kicking their cowboy boots up on the desk could handle a young woman as a secretary, but as an equal? I didn't think so.

Add on top of those two challenges the third strike of what many would call an alternative lifestyle, and it may be downright impossible to succeed with your own enterprise.

I recalled how Francine mentioned *the* room in the Seagull's Nest. Online travel reviews said the little inn was lovely, especially the rooms, all of which were outfitted with queen-sized beds. Francine had said *room*, not rooms. I had deduced Francine and Tricia had more going on than just an employment relationship.

* * *

With the catering done for the day, it was time to concentrate on the suspect or suspects *du jour*. The judges would be arriving at the Seagull's Nest, ready to sample the classic Southern cuisine of Executive Chef George Harrison Windsor.

Hours later, the dining room table would be set up again, that time for the more modern and eclectic cooking of dishwasher Cosmo Finnegan. As long as there wouldn't be snails on the plate, I'd be fine. Some lines were not for crossing. That's what napkins were for.

Soft, slippered footsteps descended the stairs and announced Velma's arrival. A few seconds later, my jaw hitting the floor made more noise.

"Grandma? What did you do to your hair?"

"It's a wig. What do you think?"

Velma now had jet-black hair, a huge contrast from her normal silver-gray. With a little more face powder, she would look like a cousin.

"Why would you do this?" I asked.

"In case the good old police Captain comes back for dinner, hoping to arrest me on a trumped-up charge of murder, I thought I could fool him into thinking I was still hiding away somewhere. Using this disguise, I could be my long-lost sister, Minnie."

"Let's hope you don't have to resort to such measures." I also hoped insanity wasn't hereditary.

"Look," she said, "just because your boyfriend said he tipped off the VCID about the bogus warrant doesn't mean the Sheriff of Nottingham won't stop by to see if I have returned."

"So you are afraid if he stops by, he would still arrest you? Why don't we get a lawyer from the city? They can file harassment charges to keep him away for a while."

Velma took off the wig and tousled her hair back into a decent shape. "I don't think we need to waste the money on a lawyer yet. But still, when it comes to J.B. Larson, *and* his overblown ego, I wouldn't put it past him to put the cuffs on me in front of everyone. For him, his image is everything. Always has been."

"Grandma, I think it best if you remain as you are. In the meantime, I'm on my way to the Seagull's Nest. If there's a problem, just text me a 9-1-1 and I'll come running back."

Make no mistake, I was happy my grandmother was safe. And with Tricia out of the picture for the rest of the day, it looked like I would have the time needed to prove my grandmother innocent.

I had to catch the murderer.

10

It took a block and a half of quick walking before I spotted the Seagull's Nest. By the time I arrived for George's cooking demonstration, several of the judges were already standing out in the front yard. The leader of that pack of gossips came forward to meet me.

"My dear, we are so sorry to hear your grandmother had to leave town instead of finishing the competition. So unfortunate. Have you found an attorney that will take her case yet? I have a brother in Virginia Beach; he's a lawyer, and he's good. I might even get you a discount? If you're interested, that is. Not that I'm judging, you understand."

I smiled at the well-intentioned, yet condescending woman, trying to recall if there was a minimum sentence for first-offense assault and battery.

The news of my grandmother's escape had traveled fast. I guess the old saying was true. The three fastest ways to communicate in a small town like Seaview was telephone, telegraph, or tell-a-church-lady.

"Why, no, but thank you. As for judging, her turn will be on Wednesday so just make sure you come to the Cat and Fiddle with a big appetite. I *know* you won't be disappointed."

"If you say so, dear, but everyone's talking about it. Of course we didn't like that mean old Chef Pierre, the way he treated everyone. So I don't blame your grandmother at all for killing him."

I couldn't believe what I was hearing. What church did these ladies attend, anyway? The Holy High Roller Church of Saint Better-Than-Thou? Regardless, I needed to find out what they knew about Bailey's mother and Pierre.

"Excuse me? I didn't realize Pierre knew the Babbitt family."

"Know them? Why, honey, Pierre *was* a Babbitt—Peter Babbitt. The whole family was so proud when he went on to culinary school, and then Paris. Once he came back, however, it was as if he didn't recognize his own kin. The arrogant man had even changed his name, calling himself Pierre St. Pierre. Talk about an ego."

"How disappointing for his mother," I said. "Now I understand the rub with Betty, but I still don't see how a jerk of a son could cause enough trouble to end up on the pointy end of a knife. There must be more to the story here."

As the other judges walked over to join our two-woman huddle, my conversation partner continued with the flair of a professional busybody, saying, "Well, everyone knows the story. When the stock market crashed a few years back, the Babbitt family lost a lot of money. We all did, but they had put the restaurant up as collateral for some improvement loans. When a local tractor company closed, sales went down even further. A few delinquent loans forced the family to use tax money for rent. The auctioneer's gavel was the next order up."

"That's so sad," I said. I never liked hearing tales of people who had lost everything. And since the Great Recession, there were a lot of those tales.

"Here's the bad part. As the Babbitts' restaurant was going under, they had a long-lost relative *die*, an aunt or something. Lawyers filed the probate papers to get the Babbitts their share of a large inheritance."

The other women all agreed with the story so far, adding *tsk, tsk* here and there. They were shaking their heads. I knew this story would not end well.

Another lady took up the narrative. "Betty tried to get the

auction postponed for a month or two, until the probate court could allow the release of the cash, but someone had bribed the clerk's office to push the auction to the top of the pile—in less than a week. The Babbitt restaurant had a new owner. What a shame."

I put the pieces together. "And let me guess. Pete, now known as Pierre, was the one able to buy the business on the cheap at the auction before his brother's family could get their finances straightened out."

"He had to buy it when the price was the cheapest," another judge said. "The boys in front of the hardware store told *me* that Pierre had spent most of his extra cash paying off the county clerk. The only way he could steal the restaurant out from under his own relatives without too much suspicion was to use the name of his investor's group. Once people learned who had bought the place, the family's morale plummeted." Several women nodded in agreement, augmenting with a few more *tsks*.

As I was about to ask the judges a few more questions, Chef George came out of the house to greet his guests. In a slow Virginian drawl, he announced the start of the morning's activities.

"Ladies. I am so glad you all could make it here today. And don't those dresses look so pretty? And, oh, I like your hat, ma'am. Brings out the sparkle in your eyes."

Ignoring their polite responses to his flattery, George waved his hand toward the front door, saying, "I have prepared a sumptuous picnic meal for you to sample, if you would be kind enough to step this way, into *my* establishment."

We walked up the old wooden planks of the front steps, the boards creaking and clacking as set after set of leather heels hit each board. The smell of a ham baked with a brown sugar and honey crust filled the air as did the sweet smell of sweet potatoes itching for cinnamon. I was certain everyone could hear my stomach grumble; contest or not, I hoped George's cooking was on point. Some vegetables wouldn't hurt, either.

Drake Grimsby was waiting in the entryway; next to him was his one-woman camera crew at the ready. Like a creepy robot, he turned on his toothy smile as we approached.

"Ladies, I, too, would like to say thank you for coming today. I know the contest has taken on a different dimension from what we had planned, but I am confident this will end up even better!"

Drake was always the showman, it seemed.

A judge raised her hand. "Mr. Grillsby, I have a question."

Drake grimaced. "You mean, *Grimsby*."

"Yes, Mr. Grillsby. I have a question. How can you be sure the chefs are using the same ingredients available at the fairgrounds?"

"That is an excellent question, ma'am. And it's *Grimsby*." He let out a sigh.

Drake turned away from the woman, relit his electric-white toothy grin, and addressed his own camera. "But to answer your great question, we contacted the sponsor, the *amazing* MegaFood, Incorporated, and asked them to deliver an identical assortment of food items to each location. And I have been here since before sunrise to make sure Chef George has played by the rules. And believe me, everything is on the up and up. No question about . . ."

He stopped his derailing monolog, lowered his head and laced his fingers in front of him, as if he were about to pray. "In light of the tragic event earlier this week, we wanted to make sure the contest itself was above reproach. It's the least we can do to honor the memory of such a fine chef as Pierre St. Pierre. I know we all miss him and extend our deepest sympathies to his family, wherever they are."

Drake's self-serving drivel was almost too much for me to take. I couldn't help but interrupt his monologue. "You are right, Mr. *Grimesly*, but what about having two competitors in the same kitchen at the same time? Wouldn't that cause a potential conflict?"

My new mission in life was to help as many people as possible mangle Drake's last name. The woman behind the lens didn't seem to mind it, either, being on the receiving end of much of Drake's impatience and immaturity. I could hear her giggle every time someone said Drake's last name in a new fashion.

"Miss Kepler, I didn't realize you would be here today. Shouldn't you be tending to your poor grandmother and her legal problems? Begging the truck drivers at your little slop chute—I mean café—for bail money, perhaps?" Drake held out the vowel sound when he said the word *bail* in two syllables.

Some of the church ladies started a subtle Gregorian chant of *Fight! Fight!*

"I wasn't aware she had any such problems," I mocked. "And why would she need 'bay-yell' money? Only someone under arrest would need bail money. My grandmother is a free woman, as you will see on Wednesday, Mr. *Grimesly*, when you come to the Cat and Fiddle to judge her cooking."

Seeing an opportunity to raise Drake's blood pressure further, and raise the competition bar even higher, I added, "Velma also mentioned she would invite all the local pastors. It will be a most pious event, to be sure."

The judges took the bait. Each pulled out their phone, texting, tweeting, and Facebooking the news that their own pastors would have lunch with them. This brought the event up to a whole new level in their eyes. One lady whispered this would be a grand idea and *her* pastor would be certain to be arriving first since he was the better clergyman. I decided against questioning such logic. It wouldn't have mattered.

Everyone knew the church ladies were friendly on the outside, but on the inside, they were just as competitive as a bunch of freshman football players trying to earn a spot on the varsity team. Second place was not acceptable.

With just a few carefully chosen words, I turned the Wednesday edition of the *Culinary Challenge* into the highest point of the week. And now there was nothing Drake Grimsby could do to stop the contest.

You could hear the wheels in his brain, grinding to a halt by this unexpected turn of events. "But, well. I mean. Eh. Miss Kepler, let us agree that Wednesday will come soon enough. For today, however, we will have a light lunch served by George and an early dinner served by his *dishwasher*, Master Finnegan." Drake had put a special, indignant emphasis on the word dishwasher. I assumed he was already trying to throw the contest to a new favorite competitor.

As we walked through the grand foyer of the century-old home, I watched as Grimsby fawned all over Chef Windsor. I peered in the kitchen and saw George acting as the surgeon with Grimsby as his doting assistant. Every time the chef needed a pan or an ingredient from the new pantry, his nurse would run to get it for him. There was also an inordinate amount of whispering going on between the two.

I wondered if this had been the plan all along. Get rid of the award-winning chef, gain invaluable *and free* advertising courtesy of the police investigation, and then twist the event so a local man wins. I made a mental note to see later if there was any business connection between the show's producer and the B and B's executive chef.

As the ladies waited in the front parlor chatting about everything from the weather to what the most audacious outfit worn last Sunday, pots and pans clanged about in the kitchen. I smelled ham steaks frying on a grill; the hiss of the steam rising from the slabs of meat confirming my suspicions. Lunch was about to be served. Even though I would pass on the meat, I was still hungry.

I made myself right at home, sitting in the midst of the panel of judges. The server was a young man—a teenager most likely, I thought—dressed in the typical server's uniform of black trousers and a starched white Oxford shirt adorned with a thin black bow tie. The boy entered the dining room carrying the first course, a platter of warm sweet potato biscuits. Next came a gravy boat of clarified butter and a side dish of sliced Virginia ham stacked high like pancakes. Finally, he presented a casserole dish of pulled pork barbecue.

Another server walked into the room. She was the boy's sister, judging from the identical slopes of their noses, high foreheads, and identical blue-green eyes. She was an inch taller. In her hands was a long oval tray of condiment cups filled with white wine mustard, homemade basil mayonnaise, a vinegar-based barbecue sauce, and a side dish of sliced pickles of the bread and butter variety.

The table setting looked tasty. My stomach reminded me again of how hungry I was. Thankfully, no one noticed. Either that, or the church ladies were just being polite.

The ladies started in on the food like a ravenous band of coyotes let loose on a ranch full of three-legged rabbits. After I retrieved my biscuits, I counted my fingers to make sure there were still five on each hand. So far, so good.

The sweet potato biscuit tasted heavenly, the light and fluffy texture melting in my mouth. There was no dough-like aftertaste, a common malady when biscuits need more oven time. Nothing is worse than eating a badly baked biscuit, the kind that sits in the bottom of your stomach like a wad of chewing gum. My mother had always told me that if I swallowed chewing gum, it would stay in my stomach for seven years. Nasty biscuits would top that by two or three more years. *Disgusting.*

These biscuits were perfect—earthy, yet not overpowering. Many said the natural sugars from the orange spud gave their pork sandwiches just the right amount of sweetness. While others grabbed the condiments, I enjoyed the simple elegance of another sweet potato biscuit slathered in butter.

The ham told a different story. The bluish-red meat was, by all accounts, too salty. In fact, my dining partners said it must have come from the Dead Sea. I almost apologized to my biscuit, telling the inanimate object I was sorry more of my companions weren't vegetarian.

I knew a true Virginia ham was salt-cured, and aficionados of the beast always soaked such slabs of pork in cold water for a few days before trying to do anything with them. Any less time would create crusty little hockey pucks ready to give your teeth a workout. There might even be a tad of ham-like flavor in them, but most people would not notice it. All you would taste is salt. George Harrison Windsor, a trained chef born and bred in Virginia, should have known enough to soak the preservatives out of his ham.

I offered the ladies a possible solution: with enough basil mayonnaise, the inadequacies of the ham might be overcome. The ladies tried my suggestion, and after a few bites, confirmed that my cooking hack worked.

Two servers carried in large trays filled with individual ramekins of corn pudding. We served corn pudding at the Cat and Fiddle, too, so I was familiar with the sweet taste. I tried a little on another biscuit, sort of like using a gravy. Big mistake. The corn pudding, like the ham, was beyond too salty. It shouldn't have been salty at all. Authentic corn pudding had a sweetness that surpassed the sweet potato biscuit.

I was not alone in my reaction. Looking around at the other women, I could see they were all spitting out their portions into the linen napkins. Semi-polite grimaces gave way to bewilderment as everyone complained of how salty the sweet corn had been. That's when I remembered what Francine and Tricia had to say about their own breakfast. *Maybe George just has a heavy hand with his salt shaker?*

While my mind tried to rationalize why something like this was happening, my gut said I needed to usurp the power of the salt. I hoped a swig of iced tea might do the trick. The first server had mentioned the tea was *un*-sweet, meaning it was straight tea with nothing else added for flavor—no berries, no lemon, and no sugar. I picked up the nearest sugar canister and added three good shakes to my glass. After a few stirs with a long-handled spoon, I took a sip.

Blech!

I couldn't take it any longer. Tapping on my glass, I announced, "Ladies, we know the ham biscuits are too salty, as is the corn pudding. But, it seems the sugar bowl has joined the crowd."

Lifting the white porcelain sugar caddy, I poured the white substance onto the table. Dipping my finger into the crystalline powder, I confirmed my statement. "This, ladies, is *not* sugar."

I could not believe George would allow such mistakes with ten thousand dollars on the line. This required taking the matter straight to the man with the beret, the executive chef himself. I walked straight past Drake, not-so-subtly bumping the man to the side, and soon enough found the chef. He was working on his dessert.

"George, there seems to be an issue with salt being inside the sugar canisters out in the dining room. Do you know anything about it?"

"Why would there be salt in the sugar bowl? That's insane," he said. "No one makes *that* kind of mistake."

He paused, looking toward the now vacant dishwashing station. "I don't believe it."

Drake spoke up. "Chef, I always had a bad feeling about your dishwasher. This could be a matter resulting in his disqualification. I'll let the judges know." He moved back through the door toward the dining room to cause more commotion.

George shook his head. "Hold on a minute, Grimsby. Our Cosmo may be a fellow competitor, but he would never stoop so low as to sabotage food being served to guests. It's just not done.

The food must always stand on its own merit. We may differ on style, but we agree on integrity. It's a chef thing, you understand. Or, well, maybe you wouldn't. No matter. It wasn't Cosmo. I stake *my* reputation on it. Like I said, it's just not done."

George's ethical standards aside, the realist in me piped up, "Oh, Chef Windsor, when such a large prize is on the line, some things that just *aren't* done, *are* done."

* * *

Space was at a premium, which is often the case in professional kitchens. There were warming tables and serving shelves in front. Off to the side there was a long wooden cutting board, where sandwiches and cold items could be prepared. Behind all of this were a set of gas-fired ovens and a flat-top grill with four deep fryers rolled next to it. The area was clean, yet still had the immutable smell of old grease imbedded in the porous ceiling tiles.

In the back were more stoves, each with a lower oven, and a nice stone pizza oven. Stuck in every nook and cranny were freezers, coolers, and spice racks. The glare from the long fluorescent lights hanging above reflected off every surface. I needed sunglasses.

The taste of the salt had not yet left my chops. Ah, yes. The spice rack. Now *there* was a crime scene waiting for yellow tape.

As I walked over to the set of spices, hoping to give the sodium chloride container a closer inspection, I stopped short to get a good look through the main oven's glass window to see what was cooking. I had a sudden reminiscence of being a Girl Scout out camping, s'mores in hand.

"I notice you have been working on dessert. Is that a graham cracker crust I see?"

The pies were already in the oven, but George had left scads of semi-crushed graham crackers on the cutting board. Sitting next to them were several wrappers torn from sticks of butter, and a half-empty shaker containing a white powdery substance, presumably sugar. At least, I hoped it was sugar.

"Yes, Miss Kepler. If you promise not to tell your grandmother any of my secrets, sometime I will let you know how to make my famous chocolate pecan pie. I think it's so good, it has a more than decent chance to beat her apple pie."

"Well, I can't make any promises, but there's nothing better than a nice graham cracker crust," I said. Deciding to drop a hint that the chef might want to double-check his ingredients, I added, "After all the salt I found out there in the dining room, I hope no one switched the ingredients here in the kitchen. That would be a disaster, wouldn't it, chef?"

George's eyes widened. He had finally taken the hint and grasped the seriousness of the situation. Picking up his own sugar container, he dipped his finger in and took a taste. His cheeks turned red, and his eyes widened like a cat about to pounce. "Salt!" George slammed the point of his chef's knife into the cutting board.

Regaining his composure, George admitted he had been fooled. "Miss Kepler, it seems you are correct. If you'll excuse me for a few minutes. I must pull my staff into the kitchen for a pep talk. If you would be so kind as to return to your table. Dessert will be served in just a few moments."

As I made way back to the dining room, I saw the chef motion for his young team to join him in the back of the kitchen, next to the pizza oven. George picked up the sugar shaker to show his staff. I had just sat down out in the dining room when we *all* heard the yelling and screaming begin. The two young servers claimed innocence.

As Drake opened the door to see if everything was under control, the female server said, "But daddy, we would never have done it. We want you to *win*." The young man chimed in, "Yeah, dad. We know you need the money, and we're here to help you, not hurt you! We're in this together."

George needed the prize money for something beyond the usual summer vacation. Maybe he had an outstanding bill to pay. Behind on his mortgage payments, perhaps. Hospital bills, or two kids who wanted to go to college. The possibilities were endless. Whatever the reasons, I decided no one in this trio wanted to sabotage the meal.

After a long and awkward silence, Drake Grimsby checked

on the chef. Moments later, the producer returned.

"Ladies, the chef has resolved the salt issue, but I am afraid it affected the dessert. However, the last course will still be the best part of the meal today. Thank you for your patience. Give us a few minutes. Please."

Us? Since when was Drake part of the culinary team?

True to his claim, a few minutes later, the kitchen door reopened and two smiling young adults gingerly stepped into the dining room, silver trays balanced on one hand. From what I could see, each tray held several large jelly jars full of light-and dark-colored ingredients layered about an inch thick each, but no one could quite figure out what the mystery meal could be. George followed his entourage.

"Ladies, our original desserts were not of the highest standard of quality we here in the kitchen demand. Upon conferring with my staff, we came up with a unique alternative that may just be the next big thing in the culinary world!"

"What is it?" one lady asked, holding her dessert jar up to the light, rotating it ever so slightly in hopes of identify the contents.

"I'm not sure this looks right," another said. She wouldn't even touch her jar, instead poking it with a fork.

The crowd pushed their chairs away from the table. I knew right away what George had done. And I salivated just thinking about it.

"Very impressive, chef," I said. "And on such short notice, too. I would have never thought to layer a chocolate pecan pie into a jelly jar. The graham cracker crumbs for the crust? Ingenious. No need to pre-bake the crust when you make the pie this way. I love it!"

"And without the normal crust made with flour and lard, we can honestly say this sweet delight is a true lower-carb and lower-fat dessert, perfect for anyone trying to maintain their already perfect figures," George said, pandering to the judicial panel.

Once the church ladies heard the dessert was *possibly* healthy, the spoons flew. In a matter of seconds, the Jelly Jar Chocolate Pecan Pie was but a distant yet tasty memory.

* * *

Drake was busy ordering his production assistant to change the position of the camera every few seconds to capture every aspect of the meal. As the camera operator stayed busy focusing on the licked-clean plates being stacked and water glasses being refilled, Drake took a second to catch his breath.

With all the flair of a circus showman, Drake then announced, "George, I think you prepared an awesome meal, even under such trying circumstances. And judging how these prominent and lovely ladies took to your fine, Southern style of cooking, I imagine you have just set the standard for your competitor to beat."

"You mean competitors, plural, don't you, Mr. Grimsby?" I had caught the producer's intentional choice of words. "The judges still need to see my grandmother and Bailey, right?"

"Of course." Drake hesitated, squirming like a mouse caught trying to get away with the cheese. "Competitors, as you say, but don't you need to be up the road at your cat and dog café, serving scraps from a can?"

Drake was using his body to loom over me and herd me toward the front door. But as he was moving, a well-placed shoe tripped the producer, throwing him off balance and causing him to fall into the tray of iced tea pitchers.

"Gosh, Mr. Brilsey, you should be more careful," one judge said.

"Yes, Brilsey," Chef George said, moving his foot back. "You should be more careful." Turning toward me, the chef smiled. "Thanks, again, Miss Kepler, for offering your expertise in the kitchen. I'm afraid without it, dessert would not only have been a disaster, but we would never have come up with this new offering. And the best part is that my two kids helped. You may have saved my family, too."

"It's always nice when families can come together," I said. "And yes, I *should* check in on my grandmother. But have no fear, sir. I should be back in time for dinner, assuming the dishwasher returns."

George, always the true Southern gentleman, walked me to the front sidewalk. He wanted a moment away from the cameras and microphones. "Miss Kepler. Winnie, if I may. I can see you are trying to prove your grandmother innocent. Very commendable. Look, I appreciate you noting the facts and not making any prejudgments. With my history with Pete—or Pierre, as most people know him—I know by all rights I should be the prime suspect."

"Well, if not you, then who would have enough cause to stab the man in the back?"

"My guess is Grimsby, but only the competitors wielded knives up on stage. Still, it is obvious Grimsby has it out for your Velma. *Please* tell her to be careful. I don't know who killed Pete, but I don't think it was any of us up on the stage. We were focused on our cooking. In fact, the only time I talked to Pete once the cooking started was when I offered him a tissue."

"A tissue? Why did you do that?" I asked.

"Poor guy was sneezing like crazy for over an hour before the contest started. I thought he had walking pneumonia or something. It stopped after we got going, though, so I forgot all about it."

"You bring up some valid points, chef. Thanks for your insight and a big thank-you for the meal. It was delicious, even with the extra sodium. But you were oh so right; I loved the dessert. I may have to borrow that one."

"Since you saved the day by figuring out the salt and sugar problem, you deserve the reward. You have my permission to use the jelly jar pie; just give us credit for inventing it, will you?"

I had enough information on my first suspect. I gave George a wave, saying, "I will give you credit for *everything* you deserve, sir. Consider it done." And with those parting words, I wondered which salt mine had fugitive dishwasher Cosmo Finnegan's name on its mailbox.

11

I returned to the Cat and Fiddle to find my grandmother filling one of her antique white porcelain tea diffusers with dark black tea leaves. Most customers would be served a generic tea brewed using large paper satchels of leaves soaked in twenty-gallon cylinders of water. Every morning I filled those tanks, throwing the large tea bags in afterward. Velma's use of a diffuser and leaves from her personal stash were for customers with discriminating palates.

"Who ordered the special tea?"

"I did, but it's not for me. It's for the girl sitting in the corner. She seemed down on her luck so I figured a nice relaxing tea would be just the thing for her. I'm adding a few cinnamon sticks, too. They'll help soothe her wounded spirit."

I glanced across the dining room and saw the woman in question. My expression changed, from the smile of a successful morning to an uncertain frown. This was a bad omen.

"Grandma, that's Fran, my old college roommate! Here, let me take the tea. She looks terrible. I think she's been crying."

Normally a put-together woman, Fran's lack of makeup spoke volumes; she'd spent a troubled few hours. Recent hours, I assumed.

With a kettle of water just off the boil, I doused the diffuser into a teapot, tossed in two sticks of cinnamon, and walked straight away to my old friend. As I reached the table, she looked up but was almost embarrassed to see me. This would not be an easy conversation.

"Oh, Winnie. This will sound bad, I know, but, I was almost hoping you wouldn't be here."

"Frannie, I work here, remember? If you were trying to hide from me, you picked an awful spot. Listen, my grandmother made you some special tea. Want some? The cinnamon will make you feel better." I poured the fresh tea into the cup already at the place setting. I didn't bother to wait for an answer.

"It will take more than cinnamon, I think. You wouldn't have a spare gallon of vodka around somewhere, would you?"

"I'm afraid we are fresh out, but the tea will help. I'm no expert on the subject, Fran, but people say tea can warm your heart. Try it. Just a sip. Please? What can it hurt?"

"Well, it can't hurt any worse. Can tea mend a *broken* heart?"

We had arrived at the root of the problem much sooner than I had expected. The empty chair across the table told me everything I needed to know.

"I'm guessing things didn't work out with you and Tricia?"

Francine took a sip of tea and straightened her back, bringing her blank stare back up to my eye level.

"How did you find out?" she asked. "I thought we had been very discreet."

I slid into the empty chair. "You only booked one room at the Seagull's Nest, and I've been there before. I know there is just one bed in each room. I assumed you were the happy couple. Maybe not, I see now."

"We've *been* the happy couple for over a year now. I started out as Tricia's assistant but, well, you know, she's nice, and attractive, and just a few years older than me, and we like a lot of the same things. It sort of just . . . happened."

The tears flowed again. I offered Fran a cloth napkin. By the time she finished wiping her eyes, my white linen was streaked with the last remnants of her mascara. I stole another napkin from the adjoining table. *Might as well be prepared,* I thought.

I had a lot on my agenda with the job fair, plus the minor

little detail about my grandmother being charged with murder, or soon to be, at least. But Fran was my friend, and my grandmother's advice kept gnawing at me. My former roommate needed to be the priority at that moment. Everything else was beyond my control for the time being.

"So Fran, if everything was going so well, what changed? Is there another woman, or man?"

"I'm just not sure what all is going on. All I know is that everything was great until we packed up our recruiting booth at the Richmond job fair. Oh, and I don't think we, I mean Tricia, is still planning on that job fair here at your place. I'm so sorry we wasted your time, Winnie."

"You *did not* waste my time, Francine. Had none of this happened, you would have driven to your office in D.C., and I would not have sat down and chatted with you again. Whatever the reason this has all happened, I am glad we are here, right now. I'm ready to listen whenever you are ready to talk about it."

"You were always a good listener, Winnie. Maybe you should talk to Tricia. I bet you could get the truth out of her faster than I could. I tried asking her what the problem was, and she cried, saying we had to break it off. Then she left. Gone. Like we never happened."

"So she's gone? Really gone? Where'd you last see her?" I wasn't sure I wanted to know the answer to my last question. It was not as if I had time to solve another mystery. But Fran was my friend, my best friend, and I would just have to find a balance somehow.

Fran took a sip of tea; I could see her loosening her shoulders down from the tight hunch they had been holding for who knew how long.

"Tricia went outside to get something from the car and never came back. When I went out to see what happened to her, I found a note and an envelope full of cash sitting on the front seat of the car. I drove around for over an hour, figuring she would walk out to the highway to hitch a ride. No sign of her." Francine's eyes welled up again. "Then I ran out of gas and had to walk back to town. I can't even *look* for her now!"

I glanced at the envelope. It was a normal business reply envelope, a number 9 in size. An embossed watermark adorned the back flap. Below, someone scribbled a few words:

I'm so very sorry—T

I wasn't sure what the watermark meant, since it wasn't a traditional set of initials, or a company name. The emblem seemed to be a pair of diamonds, laterally offset about 30 percent in a bizarre Venn diagram. The cash? A payoff from someone. My guess, at least. I didn't know how involved Fran and Tricia's relationship had become. Joint bank account? Too soon, maybe. Then I laughed. Not a big laugh, but enough to elicit a response from my guest.

"I'm surprised you think this is so funny." Francine had a scowl that could stop freight train in its tracks.

"Oh, it's not you. I was thinking of something else."

Before Fran could put sense to my words, I explained, taking her hands in mine and telling her the news she wanted to hear.

"The good news is this: Tricia still loves you. I think she did what she did only because she thought it was the best thing to do, perhaps the only thing to do. Give it some time, Fran, and I bet we can get you two back together." I didn't know this to be fact. I was just confident in my not-so-educated guess. My fingers crossed themselves.

"Do you think so? I mean, the only place I think she would have gone is the office, but she left our only car. But then again, she could have walked anywhere, I suppose."

Panic resurfaced. "Winnie, you don't think she would hitchhike somewhere, do you? That's so dangerous. And besides, can you even afford to take time off right now?"

To her point, Fran was right. I knew leaving the area to search for Tricia, even for a few days, was neither practical nor wise. The looming probability of seeing my grandmother sent to prison made me think twice.

I couldn't ignore the bread and butter of the café, either. Money had to come in somehow, and lawyers aren't cheap. This would complicate my response to Mint Street Bankers, assuming they would ever call back. I hadn't realized it, but I had palmed my cell phone again to check for new emails. I didn't really want the office job, but their paycheck would come in handy.

"Winnipeg Marie Kepler! Snap back to reality, will you?"

I knew I had lost sight of my priorities when my best friend had to resort to the middle name call-out.

Fran didn't let up. "Well? What do you think? Is this wishful thinking on my part? Am I left with nothing?"

"It's not happening," I said, answering my own internal question as my response to Mint Street, assuming they would call again.

"Oh, I see," Francine said, looking down into the teacup, hoping that the leaves would tell her a new fortune. Not finding a swizzle stick, she stirred cinnamon sticks around the edges of the teacup as she bit her lower lip. Fran was in fight-or-flight mode and had chosen the latter. She reached down for her purse, starting an impromptu exit plan.

"Fran, I'm sorry. I'm just not *that* good a listener right now."

I had to re-establish a connection with my friend. The cell phone had to go away, and I needed to focus on Fran, her problems. The job could wait. She was a good friend; and like Velma had taught me, she was a good friend for a reason. I couldn't lose her now.

"What I meant to say was—"

Even Fran looked surprised at my inability to articulate my thought. I spewed the only words my brain could muster.

"Fran, I'm so sorry. I didn't mean *you*. Can you forgive me?"

Fran gave me the look; the same look she gave me when I tried, against her advice, those shots of tequila before our first Phi Delta Sigma meeting. I knew the look. She had forgiven me, but Fran also wanted me to know she had the old "I told you so" ready to go at any moment.

Fran muted her words enough so others couldn't hear, which was odd in my mind, since there were no other customers. "So, me. And Trish? You were saying?"

"Yes. Yes. Yes," I said. "I think you two still have something as far as a relationship goes. And I think we can get it right again, but going to her office isn't the best idea right now. I don't think Tricia is there. May not be safe."

The entirety of the situation, the murder, the unannounced visit of Fran and her now-missing friend; it all pointed to one conclusion. Time was now running short.

"Where else would she go?"

"The answer may be right in front of us," I said, giving the plain envelope another glance. "Tell me about Richmond. How were things going? Meet anyone interesting there? Maybe someone Tricia spoke with, but you didn't?"

"We have a system, Winnie. At the job fairs, I chat up the college kids who are not sure what they want to do in life. And there are tons of *them*. The pre-meds and pre-laws? Not worth our time. We go for the liberal arts majors. Art history, music, even English majors. They're smart kids but not easily mixed into the business world. Anyway, they're still kids, just a few years younger than us, and that means they're hungry."

"Oh Fran. I understand the hunger for the right career. Velma has had me shopping at that deli for over a year now."

"Well, yes, figuratively," Fran said. "But what I meant was *hungry*, as in they wanted something to eat. I'd let them know we had coupons for free food at our booth. Once they heard the word *free*, they would come over in droves."

While Fran was explaining the intricacies of bait-and-switch recruiting tactics along with the follow-on data mining exploitation, I kept looking at the embossed image on the envelope. No ink, just the raised edge of some corporate icon. Not even a return address. I had seen this image somewhere before, I just couldn't place it. Yet.

"Fran, when you were walking around, did you pick up any literature from the other vendors?"

"Oh, sure," she said. Francine opened her black leather portfolio, showing me a jumble of business cards and company brochures. "I try to find something from every company we come in contact with. You never know when we may need a contact name, and it helps if I can converse about something we all have in common. What better opening to a conversation than mentioning I liked their booth at some job fair? Anything look of interest to you?"

I felt like a newly-deputized Agatha Christie as I paged through pamphlets from accounting firms, government contractors, and more temp agencies than I cared to count. "Francine, did someone from *this* company come over to your booth?"

I pulled a fancy brochure from the pile and handed it over to Francine. Their logo matched the embossing on the envelope.

"Why, yes, but not at first. In fact, since they had such a huge booth, more like a small store, we didn't even think to stop by and see them. These guys had their own hiring department and recruiting staff, so we figured they would not need our services. They wandered over, but they only spoke with Tricia."

"Why would a huge corporation take an interest in your little recruiting company if they had their own hiring department? Perhaps they wanted to offer you both jobs, you know, get rid of the competition by bringing them into the fold. Why do you think they did that, Francine?"

Before she could answer, Velma walked up. "Winnie, someone from a coin company just called. They wanted to speak with you but I told them you were busy. He left a number, though."

"A coin company? I don't know anyone from a coin company. I only collected stamps as a kid."

"They said something about coins, I'm sure of it."

"Was it Mint Street Bankers? I never gave them the business number, just my cell phone." This put a whole new light on my priority list. Lawyers cost money, and a job with Mint Street could be instrumental in saving Velma from a long prison sentence.

"'Mint,' that's right, like minting a coin."

The news started my hand twitching again with nervous excitement. The job offer must have been superb if someone went to the trouble of finding out where I worked and then placed the call anyway.

"Winnie, you go on. At least talk to them." Francine said. "Who knows? If your train is at the station, maybe you should get on board before it leaves."

I then had one of those moments of clarity. Francine had solved the mystery. At least, one of them.

Almost dropping the teapot, I said "Francine, you're a genius. I know where to find Tricia."

* * *

I slid my phone into my back pocket. There was just enough

time. I hoped. Walking over to the cash register, I took out a few twenty-dollar bills. "Come on, woman. You're taking a little trip."

We went outside, stopping at the curb. I looked across the street, and with a simple wave of my hand, Operation Reunion started. I hailed a cab from the taxi stand outside the old Northampton Hotel, one block away. The driver was in front of us seconds later.

"Where to, Miss?"

"Oh, I'm not the one needing a ride today. But my friend here? She does. Needs to be at the Harbor Park Amtrak station in Norfolk before the next train leaves. Can you get there in time?"

"The next train leaves in an hour," he said. "We should be able to get there just before the Northeast Regional leaves for all points north."

Turning toward Fran, I said, "Go to the train station. Once you get there, walk up the ramp to the platform and move to the far right where the business passengers will be standing. Work your way down about four cars from the end. You'll find Tricia there. My guess is you will find her in the 'Quiet Car' between the business class and coach sections. She'll want to cry in silent peace."

Fran was almost crying herself. It was all she could do to drop herself into the cab and buckle her seatbelt. I knew it would soon get better, much better, for my friend. And her friend.

I forked over three twenties to the driver. "This should be enough to get there, and then bring her and her friend back here to Seaview. If it's not, come into the café. The next meal is on me."

As I watched the taxi leave, the backseat occupant kept looking through the rear window. I could see the mismatch of emotions in Francine's eyes. Happiness on the one hand, fear of emotional torment on the other. Crossing my heart, I prayed I had made the right choice.

Velma had been watching the two of us with a keen interest. She asked if the Cat and Fiddle was now subsidizing the local transportation industry. I guess I had not been too slick, or slick *enough*, when I nicked the cash out of the register. At least she waited until Fran left before she brought the subject up.

"Just greasing the squeaky wheels in a matter of the heart,"

I replied.

"Sometimes no amount of money can stop that kind of noise, Winnie. I hope it all works out. But what about that phone call? Weren't you expecting it?"

The phone call. *Will I choose an office or a lunch counter as my career and future? And can I keep the friendship of Francine?*

"Yes, grandma, but about that call. What I mean to say is yes, I'll get right back to them. But like you said, no amount of money can stop anyone's heart from squeaking. Breaking, however, may be a better word for it, I guess. And Francine's wheels have been squeaking badly. The bank can wait."

12

Bright rays of sun crossed the floor, pushing the shadows of the tables and chairs into long, thin slivers. The day was not over, but time was moving away from midday. It was already time to prep for dinner, and I wanted to get everything done so I could walk back to the Seagull's Nest. Suspect number two was next up on the menu. I had my priorities, and the bank was still not at the top of my list.

On most days, I could take my time prepping the food for the next meal. First, I would put the pot roast on the stove to slow cook throughout the afternoon, and then boil the potatoes. But today was different. I had taken the time away from my normal duties to bird-dog George in the morning, and now the dishwasher and aspiring chef Cosmo Finnegan was about to cook for the judges. I couldn't miss the opportunity to size him up as a suspect.

I tried my best to finish the prep work, but some things just did not get done. As I walked out to the front sidewalk, I picked up a dish rag to erase a few items off the chalkboard menu by the front door. Why advertise it if you can't serve it, right? Velma walked out to see what I had done. We had a short planning meeting where we agreed that Velma was comfortable handling the rush without me. As I was leaving, Velma reminded me that she had kept the place going just fine by herself *before* I came home from college. *Well played, Grandma. Well played.*

I had no spare time. The walk to the Seagull's Nest would be just long enough for me to review the facts as I knew them. Unfortunately, my plan did not survive the first contact with the enemy.

I walked by the ice cream store and spied Chef George inside, ordering a large waffle cone sandwich. With three scoops of homemade ice cream crammed between the two made-to-order warm waffles, I knew the man wasn't going anywhere soon. Why not stop to see how things had gone after I had left? I checked the time. There would be enough for a quick chat as long as a few neighbors didn't mind me cutting through their yards to get to Cosmo.

George was gracious in his greeting as I walked into the store. After the usual pleasantries, he mentioned how both he and his kids were okay with the results, but he hedged his positive attitude by saying that the salt episode had thrown his overall confidence out the window.

I helped the man retrace his steps from the moment he arrived at the kitchen that morning. It was to no avail, however. We couldn't determine how Cosmo had switched the sugar out of *all* the containers, replacing it with salt. It had to have been an inside job, we agreed.

"So you never saw Cosmo this morning?"

"No, he had cleaned all of last night's dinner dishes before he left for the evening. And I was with him the whole time. He couldn't have done anything shady then. This morning, he called in, saying he didn't think it was good form to be in the kitchen while I was competing. Cosmo wanted to remove all chance of impropriety."

I thought through the logistics of such a switch. Access would have been the first problem for an outsider. I pressed George for more information.

"Did he have a key? A pass code? Could Cosmo have come into the kitchen during the night with no one knowing?"

George laughed. "I suppose he could have, in theory, but I know he didn't."

"How do you know? Were you with him all night?"

"No, but I know who he *was* with. Everyone in town knows. I'm surprised you don't. He spent the night at the rail yard. Just ask Bailey Babbitt."

I wondered if I had the wrong set of criminals. Maybe it wasn't George in cahoots with Cosmo. Perhaps he was just collateral damage. The killer might have been not one, but two people. And Cosmo and Bailey qualified as two people.

The youngest competitors could have been running a good chef/bad chef operation, trying to shake the contest favorite down until Pierre finally ended up with a fatal ventilation slit in his chef's coat.

"Chef Windsor, were you okay with cooking without a dishwasher this morning? What about all the pots and pans? Seems like a ton of work for one guy."

The chef looked at me, his smirk telling me that of all people, an employee in a food service establishment should know better.

"As you know, Miss Kepler, most chefs do not start with a staff of any kind unless they work in a hotel or large restaurant. The Seagull's Nest is a tiny operation and for many years I worked alone. Food served in the dining room was mine, good or bad. And the same could be said of the disaster left in the kitchen. All mine."

George wasn't boasting as far as I could tell. His words were those of a professional; proud of his work from years of paying dues by the heat of the stove. He lectured me at that point.

"And you will soon find out in your own place; there is a fine art to cleaning as you work. Only a novice or an arrogant fool would do otherwise. Besides, the lad had a point. If my meal disappointed, Cosmo not being in the kitchen meant the responsibility and accountability would be placed on my shoulders and no one else's."

"Then how did the salt end up in the sugar containers? The only other people here were your two children. You don't think one of them did it?"

George froze when I mentioned his kids. I told George how everyone heard him *discussing* the matter in the kitchen earlier with his two wait staff members.

"George, I believed them when they said they supported you.

I think they are just as motivated for you to win as, well, you are. I mean, we can check the video feed since I assume Grimsby had his camerawoman follow you everywhere, but I don't see it being your kids. Cosmo may be the only logical option left here."

George nodded, acknowledging my conclusion. "They *are* good kids. They know we have been struggling for money and the ten-thousand-dollar prize money would go a long way towards the purchase of our own place."

"You want out from the Seagull's Nest?"

"Not necessarily. This place has been good to us. It's given me a paycheck, health care and insurance, and the needed time to develop my skills and ideas as a chef. But I still can't say it is *my* place. The owners plan the menu themes and I have to accommodate. I want a place where I can evolve my cooking and not just serve cheesy shrimp and grits with a side of chicken on waffles."

"If you were to build your own restaurant, where would it be?"

"The original plan, if it had worked out, was for me to go into partnership with the Babbitt family. I'd be a one-third owner of their old restaurant, the operating partner in fact, while they retired to become the silent partners. But the economic downturn hit them hard and fast. So fast, in fact, that I couldn't raise enough money to help. Before any of us knew it, Pete had bought their restaurant and turned it into a fine dining establishment. The town's first."

Now it made more sense. George Harrison Windsor, kids or not, had a pretty solid motive to kill Pierre.

"You know, George, that is a great story, but as you said earlier, it makes you look like a suspect in Pierre's murder. You now have what the police would call motive and opportunity."

George's original story told at lunch had given me hope of his innocence. Now, with such a compelling motive, perhaps I had judged him in error?

"I know. But I didn't do it. As much as I want to win, and as much as I disliked Pete for finishing first in culinary school, under such unusual circumstances, I want my cooking to stand on its own merit. That, and I have an ex-wife who has been waiting for me to slip up. It's an alimony thing, if you must know."

"George Harrison Windsor, I didn't realize you were

divorced. I guess I always assumed you were single. When did that happen? And do tell about your wife. I'm not trying to be the neighborhood gossip, but I think this could have a major bearing on the case."

I fibbed. George having to pay alimony was nothing unusual. Most of his competitors had money problems. Why enter if you didn't need the prize?

"Ex-wife, if you please." He opened his wallet and pulled out an old family photo.

"During better times," he said, his tone still harboring disappointment.

"I see where your daughter gets her looks. She is beautiful; gets her eyes from her mother and her smile from you, George. I'm sorry it didn't work out for you. How'd you meet?"

"It's a horrid story, but she came from a well-off family. Opposites attract, as they say. They were vacationing here at the beach and she went, in her own words, slumming. We got together and before we knew it, she was expecting a child. One quick trip to Las Vegas and we were married. Stayed together for about two years."

The man opened his wallet again and pulled out another photograph, this one taken on their wedding day. I could see the pride in his eyes, and the regret in his new wife's half-hearted smile. Unrequited love felled another good man.

"Local country boy marries rich city girl," I proclaimed. "Sounds like a great movie. But the country boy, in this case, didn't ride off into the sunset to live happily ever after, did he, George? Isn't that how it's supposed to go?"

"Not in this flick," George said. "After a while, she had her fill of living in a small town. I guess it's understandable when your town has limited nightlife. No social scene, no Junior League, no debutante balls—nothing but a pancake supper at the firehouse every third Wednesday and an oyster roast once a month at the Lodge. And she wanted nothing to do with the Lodge. Why *wouldn't* the big city with their dance clubs, all-night coffee shops, and nail salons on every corner draw you back?"

"And back she went," I concluded.

"Like a rat to cheese," he said. "She wanted me to go to the big South Beach Food and Wine Festival in Miami. I didn't want to go, but she insisted. Our wholesaler even came by one day to talk up the event. His company had a gigantic display at the festival and they sponsored several parties with at least one celebrity chef attending each get-together."

"So you went? What about the babies? Judging by their age, they must have been toddlers at best."

"Yeah, my biggest mistake. Not the kids. My parents watched them so we could go to the event. I thought I might pick up some new ideas on how to present the classic Southern food we specialize in here at the Seagull's Nest. And it would give my wife a few days of happiness in the sunshine. She could get a tan on the beach during the day, and soak in the neon lights at night. I thought we could go dancing at a different place every night. Boy, was I wrong."

"Too modern for you, I suppose?" I was listening to the man ramble on about the food and wine festival, but was thinking more about the contest at hand and how George could have killed his school rival, Pierre St. Pierre. My attention snapped back when he mentioned his wife's behavior at the festival.

"Did you say mermaid tattoo?" I asked.

"Yes. While I was attending the cooking demonstrations, she was off with the wholesaler having her own little festival. A day later, she showed back up at our hotel room, sporting a massive hangover and a tattoo just below her waist." George pulled up his shirt to show me the exact location of his ex-wife's ink.

"No need for any more details, George. I assume the divorce came soon afterward?"

"After we separated for the state-mandated six months. I didn't hear from her at all until a lawyer showed up one day with the divorce papers. They wanted me to sign on the spot, saying no trial would be necessary since it would be a non-contested divorce. The lawyer even tried to convince me it would be better for me to stay in town and work."

"Did you?"

"I had to. He was right. A long, drawn-out court session would have caused me to lose what little income I had. The carrot on the dinner plate was my wife having to pay *me* alimony, kind of like hush money, instead of the other way around."

"What about the kids? You still have them so it must have worked out?"

"Yes, I ended up with full custody, but it took a while. I did not sign right away. I told the man my attorney and I would discuss our position on the matter."

George was talking crazy talk. "There aren't that many attorneys in Seaview. And you mentioned money was tight. With a limited budget, who'd you see?"

The answer took me by surprise.

"Your grandmother. Velma has always been the most intelligent voice of reason in Seaview. I knew she could take a look at the paperwork and spot the traps if there were any."

"And were there any?"

"Do cats hate dogs? There was one. But it was a big one. My wife's lawyer had hidden a clause right in the middle of a standard paragraph. I think they were hoping I would just skim the document and assume the wording was generic."

"So, I imagine the sentence had something to do with custody of the kids, yes?"

George's ex-wife may not have wanted a life with him, but a mom leaving her kids would be a different story. I had no children, but if I did, I would *not* want to lose them for any reason.

"She only wanted them at full custody because she needed the tax write-off. This wasn't spelled out verbatim in the document, but Velma still figured out their little plan. She even let it slip out that if the judge wasn't too much of an idiot, I would be ordered to pay for the *upkeep* of, as she said, those stupid kids. That's when the judge awarded me full custody."

"Now, George. That may overstate the intent just a little. A mother's love is hard to understand unless you've been one."

"Says the girl without children."

"*Touché*, sir, but you understand what I mean. I bet she loves her kids as much as you do. She, however, showed it in a very different way. And, at least she pays *you* alimony. Financial support with no marital stress. You ended up on the better end of this deal."

I had to reinforce the positive with George before he ordered another waffle sandwich for mental relief. No Nero Wolfe was I, but I knew what an extra thousand calories could do to a person. *Pfui.*

"The alimony she pays might be better called her penance."

He laughed. "Just when I thought *my* life couldn't get any stranger, I found out she and her new meal ticket got married a full week before our divorce was final."

"But isn't that illegal?"

George nodded. "Exactly. To keep me quiet, and to keep themselves from being charged with polygamy, she agreed to pay me the monthly alimony. I think she must have paid off the clerk to backdate the divorce since our case flew through the court system. I thought it was awesome at that point, since she absolutely hated it, but it was her own doing. Still hates it, I suppose. And that means I love it."

"So you have the kids and a little income coming in aside from the paycheck from the Seagull's Nest. But it's still not enough to help buy your own spot?"

"No," George said. "I didn't have enough cash to buy the Babbitts' restaurant, so I lost that chance. Now, there is a rumor the Seagull's Nest may be up for sale soon."

"So winning the prize money would be very nice, wouldn't it?"

"That's an understatement. A chef in my position would do anything to get that kind of payoff."

"Anything? Even murder, Mr. Windsor?"

He hesitated. "I didn't kill that arrogant man. All I want to do is win the contest. There are others with far better motives to kill."

I checked my watch. It was almost dusk, and in a few minutes it would be time for Cosmo Finnegan to serve his contest food to the judges. I had only a block and a half to walk, but I didn't want to delay any further.

"I am sure you are right, George. And hopefully I will have time to speak with all of them. But listen, I'd love to stay and talk more about your ex-wife, but Cosmo is already cooking and I need to keep my eye on him since, well, he's a suspect, too, you know."

"He's a good kid, Winnie. I don't think he had anything to do with the mix-up with the salt. I still say Grimsby is behind everything. Maybe even the murder. The man's an open book—a checkbook, that is. He puts his allegiance anywhere he can make a buck."

As I walked out, I turned around and asked, "George, you

explained the alimony and the quick divorce, but you never told me why you two didn't share custody of the kids. More blackmail, thanks to the polygamy?"

The man put down his ice cream. "I'm surprised your grandmother hasn't told you the story. She read the paperwork and saw how much a sham it was. One call to her son—your father—and a week later we had enough evidence to show the judge that my wife was planning on having a nanny raise the kids on her family's estate."

"Growing up with privilege is hardly grounds to grant the other party full custody, George."

"It is when the nanny is an undocumented worker being held like a slave. Velma asked your father to investigate and we could not believe what he and your mother found out. Your parents gathered enough evidence to swing the judge's opinion in my favor. He awarded me full custody of the kids and then set his sights on prosecuting the family."

George had just shared the longest short version of a story I had ever heard. I shifted my feet, edging more and more toward the ice cream store's front door while he continued the tale. George came right out and asked the Commonwealth's Attorney to prove that his ex-wife's family was involved with human trafficking. The media, scenting a sensational story, published the accusation and eventual results from the investigation. The family suffered financially, but thanks to political connections somewhere, no one ended up in jail.

I flashed a smile and a wave as I left. I had no more spare time. I had to step up my pace if I wanted to get to Cosmo's dinner service.

13

Three judges were sitting inside the parlor of the Seagull's Nest. Grimsby was arguing with the camera operator, who reminded him she was a woman and to not address her as a *guy*. Judging from their scowls, I could see the two had been at it for a while. Grimsby was sunburn-red with rage; the woman's dark green eyes were intense, sending emerald beams of scorn through the thick skull of her producer. It took more than a few intentional coughs from the judges to let them both know it was time to end the drama. Dinner was about to be served, and the church ladies were hungry.

The crowd settled down, and I noticed that not a sound emanated from the kitchen. It wasn't like the old wood frame house had soundproof walls, or extra-thick insulation. You couldn't drop a spoon in the kitchen without at least a few people taking notice. Either dinner was arriving by a pizza delivery person, or the kitchen staff had gone mute. I decided this aural omission needed investigation.

A slight push on the kitchen door allowed me to take a peek. Now, I admit I had prejudged Cosmo. At the fairgrounds, he dressed like all the other chefs; here on his own turf, I half-expected to see a young Bohemian man—one still sporting a short goatee, but now wearing cargo pants turned into a pair of shorts via a pair of scissors. In my mind's eye, he would be a risk-taker in both fashion and food. Peering in, this was not the case. At all.

The kitchen was empty. However, through the kitchen's back window, I could see a man working. He was in front of what appeared to be an outdoor oven, the soft red glow lighting only the crags and wisps of his facial features. At least I thought it was an oven. And I was sure it was a man. I opened the window pane a few inches, just enough for the breeze to blow little crooked fingers of smoke inside the kitchen. The dark figure stopped and turned, having heard the squeaks from the opened window. Our eyes met.

"Cosmo? Are you the same Cosmo Finnegan from the exposition hall?"

The man nodded, then went back to adjusting dials on another piece of equipment, a strange bit of machinery sitting off to the side of the oven. *So this is the real Cosmo Finnegan.* He wore full-length black trousers, not cut-off shorts, and military-style black boots and a black chef's coat. No black beret, but the man's hair was long, dark, and wavy. He was so retro, black was the new black.

His coat looked as different as his work environment, its left shoulder epaulet adorned with a red fourragere tipped with a shiny brass nib. His left breast pocket featured a rack of miniature military-style medals. I suppose Cosmo could have been a veteran, but his current *look* did not pay homage to someone once with a buzz cut.

The left sleeve caught my attention. Cosmo was wearing a leather gauntlet, a glove reaching halfway up his forearm. The accoutrement gleamed thanks to a bank of miniature lights, knobs, and switches. His look screamed "video game controller gone awry."

"Yes, ma'am. I figured since I wasn't on display like one of Grimsby's puppets at the fairgrounds, I could revert to my standard wardrobe. Not to worry, though, the food will be the same. Better, in fact, since I get to use my equipment. That crap supplied by MegaFood was—well, it was crap. No easy way to say it, but that's the truth."

"Not something I think a chef who wants to win the prize money would want to say within earshot of the contest sponsors," I said.

"A deal with the devil it is, but what can I do? Neither of us have enough money to move forward with our plans."

"You have a plan? I thought you wanted the trophy and the bragging rights over your boss."

"Who? Georgie? I am not worrying about Georgie. Right now I am more concerned with getting enough coal into this furnace. It powers the entire kitchen."

Cosmo picked up a spade and tossed a few more loads of coal into the red-hot belly of the stove. He had a good stash piled knee-high next to him, within easy reach to keep feeding the glowing monster. Judging by the amount of dust in the immediate area, though, the pile had been much larger.

As Cosmo lifted each new load of coal, he made a grunting noise. I could hear the suck-it-up-and-do-it coming out of each utterance. I hoped he had enough moxie left to power the kitchen through the end of dinner. I was no mechanic, but curiosity forced me to look around to determine how this outdoor stove could *power* a kitchen, as Cosmo had mentioned. That's when I noticed what looked to be a large keg sitting behind the oven.

Cosmo had an interest in the keg, too. Steam hissed around its seams and pipe connections. With each puff of white vapor, I realized as long as steam kept escaping, we were safe. It was when the keg stopped spewing that we would need to run.

After checking a few dials on the keg, Cosmo walked over to an old pitcher pump by the back door. The faded red paint on the handle told me the water well was probably an original fixture of the historic old house. I could see the sweat dripping from his face as Cosmo cranked on the handle, pumping water into a large carafe. However he designed his kitchen, this was a labor-intensive gig, and the poor man was not catching a break.

With full pitcher in hand, he poured the water into a funnel protruding from the side of the keg. Cosmo then secured the lid on top, twisting clockwise the brass knobs whose shine had long since rubbed off through years—no, make that decades—of use. The alchemist-chef adjusted an air intake valve on the oven, allowing the yellow-blue flames inside to push the keg's pressure gauge to its highest setting.

Cosmo pointed to the red zone on the dial. He looked at me and mouthed the word *bad*. Like I needed to be told that?

He pressed a few buttons on his electro-glove. Whatever he was looking at, it met with his approval. With a sense of confidence only a mad scientist could possess, he lowered the flames.

"No," Cosmo mused, "Georgie will win now that old Pierre is gone. I had a chance until I found out the judges were those prim ladies. For them, it's deep-fried or nothing. My style of cooking just doesn't mix well with such modern appetites, unless you have a more, how you say, *worldly* attitude?"

"So you are telling me you *don't* want to win? That makes no sense at all. You must have your reasons to want to win, don't you? Everyone does. You said something about a plan?"

"Unlike the others, I will never compromise my cooking philosophy just to win some stupid contest, but I do have a use for the prize money. Rings are not cheap, if you understand what I mean."

"I like the shade of lipstick you wore at the fairgrounds, Cosmo. I think I have something similar at home."

"You don't miss much, do you?"

"Oh, I do okay, but I'm kind of at a loss for the purpose of all this gear. It almost looks like your pressure cooker is connected to something from underneath an old pickup truck. And it all leads into the kitchen here."

"Every pipe has a purpose. Here, let me start at the beginning of the process. You'll understand once you see how the energy transfers through the conduits. It's all very molecular."

That was a head-scratcher for me. I had no clue what he was talking about, but didn't want to let on. It was time to redirect the conversation.

"All very interesting, but I'm hungry, so I am hoping food is somewhere in your mechanical blueprint."

Cosmo checked his pocket watch, its silver chain lashed to an anodized gold button on his coat. "Oh, *hellz yah*, baby. It's just about time."

The man flipped a red switch on the keg and then sprinted into the kitchen, closing the back door and motioning me away from the window.

"Is everything okay?" I knew little about mechanical things, but assumed a red switch was one you never wanted to flip.

Cosmo looked at his watch again. After a few seconds, he exhaled. "Probably. These things have blown up before and there is no need for anyone to wear dinner."

Probably?

The chef lifted his gauntlet and pressed more buttons and turned knob after knob. The bank of lights imbedded in the leather glove flashed in sequence. It reminded me of Christmas lights wrapped around a tree. Within a few seconds, a rumbling and rattling sound started deep inside the outdoor pressure cooker.

"You mentioned *blow up*. Shouldn't you check the safety valve on your pressure cooker? Those things can make a nasty mess." I related a story about how my grandmother had once splattered a good beef stew all over the kitchen when the safety valve on her pressure cooker malfunctioned. Cosmo ignored me.

"Here's the best part. Hang on," he said, interrupting me.

We watched from a distance as the needle on the pressure gauge rose well into the red zone on the dial. Without realizing it, I stepped back from the wall, unsure how this would end up, except badly.

Cosmo pressed a red button on his sleeve-bound control panel. Within a few seconds, I heard a hiss behind me. It was the metal safety cover lifting off a deep fryer. A metal pipe descended from I don't know where, its spigot dropping golf ball-sized globules of dough into the vat of hot oil below. My brain couldn't fathom what was cooking; however, my nose told me it was hush puppies!

Huzzah! Who doesn't love hush puppies?

Another click, and this time an electric grill arose from within a cube-shaped metal cabinet. The thick metal bars of the grill glowed red as Cosmo hit another switch. A ceiling panel opened with a gush of cool fog rolling down. Cosmo had a refrigeration unit above! One more tug on his switch caused a big slab of beef brisket to be lowered to an inch above the hot grill. I could see a set of cogs and wheels rotating the meat, evenly cooking the whole thing.

The chef pressed a few more controls, activating a nearby steam hose. The increasing pressure sent the hose twisting like a snake caught by its tail. He grabbed the end nozzle, and after taming the wild beast, spritzed the meat with green-tinged shots of steam.

My nose twitched; a sneeze erupted. I knew that now was the time to leave the kitchen.

"Bless you. And sorry about that," Cosmo said. "I should have warned you. You are smelling a mix of cumin and chili powder. Guaranteed to make you sneeze the first time you smell it. Happens all the time. And I think it happened to old Pierre at the contest, too. He had quite a case of sniffles at the start of the day, you know."

I agreed, saying I had heard something about Pierre's problems with his nose. I wasn't sure Cosmo's spice had caused the issue, but I couldn't rule it out.

Cosmo stuck his finger into the mist and then gave it a taste. "Gives the brisket a great flavor. But the cool part is the entire surface gets coated with the seasonings, not just bits and pieces. And, it's an instant marinade, since the steam is powerful enough to penetrate the meat."

"You picked a rather tough piece of meat, Cosmo. Wouldn't a decent chicken give you more to work with? Everyone likes chicken."

"And that is why I am using this brisket instead of chicken. Everyone uses chicken. Pardon the pun, but it tastes like chicken, you know. Where is the challenge in that?"

"Cosmo, I can see you have skills here. In the chef department and with construction, too. I'd even say your mechanical skills are far better than the handyman's who stops by to fix the equipment at the café. But why go through all of this trouble when you can just marinate the beef in a freezer bag for a few hours and get the same effect?"

"That is the second part of the plan. In most restaurants, the dining experience is not about how the food gets cooked, it is almost always about how the food tastes."

"And your restaurant, assuming you want to start one with the leftover prize money, won't have good-tasting food as the number-one concern? I'm not sure how well that will compete in this town." I was thinking of George. His culinary school technique resulted in superb flavors. Not as good as Velma's, but still, very good. Cosmo needed to step up his game.

"In our restaurant, the dining experience will be just that—an experience. People will come for the food, but what will set us apart is the visual. No one else will have twenty-first-century food amidst nineteenth-century industrial-steampunk working decor. It's a culinary show where, in today's case at least, the final act is the food being served to the diner by way of a conveyor belt of sorts."

"Right out of *Metropolis*," I added.

"I love that film!"

"Figured." I pointed behind the chef, asking, "Cosmo, is black smoke *supposed* to come out of that cabinet?"

Cosmo whirled around and, seeing the smoke, grabbed the salt shaker, hoping to put out a small fire in the warming cabinet with it. I thought about telling him about the salt and sugar mix up, but Cosmo was moving so fast, the show was over before I could say another word.

The smell of burning bread permeated the air. Cosmo opened the back window and directed his seasoned steam spray at the approaching clouds of smoke. He was using the intense vapor to create a miniature high-pressure weather system. With luck, it would push the smoke out the window.

I doubted his plan would be successful. Thankfully, no one told Cosmo it wouldn't work. The smoke soon cleared, but left a smell that might last for days. Cosmo gave me a confident fist bump.

The source of the foul cloud became apparent after the air cleared. I took a look at the chef, half-expecting him to quit the competition after seeing the burned food. It could have been worse, I suppose. At least the keg outside hadn't exploded. At least, not yet.

"I hope those rolls were not a key part of your dinner plan, chef. They look beyond help."

"Oh, *that* is where your traditional thinking is all wrong."

Holding up a charred roll about the size of a baseball, Cosmo explained. "You may see a burned roll, but I see a handheld, carbonized bread vessel suitable for holding a salsa or dipping sauce, or maybe even a homemade barbecue sauce. In fact, that's a great idea. I can make my sauce in a few minutes." Fueled by his new idea, the chef ran to the soft drink cooler and grabbed a Dr Pepper.

Instead of drinking the soda, Cosmo put the liquid into a small saucepan on the stove, adding a few cups of brown sugar and a dash of spices. He whisked with verve until the batch of sweet-smelling sauce turned into a reddish gravy, one with just a hint of smoke.

Cosmo walked over the pan of burnt rolls and carved out a small concave opening in the top of each, removing the most blackened bits. Using another hose, also connected to the jumble of pipes, the chef-inventor-mechanic-visionary siphoned the Texas-style sauce into the burned rolls.

"That," he said, "is my *basic* barbecue sauce. You can't go wrong with something made with a hint of Dr Pepper. Better than plain ketchup, I say. This stuff works on everything from guinea hen to turkey."

"And with brisket?" I interjected. "Listen, Cosmo, I think it's time I stop distracting you. I've learned almost everything I need to know here, and I think it is time I go see if old Drake still has a cameraman."

I clicked my heels together and gave Cosmo a salute, a respectful hail and farewell to the kitchen commander.

Cosmo gave a quick gasp as if he had forgotten something, and then, with eyebrows raised, stopped me. "Wait a minute. Do you like cheese?"

"I prefer nutritional yeast myself, but I know I am not the norm. Most people love the stuff. Why do you ask?"

"Look over there—you'll see. This will be so awesome!"

Cosmo pressed another row of buttons on his leather gauntlet; a bicycle wheel mounted on the wall spun. A chain connected to a sprocket wheel rotated, powering a broomstick now pumping up and down into a wooden barrel.

"Goat cheese, churned on the spot. It's as fresh-made as you can get," he said. "We have a small herd of goats out back."

The complexity of the machinery created by someone as young as Cosmo stunned me. He had an artist's vision and an engineer's mind for functional detail.

"You have got quite a show going on here, Cosmo. But all of this showmanship has made me ravenous. I better get to my seat before the cameraman takes my place."

Cosmo raised his finger as if to tell me he had just one more bit of wisdom to impart. "Ah, look, Winnie. Do yourself a favor and call her a camera*woman*, or person, or whatever. Anything but a camera *man*. I've seen that mistake with my own ears and I saw her response, today in fact. It was not a pretty sight, but then again, it was just typical Drake Grimsby. He never had a clue about the big picture. And such a shame, too."

Aha, Cosmo knew something. More than just cooking and welding. Even though no one liked Drake, I moved Cosmo higher on my list of suspects. At the least, Cosmo Finnegan was a person of interest. And not just his girlfriend's interest.

"What do you mean by that? Why such a shame?"

"Look. Grimsby's mom was an excellent cook. She taught me how to cook when I was a young man of fourteen. One day, she let it slip that years ago she tried to teach Drake, too. Apparently, he did not get along well with his mother telling him how to be patient in the kitchen. Rejecting the discipline she required, Drake began coming up with screwy scheme after scheme. Get rich quick. The oldest dream in the world, he had. Get the money without doing the work. Who wouldn't like that?"

"Nice dream, Cosmo, but you and I know the reality of life. Nothing's free." If there was anything I could relate to, it was that nothing is served on the house on the dinner plate of life.

"What I mean is that he never took the time to learn a decent, marketable skill. Now his mom is gone, and I think he is regretting many of his past choices. Probably why he has it out for your grandmother."

"I see. He's trying to make up for lost time. Is that is what you are saying?"

"All I'm saying is the food and beverage industry is full of two-faced crooks either out to get your money or prevent you from making it. I won't accuse the man of murder, but I'm not saying he's innocent, either."

"What about Pierre St. Pierre? Would you have trusted him?" I plied the young chef for information that might lead to a motive in Pierre's demise.

"Well, it's no secret he and I had a public argument last month. But, I didn't kill him, if that's where you are going with this."

"It depends on who said what to whom. What was the argument about?"

Cosmo ignored the question, instead opting to insert a large screwdriver into a slot in the wall. Twisting the tool clockwise, he set off a steam-powered engine powering a bevy of gears and wheels. As the puttering from the engine increased tempo, Cosmo dropped the screwdriver and ran to a control switch on the wall. As he pulled the switch down, I could hear the hiss of steam escaping from the now-opened valves. The engine and gears both came to a halt.

"Phew! That was almost a huge mistake," he said. "Timing is everything in my business and I almost ruined the surprise. Look, I'm sorry, Winnie, but I need to concentrate a little more on food and less on your inquisition."

"Apologies are due from me, I'm afraid. Not your fault at all. I thought you might want an opportunity to explain your relationship with the murder victim. The more I know now, the more I could help you later when the true story comes out in the official police investigation."

Cosmo looked resigned to spending a few more minutes with a nosey neighbor.

"I see your point. Well, George here is primed to take over the bed and breakfast, though he needs a little more money. The owner wants to sell it to him at a price well below market value, but his kids are going off to college, so he's got to hire more staff. It all takes money. I offered to become a partner with him but he has no desire to veer away from his own style of cooking—and he clearly does not like mine."

"Sounds like professional jealousy," I added.

"I think the real issue is that George knows he can either manage or cook, but he can't do both. He's a Southern gentlemen chef, through and through. He'll never change culinary style, nor will he allow someone under his charge to change it, either. But he can't run both the front of the house *and* the kitchen. It's a trust issue, and he doesn't trust me."

"That's not what he told me. But how does this play into your argument with Pierre?"

"The day George turned me down as a partner, my potential for success at the Seagull's Nest dropped. I needed to go somewhere new, a place where my new ideas of combining modern cuisine with retro techniques would be welcome."

"Somewhere upscale, where a more *modern* chef would welcome your ideas?"

"I went to the new restaurant in town, P-Squared. I figured Pierre, being trained in Europe, would have a broader perspective, a friendly attitude toward the diversity of my cuisine. He had traveled; I assumed he at least *knew* all the latest trends. If anyone, the mighty Pierre St. Pierre should have been open to a different culinary viewpoint."

"It didn't work out that way, I assume? And so I guess that's where you had it out with Pierre?"

"Yes, we argued. But it was less than a minute of loud and spiteful words. My words were not much better."

"Sounds awful. What did he say?"

"I went into the restaurant and presented my ideas to the chef, and do you know what he did? He laughed me right out into the street. Pierre had the audacity to say I was a 'lost little cook, looking for my broken-down food truck.' And he said it in front of all of his customers. They all got a good chuckle at my expense."

"And what did you say?"

Cosmo looked down with embarrassment. "This will sound bad, but I told him I hoped he dropped dead from all the nitrate-filled bacon grease he used in every recipe."

"You are right. That doesn't sound good."

At this point, I didn't think the lad was guilty of killing the arrogant old chef. Getting tossed from a restaurant wasn't the end of the world, and certainly not enough to end a life. But there was still more evidence to find, more suspects to interview. And besides, I was *still* hungry. I gave Cosmo a light pat on the back and wished him well with his dinner service.

The spat Cosmo had mentioned, the one between Drake and his assistant, had subsided by the time I sat down. However, one lady whispered in my ear that she had overheard Grimsby mumbling to himself a few minutes earlier. He was planning on firing the woman after the finale. Whatever was going on, it was far from over.

The judge then pulled back her dinner napkin to reveal an envelope full of cash. Her peers, with all their impeccable credentials, were placing their bets on the green-eyed camerawoman. When asked, I declined to partake.

* * *

Cosmo did not have the same serving help as his boss; in fact, he was not much older than George's two kids. But he looked in command. Cosmo wore the same paramilitary culinary uniform as before, but now had an admiral's hat complete with the requisite scrambled eggs on the visor.

The chef entered the dining room carrying a tray of what looked like sushi, though I didn't remember seeing anything aquatic in the kitchen. One thing was certain: Cosmo was a risk-taker. Who knew if the church ladies were fans of raw fish? I had my doubts.

My guess as to the judges' reaction was correct. Complaints started before Cosmo could make it back to the kitchen. Soon there was a chorus of comments like, "I don't think we could eat something like this, young man. Is it cooked?" and "It looks raw. Is it supposed to be like that?"

Cosmo heard the uproar and mounted a hasty defense.

"Oh, ladies, not to worry. This meal is made from vegetables straight from the garden out back, and real, honest-to-goodness beef brisket from cows, not fish."

Cosmo continued his tap dance of words, trying to win over people who normally considered *haute* cuisine as any food that didn't come in a basket handed out at a drive-through window. He was having a difficult time.

I don't know what came over me. I guess I liked the kid. And seeing him outnumbered by so many obstinate personalities made me root for the underdog. I remembered the problem with George's dessert. The solution popped into my mind and went straight out of my mouth with no filter. This wasn't a culinary problem, it was a selling problem. And if my grandmother had taught me anything at the Cat and Fiddle, it was how to sell.

"Cosmo, seeing that most of these ladies are so health-conscious, and from the looks of it, doing very well watching their figures, did you remind them all that your food is low-calorie?"

Those were the magic words. As the ladies congratulated themselves on being such experts on the USDA food pyramid, Cosmo clicked the heels of his boots together and raised his hand to his eyebrow in a salute.

"Absolutely, Miss Kepler. This is typical of the food I will serve once we, ah, I mean, I have my restaurant. And watch out for the black beans. They are cooked in salsa to intensify the heat. That's why you will find a cube of nice, creamy white goat cheese on the side to sooth your palate. As they say in Mexico, *buen provecho*! Happy eating!"

Centered on my plate were four domes of Spanish rice, each surrounded by a bevy of seasoned black beans and steamed vegetables. Pressed into the top of each mound of rice was a fork's worth of tender brisket. I worked my way around the meat, but as I took my first bite of the flavorful chunks of zucchini, my nose twitched from the same cumin treatment Cosmo had used on the meat. The rice, beans, and vegetables were savory. We all agreed that the food was marvelous, and that Cosmo was a culinary genius.

Was he guilty of murder? Perhaps, but he was still a superb chef. Once the evidence played out, someone was getting a great culinarian. The only question in my mind was *who*. It would be Seaview or the state penitentiary. I knew my choice.

The brisket, a good substitute for shoe leather when cooked poorly, was so tender it fell apart on the ladies' forks. They all agreed the seasonings were there, yet not one flavor overpowered the other. This was the best Asian-infused Tex-Mex food anyone had ever tasted. As good as it was, I was not sure if it was Tex or Mex. I knew it was *not* Asian. Whatever the name, it was good.

After bringing out a second round of brisket, Cosmo explained the *proper* technique for eating his entrée. The process involved spooning some of the barbecue sauce from the roll onto the bite-sized serving of brisket. Then, using the same spoon, one was to scoop up the entire glob of rice and eat everything at once.

The judges dove in for round two. Every plate on the table was clean; there were no survivors and no regrets. I settled for a second round of vegetables, my favorite being the wedges of steamed parsnips so tasty they made potatoes jealous.

Cosmo again flipped switches on his gauntlet as he announced the dessert course was about to begin. I had only seen the brisket being prepared, not the dessert. This final course would be a total surprise.

After Cosmo cleared a double load of empty dinner plates from the dining room, the chef returned to address the final course. I noticed right away the eccentric culinary strategist walking in without a serving tray in his arms. What surprise he would have in store for us now? The answer came straight away.

"Ladies, please indulge me for a few moments while I start things in motion. The finale to your dining experience tonight begins!"

He moved a coat rack to the side, uncovering a large lever, three feet long, attached to a steel plate affixed to the wooden floor.

"Does George know about this?" I asked.

"Not yet," he answered. "Hence the coat rack camouflage. But I think he will grow to appreciate it *and* the opportunities my culinary vision can bring to the restaurant. If he'll ever see things my way." With a look of mischief, Cosmo pulled the lever.

"Goodness," said one judge. "I hope this doesn't open a trapdoor or anything."

Cosmo gave a maniacal laugh. "No, far from it, ma'am. Just wait. We should see dessert in about five, four, three, two . . ."

Everyone in the dining room ducked, slumping in their seats when train whistle started its peal from within the kitchen. Our attention focused on a dumbwaiter panel in the wall as it opened with a puff of white steam. A toy train, something about the size you would expect wrapped around a Christmas tree in December, appeared in the opening; a diminishing hiss of pressurized steam bursting from underneath the wheels.

"Cosmo, there's no track. How is the train supposed to move?" I asked.

Before he could answer, the sound of the train engine began a slow crescendo, getting louder and louder. Cosmo ran back inside the kitchen, only to reappear with a preassembled train track mounted on an ironing board. He adjusted the board's height, leveling it with the table, and bridged the gap between us and the dumbwaiter. The train chug, chug, chugged onto the ironing board and headed in our direction. I lifted my fork as I saw the last car, a caboose labeled *Whipped Cream.* Before the train reached the end of the board, Cosmo stopped it with a flip of a switch on his gauntlet.

Cosmo ran back into the kitchen. This time? He had a tray full of waffles! These weren't just any waffles—they were thick, Belgian-style squares, each about three quarters of an inch thick.

"You will love *these* waffles," Cosmo said. He restarted the train, guiding it onto the table. Once the caboose arrived at the center of the table, he shut down the engine.

Cosmo lifted a small hose from the tanker car and pointed it toward the tray. The inventor-chef then sprayed a fine mist of maple syrup, covering the waffles. After spooning a snowfall of powdered sugar over each stack, Cosmo finally topped each off with an elegant dollop of whipped cream.

"Please, help yourself," he said. "If you would like cinnamon or clarified butter, just open the two remaining box cars, the ones in front of the tanker. All aboard, have fun, and again, happy eating!"

The judges and I found ourselves delighted with the interactive food *and* the presentation. If I had to pick a winner, it would have been Cosmo and his HO gauge railway cuisine. When I mentioned my thought to the chef, he took a deep bow.

As I finished eating, I could feel the telltale buzz of my cell phone. Looking at the screen, I excused myself. Something had come up at the Cat and Fiddle requiring my attention.

14

By the time I made it back to the Cat and Fiddle, Velma had already cooked up some of her famous chicken and dumplings. The smell of the savory aromatics, little gems like garlic, thyme, and oregano, filled the air. If I hadn't already sampled the wonderful food cooked by Cosmo, I would have whipped up a tofu version before taking off my coat. Just because I didn't eat meat, didn't mean I didn't love the smell of memories.

Sitting at the counter were two weary but familiar travelers. I saw empty salad bowls next to empty bread baskets scattered with crumbs. The dumplings came next.

"You two look happy," I said. "Is it the appetizers, or something else?" What a loaded question. I knew it wasn't the food.

I picked up a clean towel and wiped down the counter. The guests were still eating as if it was their first meal in months.

Tricia spoke first. "Winnie, I don't know how to say thanks. I was at my wits' end and the only thing I could think to do was leave. When Fran showed up in the taxi, I couldn't believe my eyes. It was a sign, I was sure of it."

"Yes, Winnie. Once the hug was over, we looked at each other and said the same thing. We knew then everything would be just fine with you having our back." Fran was trying to speak *and* eat. It was not going well. She was stabbing at the chicken and dumplings, watching pieces fall from her fork as she was speaking. I decided against laughing for the moment.

"Slow down, you guys," I said. "I am getting tired just watching you. Anyway, I am glad my hunch about the train paid off."

"Us, too, believe me," said Tricia. "But, once MegaFood finds out we didn't finish their little plan, I am afraid things might get a little sketchy for everyone."

"How so? And what plan?" I asked.

"You don't just take two thousand dollars in cash and then *not* do what you are told," Tricia said. "The MegaFood guy didn't give us a choice. He said he knew people who would be happy to convince us if we balked at his direction."

Shaking her head, Francine offered a countering opinion. "But we don't have to worry now. Soon enough these idiots will learn they can't use our relationship as a blackmail threat. That's all done now."

"Are you sure? Going public may run off some of your customers." Seaview was still a conservative town. So much so, that when the café added a vegetarian section to the menu, it was the talk of the hardware store for months. Who would want to eat such a meal, they asked? No bacon, either? Sacrilege, they said. A few months later, people requested the tofu chili. I was amazed. Some ate the chili, liked it, and *then* found out it was tofu. Regrettably, I haven't seen them come back.

But it might take years for a few of our residents to accept that some women were fine with being lesbian *in public*. And that they might live in Seaview. As if there weren't others already. People are so stupid.

I continued my benevolent interrogation of Tricia by asking, "And what about those goons you mentioned? MegaFood is a huge corporation with deep pockets. They didn't seem to have a problem coming up with a few bucks to pay you. More cash paid to some thugs could prove their point. Are you sure you are up to taking on the risk?"

Putting my feelings on the line, I admitted something to myself at the same time I spoke the words out loud. "Fran, I just found you again; I don't want to lose you." It was all I could do to not cry at that point.

"Gangsters aside," Fran said, "you were right in that our biggest concern was the business. But on the way home we had an interesting chat with your taxi driver. Did you know he was from Sicily? Anyway, now the question of the impact on our business has been answered."

Tricia continued. "We asked the taxi driver what he missed the most since he moved here. He said decent pizza. He told us all about how back home, his mother made them from scratch."

Fran spoke up with enthusiasm. "And he was so nice. He gave us his mom's recipe for the dough. And with all the fresh tomatoes being grown here on the Shore, pizza was a natural choice."

"So you're opening a pizza joint?" All I could think of was hundreds of little kids running around screaming and playing silly games for paper tickets—all to buy a stuffed toy worth less than the cost of a side salad. Harried parents cowered in the corner booths, attempting to eat a cold, stale slice of pepperoni pizza pie.

"Absolutely," Tricia said. "But we want to make it a nice place to take your date. We also wanted to provide convenience so we thought a delivery service would be nice, too. And now we know a taxi driver who likes pizza! I'm sure a deal could be made."

Fran put down her spoon and asked, "You haven't said yet, Winnie. What *do* you think?"

I thought about the unintended consequences of their decision. "And the guy from MegaFood? He's okay with this deal of the century?" As exciting as it was to hear of their new business venture, and their new commitment to each other, I reminded them about the reality of corporate greed and corruption.

Tricia picked up her cell phone and after a few taps, showed me the electronic record of a phone call made a half hour earlier.

"Far from it," she said. "Once we had sold our business, his money was of no use to us anymore. On the way here, we found a grocery store with a Western Union desk. Two minutes later, the money was returned. And MegaFood has already posted a receipt online. We are free!"

"And it's all because we are now about as *out* of the closet as you can get, and did that news make the man upset," Francine said. "But there may still be one problem. Winnie, have you heard anything new about your job offer? It was from a bank, wasn't it?"

"Sort of, yes. From a financial management company called Mint Street Bankers. A project of sorts designed by a well-intentioned grandmother. Why do you ask?" I noticed my hands were twisting a napkin into a crooked magic wand thanks to the tension building throughout my body. In all the excitement, I had pushed thoughts of my being cajoled into accepting an executive career back into the far reaches of my mind, waiting for a better time to be brought forth. Or not back at all.

"Well, there was a newspaper in the back seat of the taxi. It was today's edition of the *Seaview Times Herald*. On the back page, next to all the vacation rental ads, there was a small article about how your company, Mint Street Bankers, had just became the major shareholder of three or four big companies. And MegaFood was one of them."

I shrugged my shoulders. My anxiety level subsided with the news, much to my surprise. "Mint Street isn't *my* company. And I don't think I need to be concerned about a transaction at such a high level. MegaFood is one of the biggest companies around, and if Mint Street could buy *them,* I doubt they would know a little girl like me even exists. Thanks for the concern, though. But are you sure this is over?"

Tricia explained. "All he wanted us to do was cook up a phony job fair at your place. And do whatever it takes to use up your time."

So, MegaFood had something to do with Pierre's murder. This was a new turn of events. A turn for the worse.

Fran added that she thought the man was just a lower-paid henchman. "Someone's pulling the string on his back, telling him what to say and what to do. He looked kind of, I don't know, kind of sheepish at the Richmond event. An order-taker, not an order-giver. But that's just my opinion. Tricia did a good job of telling him off."

"Tricia, did you threaten him?" I asked.

"I reminded him that we never shook hands and did not sign a contract. And I *may* have mentioned there were customers in your diner who not only liked you and your grandmother, but they could also shoot the tail feathers off a duck at three hundred yards *and* field gut a deer in a matter of minutes," Tricia said.

Fran interjected. "We heard guys talking about their hunting trip. As long as they and their friends like your grandmother's barbecued venison pizza, I think we will always have support if we need it."

Tricia concluded, "He hung up after that comment. I would be surprised if he ever crosses the bridge to our little sliver of Virginia."

I had underestimated the bond these two women had with each other. When I complimented the couple on their honor, courage, and commitment to each other, they said it wasn't as much a sense of duty to each other, as it was just *love*.

I raised a glass of ice tea and offered a toast. As the words about love and commitment were flowing, in the back of my mind I was hoping I could find the same feeling someday. I was thinking about Parker.

* * *

Velma came over to our table, hoping to clear away the dishes. She asked the girls if they wanted anything else. Velma held out a small plate showcasing a slice of her apple pie. She bragged a little, saying it would be the crowning touch on her picnic meal tomorrow.

"Grandma, you have to cook for the contest *tomorrow*?" I asked. "I thought it was the next day."

"Drake *Brigsly*, as I heard a customer refer to him today, called and said the judges wanted to do two meals in one day. They had such a good time with George and Cosmo that they wanted to try the same format again. So lunch is at the rail yard with Bailey cooking, and dinner is here at the old Cat and Fiddle with yours truly behind the frying pan. And they mentioned something else, too. Do you know anything about extra guests?

Pastors, I think they said."

Ignoring her comment on the extra diners, I offered, "You know, grandma, instead of apple pie for dessert today, we could save it for tomorrow and try something new. Something like a chocolate pecan pie in a parfait glass? Don't worry about your apple pie. It's a winner; you don't need our vote."

Everyone thought the chocolate pecan pie was a great idea. I recounted how I had learned the recipe from George after he had to make the culinary detour due to the spice switcheroo. We made it a team project, with all of us bounding back into the kitchen to try our hand at making the layered dessert.

There was non-stop laughter and the occasional cloud of flour rising from the prep table. I even had to referee a debate about how to pronounce the word *pecan*. Tricia said the Southern way to say the word was something akin to *pee-can*. Francine disagreed, saying that when she was a little girl in Texas, her kindergarten class would often go for a walk around the neighborhood, picking up *puh-cahns* that had fallen from the trees lining the streets. After I noticed Tricia's pronunciation mimicked the slang word for a chamber pot, everyone agreed that we would go with the Texan version.

15

Velma had already worked for an hour before my feet hit the floor the next morning. She had been wanting to sharpen her wooden skewers, but realized she had forgotten to order them. Instead of placing an emergency call to the closest food supply warehouse, Velma improvised. When I walked down the stairs into the kitchen, I found her rummaging through the back storeroom.

I sat for my first cup of coffee as clangs and bangs emanated from within the storeroom. A sombrero flew out of the door, followed by several green-and purple-feathered boas. That's when I heard my grandmother cry, "Found it!"

"Dare I ask?" I had no idea what to expect.

"Chinese New Year, 1952. These chopsticks are genuine bamboo; perfect for the fried chicken on a stick. I figure as long as it's a stick, the advertising is true. Who knows? Maybe I'll add some peanut sauce and call it Far Eastern Chicken on a Chopstick."

"Well, I think you should *stick* with the good old fried chicken you had planned. Everyone likes fried chicken; and when you are famished, there's nothing better than fried food on a stick. If you could add corn dogs and mustard to your menu, you would be all set."

"You're right, Winnie. I'll play it safe, so to speak, and keep the presentation simple. When are you planning on visiting Bailey?"

"Once I get this last bucket of chicken submerged in the marinade. I am curious as to her cooking skills. When she worked for her parents, at their old restaurant at least, the only thing they would let her do is decorate. I heard she even caught a milkshake on fire once."

"Now *that* is a talent. But in all honesty, I hope she does well. Even if she doesn't win, it sounds like her cooking reputation could use a boost." Velma was always the positive one, trying to boost everyone's self-esteem.

"I imagine Cosmo will be there, too," I said. "And judging by the lipstick he seems to wear every time I see him, I might need the fire extinguisher for more than just the milkshakes."

"Winnie, you are bad. Atrocious," Velma said with laughter. "But Parker *could* stand a lesson or two in courtship from Cosmo."

My grandmother just loved to drop hints about how to manage my social life. Velma's advice always ended with her trademark throw-away remark about how she wasn't getting any younger. That, and how she didn't want to die and leave me alone in the world. As if that would ever happen. I had parents. And Fran. And I could always get a puppy.

"Well played, Grandma. Well played. But let's just worry about the Saucy Skillet trophy right now. And once I have the job locked in with Mint Street, I will speak to Parker about his intentions. But remember, we barely know each other right now. These things take time."

"Don't wait too long, girl. I won't be around forever, you know."

"He hasn't even asked me on a date yet. Let's not get ahead of ourselves. You'll just need to hang on for a little while longer. Love is like a pot of water warming on the stove. It's got to get steamy before it boils over."

I stopped the conversation, hoping to change the subject without my grandmother noticing. Velma looked right at me. We both knew this was the first time I had admitted my burgeoning feelings for Parker, using the *L* word. The words that just came pouring out like Cosmo's syrup on the pancakes would dry up and blow away in the breeze.

The best plan I could come up with involved a fast exit. Pivoting on the heel of my right foot, I aimed my body toward to the front door and started walking. If I kept moving, Grandma wouldn't be able to continue the conversation.

"Well, the marinade is all done and the chicken will be ready for breading by the middle of the afternoon, and I should be back by then to help."

"You better go." Grandma tasted the marinade. "May need more salt."

"Yes and no. Yes, I'm on the way. And no, I'd add white pepper instead of salt."

"Will he be there?"

"No, I don't think so. He has to work at the station."

"Too bad. Maybe I'll drop by with a plate of cookies for the boys."

"Grandma, you want to tell him what I said, don't you?" We both knew the answer.

"I wouldn't interfere with your love life. Not my place, dear."

"Make sure you don't. Please."

She walked toward the kitchen door. "Just run along. Give my regards to Bailey. I will want a full report later. And white pepper? Too much. A pinch of salt it is."

"Do I need to call the station and warn Parker?"

"The cookies won't be *that* bad. The salt is going in the marinade, not the dough."

"That's not what I'm talking about, Grandma. You know what I mean."

"Winnie, I said I wouldn't."

"Please make sure you don't. I'll talk to Parker about a date— when I'm ready."

"If you are near the Dollar Store, check on prices for new canes, would you? Mine is getting kind of rickety."

"Your cane is fine, and besides, you don't use it. Plus, everything in the Dollar Store costs a dollar. That's why they call them dollar stores. Now, shouldn't you be working on the potato salad now? If you want it to be chilled, it should go in the cooler soon."

"Winnie, the spuds will be fine; I know what I'm doing. Run along now."

"Yes. And one last time, please don't talk to him."

"Grandchild of mine, relax. You know I'll do the right thing. Now go on."

I would not win this war, and we both knew it. I gave her a kiss on the cheek and left. As I walked across the grass field to reach the rail yard, I replayed the last conversation over and over in my mind. What *was* the right thing? Did Velma know what was right for me?

Gads, did *I* know what was right? Could me blurting out the fact I may love Parker have been my heart speaking? Before my brain's defense system could activate? This relationship crap was becoming way too difficult.

I came up with a plan. When this Pierre drama was over, I would pull Parker by the collar down to my level and ask *him* out. Next, lay a big kiss on him. A full-on frontal smack on the lips. Depending on his response, I'd either kiss the man again, or drag him home like a cave girl. Deep down, I knew I would have him one way of the other. Was I becoming one of those obsessive stalkers? Not me.

16

Seagulls wandered the rail yard, scavenging for insects among the mismatch of abandoned track, empty boxcars, and rusting maintenance equipment. The doors of a dilapidated tin storage shed flapped in the gentle breeze, their hinges creaking in harmony with the birds' cawing.

I had to sidestep many a gull who had mistaken me for a tourist with pockets full of bread crumbs. They hopped about in front of my path, and then, receiving no satisfaction, retreated to the safety of nearby flatcars.

There were more insistent birds, too. Those I shooed away with short kicks, never actually touching the birds. I just hoped to keep my shoes guano-free. Nothing would be more embarrassing than to show up at Bailey's place with nasty, splattered leather shoes. In short order, I found the warehouse containing her pale blue caboose.

Checking the time on my phone, I found I was actually early. After pressing the loading dock door buzzer, I counted twenty seconds before a tiny little voice emanated from a speaker mounted on the door frame. A voice pushed through crackling static, telling me to stand back as the door opened. I was invited.

For a building abandoned so long ago, the door lifted without a sound. I could see the drips and drabs of fresh grease applied to the hinges and gears. Maybe Cosmo had something to do with it? Bright white hanging incandescent lights glowed, obscuring my vision as I stooped under the still-lifting door. As soon as I had made my way inside, I flinched as a loud Klaxon horn sounded, warning me of the door's imminent closing.

Something appeared from the shadows beyond the beaming lights above me. It was small and it ran fast. Before I could turn, the creature was gone.

A female voice yelled, "Tinkers! Bring that moustache back!"

Moustache?

"Hi, Winnie, I didn't expect to see you so early. You didn't see where that klepto-cat went to, did you?"

I saw Bailey standing on the back landing of the caboose. Looking around and seeing no cat, I replied with hunched shoulders. "Ah, sorry. I think she went toward the flatcars? She's a fast cat, you know. Did you say moustache?"

"Never mind, I have a spare," she said. "Come on in, will you? Watch your step though. I spilled a glass of wine on the steps when Tinkers ambushed me."

"I didn't realize Tinkers was such a commando," I said.

Bailey brushed fur off her shoulder. "It was like she was hiding on the roof, just waiting. Once the door opened, that's when Tinkers launched her attack. The fur on my shirt, I can deal with. The claw marks, not so much. And I still don't know how she ripped off my fake moustache. The cat's a menace! And now I need more wine for the sauce I'm reducing."

I climbed aboard, then stopped to look around. I had never been on an old-fashioned steam train before, and Bailey's caboose was the tail end of a four-car set. Leading the way was an antique steam engine, its brass fittings shined and bell poised to ring whenever the conductor pulled a one-foot hemp rope.

The coal car followed, its box almost full of the black stones needed to power the engine. My guess was that this load was from the final order received before the railway went bankrupt. I could see the handles of a pair of shovels half-buried in the coal by the last person to work as the stoker.

The dining car was third in line; a two-toned blue conveyance still smelling of fresh paint. This car was lit up from the inside, a romantic, soft ivory glow coming from small table lanterns. I strained my neck and saw twin rows of tables inside already adorned with white tablecloths and centerpieces of mums and baby's breath. Bailey had done well.

The last car was the iconic blue caboose. I assumed it served as both the kitchen and the sleeping quarters for the crew. And by crew, I meant Bailey.

"Is there anything I can do to help, Bailey? Set a table? Greet the judges?"

I then realized I could smell nothing cooking. Perhaps I needed to help the girl light a stove?

"Bailey? Do you have anything started yet? Your lunch doesn't come out of a can, does it?"

"You are so funny, Winn. In fact, I am almost all done. Here, let me give you a tour of my new *restaurant*."

Restaurant? Unless the train could pull around a fast-food place and fit under the drive-through window canopy, I couldn't see it. We walked past the engine and the coal car, then scaled the black metal stairway rising to the dining car.

"I like your train car's name. *Southern Comfort* has a nice ring to it. Reminds me of the days when I would come visit my grandmother. You may have a winner here, Bailey. I hope the food is just as comforting."

"I like to think so. The final menu is still under development, but today's offerings are a good start. This will be a family destination point, part historical reenactment, part steampunk science fiction fantasy. And I have something the kids will want. The only thing missing is a dog park, but I had to draw the line somewhere."

"You're serving the judges a kid's meal? The theme is all-American picnic, right?"

"Yes, but meals aren't just about eating food. I'm serving the judges *memories*. Experiences, if you like. This may not be the fanciest meal they will have had this week, but I think it will be the one the judges talk about the most, and for the longest time."

I wasn't sure if Bailey was a future James Beard award-winner, or someone destined to work on the line at Mrs. Baird's Bakery.

"So, Bailey, let me ask you, if it won't interfere with your cooking, so to speak, about the murder the other day. You've had a run-in or two with Pierre, yes?"

"Oh, you don't know the half of it, Winnie. When my parents and I heard Uncle Peter was coming back to town, at first we were happy. We thought Seaview would finally have a four-star restaurant. A fine dining place would bring more tourists, and that would benefit everyone. Uncle Peter had the skills, the experience. He could even speak French. That was '08, just before the economy went sinking right into the bay."

"That's when the tractor company closed, right?"

"Yeah," she replied. You could hear the letdown in her voice. I was such a fun-sucker.

Bailey paused for a second, and then perked right up like a cheerleader whose team was starting a comeback rally.

"The tractor guys were our best customers. Without them, we lost money right and left. And I knew it would be hard even for a chef as experienced as Peter to get something exquisite going from scratch. Our own, well-established family-style place was already serving a negative profit margin; one in red double digits. How could a new place survive? I think the only reason your grandmother's place survived was the fact that she lived there. For us, we had two monthly mortgage payments. We couldn't set up tents in the dining room so the decision was made to sell the restaurant."

As the sad tale continued, we wandered into the dining car. I picked up a wine glass and checked it for water spots. It was perfectly translucent. Even the salt and pepper shakers glistened. Knives, forks, and spoons were aligned with the lowest edge of the plates. Nothing seemed left to chance.

"But you all ended up here. How'd that happen, if those were your two choices?"

Bailey clasped her hands as if to pray. "Providence. You ever have something in mind, something you want, some—I don't know—*thing* that you believe if you have it, or at least will soon get it, that your life will be so much better? That was us and the new four-star restaurant. We were so sure we would be okay if the restaurant could just hang on long enough for dad to make a deal with his brother."

"But it didn't happen."

"No, it didn't. My dad had put all his hope in Peter, assuming he would give up on his own plan and want to buy into our restaurant. We would make him the operating partner so he could develop the place into his own. My parents were in their sixties, Winnie. They didn't want to be washing dishes anymore. They were ready to hand over the keys in return for a little financial security in their old age."

I waved my hand to the row of two-top tables covered with white tablecloths, fine china, and little tea lights serving as ambiance. "What about you? Did your parents ever talk to you about taking over the family business? From the looks of the dining car here, you seem to have a handle on presentation."

Bailey smirked with a sense of resignation. "They did, but I was never a great cook. One time I scared the neighborhood dogs *and* cats when my potatoes exploded in the oven. I never knew you had to stick a fork in raw potatoes before baking them. Did you know that? I never knew that. Someone should have told me," she said.

"I think I may have heard that somewhere before," I said uneasily. "So if not a chef, what *was* your plan? How did you end up here? Doing this? I may be crazy, but it looks like, for as bad a cook as you say you are, you're doing well impersonating a chef."

"Uncle Peter's selfish behavior made me sick to my stomach. I had studied hospitality management in high school, and I had taken a few classes over the Internet. I mean, I'm all for running a place, just not cooking for it. If it weren't for my, my parents—"

Bailey couldn't finish her sentence.

"I'm so very sorry."

"Thanks," she said, wiping away tears. "But they are much happier now, I'm sure of it. Much more so than during the last few months. Mom went first, may she rest in peace. Stress. Disappointment. Heart attack."

"How'd you handle all of that? You must have an amazing sense of self."

"Oh, yes, I handled it *so* well. Not. I locked myself in this caboose for three weeks, crying. Some amazing hero, huh? I often wonder what would have happened if I had focused on the back of the house, cooking, rather than the front of the house. Would the family business have become *Bailey's Bistro?* Would my parents still be here? Their deaths could have been all my fault."

As we walked from the dining car to the caboose-kitchen, I tried to change the mood of the conversation back to the positive. "Listen, Bailey, I don't blame you at all, so don't you dare blame yourself, either. I'm just glad you have bounced back and have a plan, with or without Pierre."

"My parents had bought life insurance policies when they married. A week after my mother had passed, a man from the insurance company showed up here at the caboose. Beats me how he found out where we were staying, since we were trying to keep a low profile. I mean, we *were* squatting, so who'd want to draw unwanted attention, you know? But anyway, the guy hands me a check. I didn't know what to do, so I held on to it. After dad went, another check showed up. That's when I went to the bank and then to a lawyer straight away to buy this train. I have legitimate standing to be here now and no one can take that away from me."

"Wow, that's a great story, except the parents-passing-away part. So now it's just you living and working here?"

"Worked for your grandmother, didn't it? And she's one of the smartest people I know. Why fool with a plan that works?"

"Good point. So you bought the train; I love the concept. It'll be great once the tourist season starts again. I imagine the prize money will help a lot with more remodeling."

I looked around the caboose. This final railcar held the sleeping quarters in the rear third, the remaining two-thirds reserved for cooking and storage space. Every square inch served a purpose.

"Yes, I have a few more things on my list; upgrades I would like to do to the old car here, but most of the money will buy space on the rail. I have enough coal to last about a month if I make one run a day from Seaview to Chincoteague and back. But the real money goes to Norfolk Eastern Railway. They bought the rights to the line, so I can sit here all day at no charge, but if I fire up the engine and steam out past the town limit, I am forced to pay them by the linear foot."

"And it isn't cheap?" I asked.

"Let me put it to you this way, I'll need at least a half-full train of paying customers each time to break even. Hopefully, I'll fill more seats; I need to build up a cash reserve. It will take a lot to keep this train wreck moving through the winter. More coal, too. It all costs money."

"Well, then. Let's focus on today, shall we? What choice caboose cuisine are you cooking today? I noticed the stoves aren't lit. Going with sushi? Raw foods? Maybe smoked salmon?"

"It's all hush-hush for now, Winnie. But I will show you one thing. I'm proud of Cosmo for making it. We're an item, you know."

"So I gather. He spoke about you when I was over at the bed and breakfast."

"Not *too* much, I hope." She giggled. "Some things just need to remain a secret, right? Anyhow, hand me that bag of peanuts, will you?"

I reached up to a high shelf and secured the brown paper bag labeled *Authentic VA Peanuts*. There were many crops grown in the Commonwealth of Virginia, but the most acclaimed—aside from the now out-of-vogue tobacco leaf—was our tiny peanut.

"Ah, going with Asian cuisine, very different, yet somewhat reminiscent of Cosmo's style."

I was guessing the ethnicity of Bailey's menu. She could have been creating in several culinary genres.

"Very different as in atrocious?" Bailey had a look of panic. I didn't realize she was hoping for my approval.

"No, Bailey. I think a little Far East cooking is a great idea. Anyway, no one has served a true ethnic food yet. Cosmo was close, but it was Tex-Mex wrapped in an Asian package. Yes, I think you should stick with it, Bailey."

The cook laughed. "You are so funny, Winnie. I never said I was cooking Asian food. Here, let me show you what we're doing here." Bailey poured the peanuts, shelled and roasted, into a metal canister. She then added a cup of vegetable oil and a half cup of mixed spices.

I looked at the plethora of wires and hoses hooked up to the canister and knew who was behind this operation. "This has Cosmo's name all over it. What does it do?"

Bailey just smiled, remaining silent as she opened a circuit breaker box and pulled down the main switch. The lights in the caboose dimmed for a second, and then returned to full brightness as we heard hidden machinery come to life.

"In about ten minutes," Bailey said, "you will have the most fab peanut butter sauce ever. Care for a drink of watermelon?"

"Excuse me?"

"Here, just try it." Bailey poured a glass of chilled water, pinkish in hue, and topped it with a small mint leaf. As she handed me the glass, Bailey counted on her fingers.

Being unsure of the drink's content, I held the glass up to the light of the nearby window. Seeing nothing life-threatening, I took the chance and brought the glass up to my nose and took in a deep breath.

The sweetness of the watermelon was evident; the mint's light and delicate fragrance danced about. After a test-sip, I chugged down the remaining drink. I opted not to belch for propriety's sake, but I am sure my long exhale told the truth of my contentment.

"That, my dear Bailey, is a winner! Refreshing, cool, sweet but not too sweet. You *are* serving this for lunch, right?"

"I'd be foolish not to. It will be a nice complement to the entrée."

"Which is?"

"Try this." The chef handed me a wooden spoon with a dollop of the homemade peanut butter.

Again, I crinkled my nose with two quick sniffs of the spoon's cargo. And just as I had enjoyed the refreshing aroma of the beverage, I enjoyed the olfactory avalanche caused by the spices used in the peanut butter. Perhaps I underestimated the skill of this young competitor.

I complimented Bailey on the recipe, and then walked back to the dining car to prepare myself for the meal. Once I found a seat at the end of the car, I realized what had just happened.

Bailey Babbitt, a girl who appeared to be so innocent, one with a sob story that'd make a cemetery's stone angel cry, wasn't as naïve as everyone thought. No, far from it.

I had just spent twenty minutes alone with a suspect, and what did I have to show for it? *Nothing.*

Soon enough, the judges arrived. After most of them had made it up the stairs and had found their own seats, Drake and his one-woman camera crew arrived.

As Drake stood to make his usual remarks, we found out today would not be like the day before. Not even close. With the flair of a circus barker-turned-preacher, Drake began what he hoped would be his best performance.

"Ladies and gentlemen, as we begin a new day with a new competitor, I would like us to take a moment to remember that one of our own, Pierre St. Pierre, is no longer with us."

Turning to face the camera, he continued in a much more somber tone. "Today, I shall ask that we have a moment of silence, after which we will move on to Bailey Babbitt's lunch offering."

The dining car fell uncomfortably silent. After thirty seconds of people shifting around in their seats, coughing, sniffling, and looking around hoping to find something to push life forward, Drake broke the tension.

"It's no secret that the killer is still on the loose. This morning, the VCID ruled the cause of death as shock caused by massive blood loss due to a single knife wound in the lower back, left side."

Judges looked at each other, their faces blanched. Grimsby's graphic description of the crime only became worse as he continued.

"And given the fact that the only people in the area at the time of the murder were the competitors, it is with a sense of danger, intrigue, and dare I say risk, that we today dine in the abodes, the veritable lairs of the last two suspects. Ladies and gentlemen, I make no guarantee as to our own safety today, but I promise you this: today's episode will be one you will *not* soon forget."

I couldn't believe my ears. The man was playing to a future television audience, trying to build suspense *and* ratings at the expense of every decent cook in town. The only way Grimsby could have added more melodrama was if he had brought in someone to play old soap opera music on an equally old pipe organ.

Lunch couldn't have come quick enough for me. With Grimsby rattling on about nothing in particular, I wondered if the dining car came equipped with barf bags.

A small bell rang. A hand appeared from within the side of the curtain; it pulled the eggplant purple velour back to show a dark passageway leading to the caboose. Cosmo, dressed in black trousers and a starched white button-down shirt topped with a bow tie, side-stepped to the center of the door. A comically fake handlebar moustache framed his smile.

As for our host, there was still no sign of Bailey. Her partner steadied his gait by latching on to the aisle-side chairs as he walked forward. We were all certain he would lose his balance and drop the tray full of tallboy cocktail glasses he was carrying.

The rays of sunlight from the windows bent as they pierced the glass and reflected off the ice cubes. A panorama of rainbows appeared on the interior walls of the dining car. I inspected my drink's bouquet with a quick sniff and knew right away what sloshed about inside the glass.

Giving Grimsby a quick, insolent look, Cosmo said, "Ladies and *others*, let me offer you a refreshing drink. This is a watermelon spritzer, perfect for waking up those taste buds before you start your afternoon meal. Please sip, don't gulp. And remember, you will want to save room for the picnic basket to be served next."

As slurping sounds of happiness echoed throughout the dining car, telltale clinks of ice cubes signaled that glass upon glass were being emptied, regardless of the warning. Cosmo, as he was returning to the rear galley, stopped and said he would get another tray of refills. I wasn't positive, but I thought I heard him say under his breath that Bailey would need to step it up before someone loses a hand.

Minutes later, the second round of watermelon spritzers arrived, and by the time Cosmo finished, he was thankful the main course was on its way. The bell rang again, and like Pavlov's dog, everyone turned to see what would come next through the curtain. Even though I had tasted a sample of the savory peanut sauce, I had no idea what was to be served.

Instead of the tall, lanky Cosmo, however, a much shorter and more feminine figure appeared. It was the chef du jour, Bailey Babbitt. She was wearing a uniform similar to that of her co-conspirator Cosmo—and she also sported a fake mustache. I prayed it was not the same hair piece, but vowed to not think about it again. If that were possible.

Another silver platter balancing act. This time, however, there were no tall pieces of glassware defying the laws of physics. I noticed several small packages, each wrapped in wax paper, tied with colored ribbon. The tails curled, making for a frilly lunchtime present.

"In keeping with the picnic theme, I have prepared a classic, almost iconic piece of picnic fare, the humble peanut butter sandwich." Bailey gave a slight bow, raising back up with a hopeful expression.

Her face changed when she heard the low mumblings of discontent. Comments echoed off the hard maple floorboards.

Bailey went into damage control mode. I had to give her props for perseverance.

"But as you will see—and please open your packages now if you have not already done so—this is not your ordinary sandwich. This was one of my mother's favorites: the Peanut Butter Pickle Banana Crunch Sandwich. Complementing the homemade peanut butter are a few slices of fresh banana, a drizzle of honey, and a special topping of potato chips and pickles! Sweet, creamy and smooth on the one hand; crunchy, salty and tangy on the other. Perfect for an outing to the lake, the woods, the beach, or even on a train ride back into history. Please enjoy. Dessert will be forthcoming, surprising, and delicious. I promise you."

Bailey, to my surprise, succeeded in quelling the uprising. The negative comments had stopped and now the only sounds being heard were the crumpling of wax paper. Soon enough you could hear everyone speaking about the amazing concept of adding pickles and potato chips to a sandwich.

I wondered if anyone else noticed that so far, nothing had actually been cooked. Sure, making the peanut butter with all the extras was a nice touch, but I had always equated cooking to the scientific process of adding heat to ingredients to create something new worth eating. Maybe I had become a food snob, a dreaded *foodie*, and it had taken Bailey Babbitt and her deluxe PB with no J sandwich for me to realize it. All I had ever done to a peanut butter sandwich was to add bacon—back in my meat-eating days.

As we finished eating, Cosmo returned to clear away the discarded wax paper and twisted, knotted clumps of ribbon. He stopped long enough to catch everyone's attention, asking if anyone would care for some chocolate.

Who wouldn't want chocolate?

Cosmo pointed his index finger up as if to tell the diners to wait one more minute. He then checked his pocket watch. A few wild hand and arm signals later, we understood he would be right back with his partner, Bailey.

If my single-moustache theory was to be proven true, I would soon know. The answer came unexpectedly, when to everyone's surprise, both Bailey and her sous chef Cosmo returned on a tandem bicycle.

Laughter and clapping erupted as the two period actors rode the bike up and down the narrow aisle. Cosmo was in the back providing the pedal power and Bailey sat in front, steering with one hand and tossing out wrapped desserts with the other.

I caught my tasty treat as the two eccentric cyclists tooled by a second time. With the anticipation of a child opening her first Christmas present, I tore through the tape holding the four corners of the three-by-three-inch cube.

As the sides unfolded, I found myself face to face with a nice, dark, chewy fudge brownie. After the first bite, no one cared about the theatrics. Every diner enjoyed the dessert course. Nary a crumb remained.

As the lunch presentation drew to a close, the two cooks came out from the caboose once more. Holding hands, they bowed in response to the vigorous applause from the judges. A gentleman above all else, Cosmo pulled away from Bailey, his hands upturned to present her as the mastermind of the entire lunch experience. He then joined in the applause. I then remembered what the young female chef had said. Her lunch may not be as fancy as the others, but it would be the most memorable experience of the week. She was correct.

And as much as I loved my grandmother's cooking, I realized that she may not win the Saucy Skillet trophy this year. Regardless, I wanted—almost needed—to see how Bailey made those delicious brownies.

Could Bailey have killed her own uncle? At this point I knew she had motive, but the cooking and presentation alluded to more naïveté than guilt. Maybe I was reading too much into it? People said my parents were cynical and jaded; perhaps I had inherited the same traits.

Drake and his ever-increasing ego pushed everyone out of

the dining car. He said they needed time to set up at the Cat and Fiddle and could not, in his words, *dilly dally around some old train car.* Talk about looking a gift horse in the mouth. I couldn't believe he was dismissing the awesome lunch and performance art we had just witnessed.

But to his point, the contest had to go on. Everyone agreed to meet back at six that evening. I had just five hours to tell Velma about today's simple yet outstanding lunch and hope we could—or as I should say, *Velma* could—deliver an even more spectacular meal, an easy task, as long as she wasn't in handcuffs. As I was saying my goodbye to the chef, I noticed Grimsby flip open his phone and call Captain Larson.

17

It wasn't too far a walk across the rail yard from the *Southern Comfort* to Front Street. With a few spare minutes, I stopped by the ice cream store to say hello to the owner, intending to sample an ice cream waffle sandwich. However, the sound of an ambulance's siren caught my attention.

Gazing up the street, I saw a large white box-like vehicle with blue and red lights flashing, racing along the street and making a beeline for me. The driver was waving, trying to get my attention. Up to that point, I had felt fine and, unless someone had just learned Bailey's brownies contained something other than chocolate, I did not understand why the ambulance was approaching *me*.

As the vehicle slowed and pulled alongside the curb, the driver rolled down the passenger side window and leaned over, asking, "Are you Winnipeg Kepler?"

My eyebrows raised and my jaw dropped. I stammered, "Yes?"

"Get in the back, hurry!"

I ran around to the double doors in back. The attendant inside had just opened the doors, allowing me to see the patient, *my grandmother*, strapped to a gurney; she had an assortment of wires, electrodes, and tubes attached to her body.

"Holy bah-joh-lee!" I said, jumping into the van as it pulled away. "What's going on here? Grandma, can you hear me? What's wrong?"

The emergency medical technician answered, But I ignored him as Velma lifted her one free arm and motioned for me to come closer.

"I'm okay; just a little chest pain," she whispered, her voice barely audible above the sound of the sirens. "I told them to stop and pick you up if they saw you."

"Chest pains? Grandma, we need to get to the hospital right away!"

Seeing my grandmother fade back into unconsciousness, the EMT transmitted the woman's vitals to the hospital's emergency department awaiting for our arrival.

"Grandma?" I exclaimed. "Are you okay? Is she okay?" Unfairly, I was holding the poor technician personally responsible for the health and welfare of my grandmother.

"We should be at Eastern Shore Memorial in a few minutes," he said. "Her heart is still beating strong. I think she took a nap? All the vitals are looking good."

"But there's *something* wrong, otherwise she would not have called you, right?"

"She didn't call. Doc Jones called us."

"Will he meet us at the hospital? Doc Jones has been the family doctor for years."

The technician laughed. "Doc Jones has been everyone's family doctor for years. He retired about five years ago. Said he didn't want to pay another month's rent for an office he never used."

"So he can't practice medicine anymore?"

"Oh no, he can still practice. In fact, all the doctors at Shore regard him as the authority on just about everything. He just doesn't have an office now. Only makes house calls when he feels like it. Your grandmother was lucky he stopped by for lunch when he did."

I held my grandmother's hand, watching her chest rise and fall, a comforting sign the lungs were still working. Time passed, although I had no concept of how much, thanks to the adrenaline racing through my system.

The ambulance jostled front to back to front again as it came to a stop in the rear of the small county hospital. Ubiquitous red and white signs clamored that we were now at the Eastern Shore Memorial Emergency Department.

The doors swung open as the crew extracted the gurney and my grandmother along with it. As they wheeled her through the bay doors, I sprinted around to the waiting room, looking for a receptionist to see what else had to be done. I slid my finger through my phone's contact list. I would have to call my parents, too.

The woman behind the desk was pleasant and empathetic. That said, she held up a ream of paperwork. Before I could finish rummaging through Velma's purse to see if she had her insurance card, the charge nurse came out of the treatment room. She told the receptionist to put away her paperwork. This would be a pro bono case per Doctor Jones. He was our guardian angel.

The nurse's words left me with a little less weight on my shoulders, but I still needed to find out what was wrong with my grandmother. I flagged down the RN as she was leaving and asked if she knew anything yet. I knew it was early, way too early, but I needed answers and I would not stop until I found them.

"Ma'am, you must be Winnipeg. Velma told us you would be worried. Come this way and I will explain what is going on."

We went to a small unoccupied office. I toyed with the pencil holder on the desk while the nurse spoke.

"Ma'am," the nurse said, "it looks like your grandmother's heart is fine. But something triggered her to faint. When the rescue squad arrived, she was holding her heart and talking about palpitations. Then Doctor Jones called to let us know he was on the way, too. Said he had never lost a patient, and he wasn't about to start now."

"So, no heart attack? Then what else could it be? Anxiety attack?"

"Could be," the nurse said. "Has she experienced greater than normal stress?"

"Well, there is the police harassment and a bogus murder charge." I could feel my own heart rate spinning up.

"I'll just put down *yes*," the nurse said, rolling her eyeballs at yet another irrational relative.

"Just put down that Velma Kepler's granddaughter blamed the chief of police, Captain James Billy Larson, for any and all undue stress and anxiety placed upon her grandmother."

As my inquisitor gave me the stink-eye for being so forthright, another nurse walked into the office to let us know that Velma was now stable. Taking the statement as an invitation to invade the secure confines of the emergency department's treatment area, I thanked the nurse and left before I even knew which exam room to infiltrate. Fortunately, the Eastern Shore Memorial ER only had eight beds.

I didn't need a crystal ball or a ten-dollar psychic to find Grandma. The staff used so many monitors and testing devices that her exam room was an opera of beeps, chirps, and buzzes.

Peeking around the rust-brown wrap-around curtain, I found my grandmother sitting up in bed, eyes closed. She still had the plethora of electrodes connecting her to a heart monitor, and one tube ran a saline drip to a port in her right arm.

"Grandma, CAN YOU HEAR ME?"

"Dear, I had chest pains, not wax in my ears. No need to yell."

"Sorry, Grandma. I thought you were in a coma or something."

"That's silly, dear. I'm fine, but the good doctor didn't believe me."

"Can I get you something? Have you eaten? Are you allowed to eat?"

Velma motioned for me to come a little closer. "The nurses want to take real good care of me since they think I am a fragile little thing. So I figured I would let them for a few hours. I need to ask you a favor. But only if you have time. I don't want to interfere with any job interview you might have lined up."

"Grandma, I know you want me to take that job with Mint Street, and yes, a job's important, but not as important as you. What do you need me to do? Call Mom and Dad? Fluff your pillow? Another cup of ice chips?"

"Calm down, Winnipeg. I'm fine. Like I said, just a little chest pain. Heard some unexpected news from Doc Jones, that's all. Took the wind right out of me. But look, I need you to do something. Two somethings, actually. Can you do it? Them, I mean?"

I looked at my grandmother with the eyes of a baby duck ready to follow its mother for the first time. "I'm ready to help. What do you need?"

Before the patient could say another word, a nurse walked in pushing a computer cart. Like clockwork, every patient had their vitals recorded every three hours. Now it was Velma's turn. She started to record Velma's vitals. Temperature. *Check*. Blood pressure. *Check*. Blood oxygen. A bit low but still *Check*.

Afterward, the nurse almost demanded I leave "to allow your grandmother to get some needed rest."

I fluffed the pillow beneath Velma's head and said, "The nurse has a point, you know. Now, in one hundred words or less, tell me what two things you need me to do. And they need not involve the café. I'll just post a note on the door. People can go up to the gas station diner on the highway and get a burger if they're hungry. We can stay closed until you return."

Grandma chuckled. "Winnie, did you forget the contest? I prepared the food, it just needs to be heated and served. Dinner's at six tonight. I know you can do it."

"I can do *that*. I'll just need to call the taxi and have him come get me. Shouldn't be a problem at all, as long as I'm back by five. What's the other thing you need help with? Do you need me to tell old J.B. Larson off? I'd be happy to do that, you know. That's a freebie."

Grandma said something about the police captain, but her words slurred; she was dozing off. I had assumed the events of the day had now taken their toll on the aging woman, but then a multitude of warning lights blared. Her vitals were crashing.

I ran past the curtain, hoping to catch the eye of any nurse or doctor in the area. Over the years, I had been in enough hospitals with my dad—a hazard of having a private detective for a dad, I suppose—to know there are many times when there are no spare nurses to be found due to budget cuts and staffing shortages. I said a quick prayer, asking that this not be the case today.

Before I could say *amen*, a trio of nurses rushed into the room. The decision was made to take Velma up to the second floor, the surgical wing.

"Winnie," a tiny voice said. "I need Winnie."

The nurses told my grandmother to relax and that everything would be okay. Another voice came over a nurse's radio saying that Doc Jones was already up in surgery, with a cardiologist standing by. It was as if Doc Jones had predicted this medical emergency.

The nurse with the radio pointed to me. "You can wait upstairs; there's a family waiting room. We'll keep you updated." I wasn't sure she meant it. The words left her mouth in a mechanical, scripted fashion. Like Captain Larson's cheat card of Miranda rights, I suppose she had just the one benign statement deemed safe to tell worried family members.

Hearing the gurney's wheel latches unlock, I acted fast, shoving my foot in front of the wheel.

"Grandma, what is it? What did you want to say?"

She pulled me down by the shirt collar, saying, "Tell him—"

"I'll tell J.B. you are here. No problem at all. I've got that, Grandma."

"No. Listen. This is very important. Tell him I know, and . . ." Grandma lapsed into unconsciousness.

"Heart rate is dropping," said one nurse. "We're going—now!"

I stepped out of the way just in time; my foot was still throbbing from the hard rubber of the gurney wheel. All I could do was blow a kiss as she disappeared into a waiting elevator.

What does she know? And how is this J.B.'s fault?

A tear formed in the corner of my eye. My mounting anger toward Captain Larson, however, prevented it from falling. I did not know what caused my grandmother to be in this precarious situation, but I knew Larson must have been the trigger.

Larson would pay. Yes, he would.

* * *

I found my way upstairs to the waiting room. The next hour was tense; no word from the charge nurse, nothing from the operating theater. For distraction, there was a smattering of well-worn books and magazines, the kind you see in doctor's offices but never on the supermarket shelf.

Just to stay busy, I found a tissue and dusted the few plastic plants set about to make the room look more like home.

Old habits never die, I guess. I reverted to checking my cell phone every few minutes. No call from Mint Street Bankers today, either. Perhaps I didn't get the job after all? Maybe they tired of trying to reach me? The way today had gone, why should I have expected anything other than more disappointment? And why was I disappointed? I liked working at the Cat and Fiddle.

The cardiologist walked in, looking around the vacant waiting room as if there might be someone else there waiting for news. "Are you . . .?" The man hesitated, looking at his chart before he finished his sentence. "Are you Winnipeg Kepler?"

"Why, yes. How is my grandmother?"

"She's fine. Doctor Jones gave me your grandmother's chart, and when I saw the heart cath data, I decided it was time for a stent. The procedure went fine. She's practically hop-scotching trying to get released now, so I think we found the cause of her problem."

"Oh, I am sure she wants out of here, but is that the wisest idea? Shouldn't you keep her for observation or something?"

"Our policy is to keep a patient for at least six hours after any procedure such as inserting a stent, just in case something unexpected crops up. The real problem is that once we release Ms. Kepler back to her room, she could, in theory, refuse further treatment and walk out of here. In fact, she already told the nurse she would do it."

"That's my grandmother. But I know a way we can keep her here until tomorrow, if you think she should be here that long."

"Wouldn't hurt," the man said. "Doctor Jones and I both think a night of observation would be the best choice, but other than chain her to the bed, what can we do?"

"You worry about the medical issues, I'll take care of the rest. Hold her in the recovery room for at least an hour more, will you? Then you can send her back to her room. And you better tell the cook to prepare her dinner. She *will* stay overnight."

The cardiologist agreed to the extended stay. He left without asking how I planned to accomplish the task. Plausible deniability, I think they call it.

As I returned to Grandma's room, I knew it was time to call a taxi. After several unanswered calls to the Eastern Shore's only car service, I hoofed my way to the highway. I had a trash bag full of my Grandma's clothes slung over my shoulder, and upon reaching the highway, I took shelter under a covered bus stop. The canopy and accompanying bench were provided by the Shore's only bus company, which did not want its over-the-road coaches to pull into town. Drivers could just stop along the highway and gather cash-paying customers on a milk run or trying to get to work. There were lots of poor people in these parts without the financial means for a car.

With only a few dollars in my pocket, I wasn't sure I had enough to pay the fare to Seaview. Then, I saw my white knight approach, white clouds of steam billowing on the horizon.

The *Southern Comfort* was on its way to the rescue!

The train track ran parallel to the country highway. In years past, the railroad provided passenger service up and down the entire Eastern Shore. The trains connected the local working families to the big cities of Washington, D.C., and New York; even Boston, if you were of exceptional financial means. Today, however, the only train running the rails was the rolling diner belonging to the Babbitt family, all one of them. And was I ever thankful.

The train's bell rang, and I could see Cosmo and Bailey almost falling out of the conductor's window as they tried to wave. The hiss of the steam made it impossible to hear what they were saying, but their frantic movements told me the two culinary Casey Joneses had received my voice mail.

The train slowed and soon came to a full stop. The steam engine was still firing its boilers, so I had to wade through clouds of damp white vapor to reach the black metal railing leading to my chauffeurs.

"Going my way?" I held my thumb out like a hitchhiker.

"Permission to come aboard granted, but we must turn around in the next roundhouse," Cosmo said. "We can have you back at the Cat and Fiddle in less than an hour, if that works for you? Not that you have much choice." Cosmo finished with a chuckle. He knew what needed to be done, and his confidence rivaled that which I saw when he was commanding his mechanical kitchen devices.

I checked the time. If we made it back in an hour, I would have just enough time to heat the chicken and the pie. Any later, and the judges would suffer with nuked leftovers. I was proud of my grandmother's cooking; I wanted to ensure all the food had, at the very least, a decent shot at winning. No one entered a contest of any kind hoping to get second place. That's why it was called winning. Given no unexpected delays, I determined an hour of travel time would work; an hour and a half would not.

Soon enough, the train's engine roared back into high gear, its tanks churning with boiling hot water fueled by the coal shoveled into the furnace by train engineer and budding chef, Bailey. That girl was wiry, but dang if she didn't have some muscle on her. I guess refitting a train on your own does that to a person. *If things get nasty with Drake later, I could enlist the help of Bailey as my tag-team partner. I'm sure we could take him.* Heck, Bailey looked like she could put the slimeball into a headlock with no problem.

The next roundhouse was up the road about a mile. By the time my legs grew used to the unsteady rocking of the train, our little train was pointed south and chugging back to Seaview. I checked my cell phone at every intersection, almost hoping to see something from Mint Street. No such luck. On a positive note, there were no calls from the ER or my grandmother, either.

I recalculated the travel time, a moot point given there was nothing I could do to make the train go any faster. But it gave me hope, so I kept on, trying not to be too obvious. Again, no such luck.

The train pulled into Seaview, but before coming to a complete stop, I jumped off like a Hollywood stuntwoman. God's grace and soft grass allowed me to land on both feet. It was a risk, but when you're in your mid-twenties, that's what you do.

I waved back at Cosmo and Bailey, thanking them for the ride. It was a quick wave, though, since my self-imposed deadline was looming. I started walking, then picked up my pace, bolting for the café. Even from that distance, I could see the judges, their pastors, and the one and only Drake Grimsby already waiting outside the locked front door of the Cat and Fiddle. As I approached, Grimsby glared smugly.

"Winnie, I'm afraid we will have to disqualify your grandmother. She's not here, and it's time for the judges to make their decision."

As I unlocked the door, I turned around and said, "I understand, Mr. *Grillsbut*. Why don't we all go inside and I'll whip up a batch of fresh *and healthy* cinnamon streusel-crisp cookies for everyone? You and these fine judges can snack for a few minutes while I plate up the food my grandmother cooked for you today. If you would rather leave hungry, I'll just eat the cookies myself."

The judges, hearing the optimal word *cookies*, said that leaving would be the utmost in poor manners. An unofficial leader within the group spoke for all, saying they decided it best to wait for the food to warm up. And the cookies, while unexpected, would be more than welcome, another commented. A third judge, a rather large woman concerned about the healthy aspect of the snack asked me to reassure her that the cookies were not just sugar and flour.

"Oh, perish the thought," I replied. "These cookies might actually be good for you. The cookie itself is, yes, a basic sugar cookie, but it is a proven fact our bodies need sugar for energy. As long as you don't eat more than a half dozen at one sitting, your blood sugar levels might be fine." I was being careful to not promise anything.

I continued, "And then there is the cinnamon and the crushed pecans. The spice has proved to have a possible effect on lowering blood pressure. Wouldn't it be great if we could all stop taking those silly blood pressure pills just by having cookies? You should check with your doctor first, but I would think so. And the pecans; well, we all know nuts have numerous health benefits."

"So these cookies are good for you? Every bit of them?" I think three judges asked this same question at the same time. Nothing motivates rationalization like a decent cookie.

"Well," I said, "the caramel sauce drizzled on top is the only part of the cookie that might be just a little too much. But when I make them, I'll just use the sauce sparingly. No worries."

I didn't think I did that good a job with the sales pitch, but as the judges entered the café, one of them whispered into my ear, "Now dear, don't be too stingy with that caramel sauce. I think we can all handle it."

My plan worked. Drake could try to make Grandma look bad, but the judges' intense desire to eat tasty food prevailed. These were formidable women, bent on a culinary mission; they would force him to go along. Now all I had to do was bake those cookies and hope they lived up to my promises. If only I had a recipe.

If grandma fooled them with her apple-free apple pie, I can get away with an improvised cookie. My confidence had returned as if Velma was standing next to me.

As the judges made themselves comfortable, and Drake sat at the soda fountain bar looking like a poor, unloved dog without a bone, I went back to the kitchen and assembled my new creation. The camerawoman tagged along, which was fine. I think she wanted to get away from her boss. And that made sense.

Seeing me put three cans of sweetened condensed milk into the dishwashing machine, she put her camera down and asked, woman to woman, "Is this a real recipe or did you make the whole thing up to get people to stick around?"

"Sometimes you do what you have to do, right?"

"Are you even a baker, or a cook? You seem different. Smart. Smarter than these people. And conniving, perhaps? You don't fit in this town, Winnie Kepler—and *not* in this diner. You, woman, are not all you appear. What's your game here?"

"Oh, I'm just a poor college grad trying to make her first million one blue-plate special at a time. But don't let the dirty dishwater fool you, I'm just hoping to serve up chicken on a stick and call it a night. It's been a rough day," I admitted.

"We all have our problems," the woman said. She nodded her head toward the front of the house where her boss sat with his back to everyone as he played card games on his cell phone.

"Don't I know it," I said. "You know, once this is all over, I think you and I will have a much better understanding of each other."

The oven's warning buzzer sounded, letting me know there was no more time for small talk. That could come later in the guise of plotting the downfall of the camerawoman's chauvinistic boss. Regardless of the fun in that, the first batch needed my attention. The cookie crisps were done, their tops browned with little reflective hints of sugar and cinnamon.

I removed the pan, trying not to burn my fingers. Once I transferred the cookies onto a wire cooling rack, I removed the steaming hot cans of condensed milk from the dishwashing machine. The bath of hot water had turned the sweet milk into a luxurious caramel sauce. After spooning the sauce across the baker's dozen, I knew there was enough decadence in, and on, each cookie. No judge would complain today.

With chicken warming in the oven, and some bacon dressing coming to a simmer in a saucepan on the stove, I felt comfortable enough with the time remaining to arrange the cookies on a nice platter.

Seeing their pastors gathered in a conversational huddle, a practice universal whenever men and women of the cloth get together, I waved the cookies in their direction. The treats were as a beacon, lighting the way for them to find their chairs at the table.

I returned to the kitchen two more times to replenish the cookie platters. The plan was working. Several pans of cinnamon streusel-crisp cookies later, the chicken was ready for phase two. I walked over to the prep table and stabbed—well, maybe that was a bad choice of words? Perhaps something else? *Thrust*? Yes, much better. I thrust the sharpened chopsticks through the long, thin strips of boneless chicken.

Holding the oven-fried chicken stick up like a sword, I liked what I saw. Great flavor without the mess. Nothing gets on the hands; nothing to wash later. Almost the perfect food, but after a quick sniff, I realized it still needed something.

Heat and sweet. That would make a good dish even better. I knew my grandmother wouldn't mind if I spiced things up. Perhaps I was bending the rules of the contest, but after the events of this week so far, what *were* the rules? Complaints could be addressed to the dead guy. I might have been cooking, but I was still on the case.

I threw together an Asian-style sauce made from a little soy sauce, brown sugar, minced garlic, and chopped pineapple. A few pulses in the old blender followed by a minute in a saucepan over high flame, and this sauce was ready for the poultry on a pole.

I soaked the oven-fried chicken strips in the warm sauce, leaving the handle end of the sticks up to help make removal a little easier. While they were marinating, I plated the potato salad Grandma had premade and cooled in the refrigerator. Hot bacon dressing would be added just prior to serving.

The only item left on my grandmother's championship menu was the apple pie, *sans pomme*. I had eaten this pie at least once a year over the course of my entire life and never knew the pie plate had yet to see an actual apple. Was Velma more magician than cook?

I warmed the pie up by setting the plate on top of the shelf above the flat-top grill. The warmth from the pilot lights under the grill's steel deck made for more than enough heat to take the chill away.

Timing was everything, and I knew it from watching my grandmother work the Cat and Fiddle day in and day out. I knew I should visit with the guests one more time before I put myself into overdrive putting the finishing touches on Velma's contest entry.

As I walked out to the dining room, I saw a sullen crowd suffering from the constant rants of a crazed television producer. This would not do in my place. I had to do something.

I approached the judges and, freezing in mid-stride with my arms out, I asked the guests a question I am sure they had not expected.

"Is anyone here afraid of fire?"

The judges looked at me like I was a non-union cook who had crossed the picket line to save management from a service worker union's strike. One woman raised her hand, unsure if she should, or if anyone would join her.

I now had their attention, which was the goal. "Not to worry, then," I said. "You are *probably* safe. I'll be right back with the best food you will have eaten this week."

As I walked back to the kitchen, I poked my head out the swinging door one more time. "You girls in the front may want to scoot back about a foot. And one of you fine pastors may want to say a quick prayer. Never hurts, you know. But be quick about it; this will only take a second."

I was trying to keep the ladies' attention away from Drake and his self-imposed soap opera. And, seeing this was still a contest, I wanted to build culinary suspense without having another person getting stabbed in the back. A heightened sense of danger might keep everyone's attention on how well the food would taste. At least, that was my plan.

* * *

The kitchen door opened with a bang as it hit the side of the wall. Before anyone could register what was happening, I was upon them, pushing the large stainless steel prep table. This was known, on a much smaller scale in fine dining restaurants, as *table service*. I had to improvise, going one step further by bringing in the entire table. This was beyond big. I was pushing a twelve-foot long, stainless steel, squeaky-wheeled table. I needed the space in the kitchen, anyway.

"The main course is Velma's famous chicken on a stick, à *la flambé*."

I needed to make this a show to remember. With one hand, I removed the chicken-laced chopsticks from the marinade, laying them flat on a wire tray to allow the extra sauce to drip into a catch pan. Having borrowed a butane torch from the kitchen's tool kit, I lit the flame and seared the chicken, turning the smoldering chopsticks every few seconds. If the wooden chopsticks burned, my day, and the meal, would be over.

"Ladies, please don't try this at home. Gentlemen, be sure to call the fire department before you attempt it, since I know *you* will try it."

Nothing like playing the genders against each other to liven up the party. The ladies found the humor; the men checked their cell phones to make sure they had the right phone number for the nearby firehouse. One younger pastor started to record my performance with his phone's video camera. We were going viral.

The brown sugar in the sauce had soaked into the deep-fried breading. When the blue flame caramelized the sugar, a crisp and sweet shell formed around the tender fried chicken. At least, I think that was the case. It was rather difficult to tell, what with all the smoke. There were times I couldn't see the chicken. Didn't matter, though. The clapping from the judges told me everything I needed to know. They would not soon forget today's meal.

The judges cheered like kids on a playground when I tossed the chicken like a set of horseshoes, chopsticks flying across the table and landing on their plates. As the last one hit the center of the farthest plate, the judges raised their hands, giving my Olympic delivery a ten-fingers-up sign of approval.

"Please, hold your appreciation until the end. There is more to come."

As the crowd scarfed down the flame-broiled yard bird, I went from guest to guest, serving the cold potato salad. After spooning hot bacon dressing on top, I could *see* the smell of seared pig wafting up to each judge's nose. One almost stopped eating the chicken to switch to the side dish when she smelled the bacon dressing. She thought better of it, instead opting to finish the chicken on a stick. She sucked the chopstick clean. Twice.

It was time for the pie. I had cut a big slice for each of the judges, garnishing the top of the crust with a dusting of powdered sugar and a mint leaf, just for the color. A few whole apples were added to the tray, positioned around the dessert plates. I was hoping they would all taste the flavor of the apples with their eyes. If they thought they were seeing apples and powdered sugar, they would assume the flavor would match—my biggest gamble of the day.

"Well, folks," I said, "You have had chocolate pecan pie in a jelly jar, brownies in a box, and even waffles steamed in by train. But now, we have saved the best for last. Of course, I am referring to Velma Kepler's world famous apple pie! And, to give it that extra sweetness, I have taken the liberty of dusting each slice with a light snowfall of confectioner's sugar. I am sure you would agree Velma would have done that herself, had her weak heart allowed it."

I placed a piece of pie in front of each guest. The edges of each slice maintained its triangular shape, and the crackers mimicked the apples to perfection. Just when the judges were about to dig in, I stopped them.

"Oh, but ladies and gentlemen, please wait for just one more moment. The pie may look good enough to eat, but there is one thing missing. A little secret sauce, if you will. I'd describe it, but I think you would rather I show you."

I pulled a red ketchup bottle out of my back pocket. You

could hear the gasps. Head fake! Instead of ketchup, I had boozed up the sauce from the cookies. To everyone's delight, a caramel-*brandy* sauce made its way onto the pie. It may have been a little over-the-top, but I tried to scribble the initials of each judge on top of their respective piece of dessert. I had more ideas flowing through my head, but decided enough was enough, and besides, the crowd was still hungry.

The happy mumblings from the judges confirmed that I had made the right choice. Even the pastors were silent, a marked feat given that they were of that rare breed of people who were paid to talk, and most enjoyed every penny of time they could get to do it. Everyone was trying to sop up as much sauce as possible.

I considered Velma's entry in the Saucy Skillet contest a rousing success. But as I cleared the dishes away from the guest table, I noticed several of the judges going back to the prep table to snag a few more pieces of chicken.

"Ma'am, if you'll give me a minute, I'll light the torch and fix those up for you," I said.

The old woman ignored me, sparking to life the butane flame using a matchbook she had dug out of her purse. Using an old bar trick to light the match, she used one hand to maneuver a single matchstick out from the rest of the book. Her thumb dragged the match head against the thin garnet strip, igniting the sulfuric yellow flame.

My curiosity must have been obvious. She played her act off like it was a common occurrence. "I used to weld aircraft carriers at the shipyard, honey. I can handle a little toy like yours."

Another judge joined her. "Yep. She's not what she seems. It's the old book-and-cover routine, kid. Don't judge us by our appearance just because most of us are over seventy."

We all had a good laugh, but their words made me think. Which volume in this shelf of book covers had committed the murder? Drake? One of the chefs? Heck, did Captain Larson do it? What about me? At this point, who knew?

As for Grandma's contest entry, I considered the effort worth the time, even though it may not have been how my grandmother might have presented it. The judges were happy they had tasted all the food, even under circumstances that they had once said were *suspect*.

As they finished their deliberation, one judge asked me to take a group photo. I positioned the camera so I could see the entire group, and then Drake tried to weasel his way into the picture like an obnoxious drunk uncle. The unwanted photo-bomber was elbowed out of the group by the welder, allowing me to click the shutter on the camera. Once the mob dispersed, I knew *who* killed Pierre St. Pierre. Just not *why*.

18

As I watched one judge use an extra chopstick to skewer her last piece of fried chicken, the entire murder case flooded my brain like gravy on biscuits. The solution to the problem of who killed Pierre—and the reason why—was now as clear as one of the ice cubes in my tea glass.

"I've got to call Captain Larson," I said out loud to no one in particular. "I know who did it." A few ladies standing next to me gave me a quizzical look but went back to nibbling on the remnants of the dinner.

In my effort to keep my alternative diet hidden from the meat-and-potatoes crowd, I dropped a piece of granola. After searching about the small cubbyholes in the desk under the cash register, I came upon my grandmother's cell phone. It was improbable she had saved the personal phone number of an obstinate old crab like Captain Larson, but I held out hope, sliding my finger across the glass cover.

As expected, the Captain's personal cell number was unlisted. I considered making a call to the police station, but I didn't want the entire force swooping down on the Cat and

Fiddle like a SWAT team on a drug bust. Parker could only do so much to protect us. Better to call Velma and hope she would be well enough to answer the hard-wired phone sitting on the nightstand next to the hospital bed. Hopefully she would have forgiven me for making off with her wardrobe.

The phone rang several times before a feeble voice answered. We spoke for a few minutes, and I learned the test results had come back proving that Velma indeed had suffered a cardiac event. A "widow-maker," she called it. I guess we owed Doc Jones once again. The stent had saved her life.

As my grandmother's inquisitive nature showed through again, I could hear the tension in her voice elevate. This conversation would not be good for a heart patient. One dead body was enough. Once she had settled back down I related the success of her culinary offering to the judges. Hoping to not raise any more suspicion, or her blood pressure, I brought up Captain Larson's cell phone number.

"Winnie, why would you think I might have his personal cell phone number? He's a nice-enough guy, but he doesn't tip well, you know."

"I don't know, Grandma. It's just I think I have solved the murder and I need to speak to him. When I looked in your phone's contact list, I couldn't find it. Maybe you misfiled his entry?" The last thing I needed right now was a grandma experiencing the onset of dementia.

Grandma was silent. As I was about to apologize, the answer came through the speaker.

"Look under *I*."

I? That was unexpected. "Shouldn't it be under *L* for Larson? Possibly under *J*, for his first name?"

"No, child. I filed his phone number under the letter *I* on purpose. He's there because he is and always has been an *idiot*."

That brought out a good chuckle, at least from me and the judges who had overheard the conversation.

Even Drake Grimsby laughed, an occurrence I had not seen from the man since this whole affair began a few days ago. The only stone-sober face in the Cat and Fiddle was the poor camera operator, who was once more struggling to keep her shot steady in all the commotion.

I said goodbye to my grandmother and then placed the call of every amateur sleuth's dream. "Captain Larson? Miss Winnipeg Kepler here. If you have a moment, I'd like to ask you for a favor."

"And what," he replied, "might that favor be? I suppose you have solved the crime already?" He let out a muffled *harrumph*. "Your parents aren't in town, are they?"

"Oh, no, sir. Nothing of the sort. I do have my ideas on who murdered the chef, though. There's just one, teeny little problem."

"Young lady, I don't have time to play games. Either you have it or you don't. Assuming you do, what are you asking me to do?"

It was time to set the trap. "Bring all of the suspects together, of course. But only to announce the winner, maybe? We don't want to scare the killer off before *you* make the arrest."

"Well, since you put it that way . . . I suppose I could help out."

The trap had sprung! "Great! Thanks so much Captain! And remember to bring those shiny handcuffs. If the killer escapes, the state boys might grab the collar."

"Well," he boasted, "no need to worry about that happening. I'll have Williams assist. We'll show those Richmond desk jockeys. You name the place and time, and we'll get the whole crowd there."

This was working out better than I had anticipated. "I'm sure you would like your photo taken at the scene of the crime, bad guy in cuffs. How about tomorrow? Six-ish? The setting sun will reflect nicely off your badge."

The Captain agreed to the entire plan. Now I had just one problem remaining. I still didn't know exactly who killed Pierre. This type of gathering always worked on television. My fingers were crossed.

My elation subsided as the church ladies instigated me to call Captain Larson an idiot to his face before I ended the call. He heard the commotion and asked if everything was okay. I said yes, it was, but declined to relay the other comments from my grandmother. Or the pious companions on my right and left. No need to ruin a good moment.

* * *

The next evening, everyone arrived at the exposition hall just as the sun was setting over the water's horizon. The diminishing light triggered the security exterior lights; their warm, orange glow painting the parking lot and steps leading to the door. It was a surreal setting reminiscent of an old movie filmed in mid-twentieth-century Technicolor.

The fairground parking lot was filled with the vehicles of each member of this bizarre dinner party. There were squad cars bookending the gathering, presumably to thwart an escape. Added to the mix were a few vehicles belonging to folks who had an interest in the outcome, including the shared car of Fran and Tricia.

I pulled into a vacant parking space and turned off the engine. My car, a very used car when I bought it from some guy needing quick money for a lawyer, clicked and clacked as the engine cooled down. It was something one had to get used to hearing. I didn't even notice the noise anymore.

I had picked up my grandmother from the hospital; now she turned to me and spoke.

"Quite the symphony of aches and pains coming out of that engine, Winnie. You bought this old car while you were still in high school, didn't you? If I could ever talk you into accepting the job offer from that bank, you could upgrade."

"As soon as the lady who owns the Cat and Fiddle gives me a $10,000 raise."

We both enjoyed that little exchange. She had a point, though. I glanced at the lineup of much newer, much nicer vehicles as if I were shopping on a dealership parking lot. The best vehicle was a new European sedan parked in a reserved parking space. *Grimsby's*, I thought. The little voice in the back of my brain reminded me I could have such a nice car, too, if I dropped all the Sherlock Holmes nonsense and just called Mint Street Bankers on my own.

"Grandma, why don't we use the side door by that equipment van? The door seems to be propped open."

She agreed, and we walked across the close-trimmed grass. After edging our way around the side of the van, its back hatch lifted high and almost flush with the short awning, we were soon inside the lobby.

"Grandma, you meet up with everyone. Tell the Captain I'll be there in a minute. I want to get a better look at this van. I just had a thought."

As she walked into the lobby, I took out my phone and took a few photos. An Internet search or two later and I was on my way to join the gaggle of suspects. I opened the door leading to the stage area and found the Captain. This time, his reception was much more pleasant.

"Winnie, everyone is here, just like you asked on the phone," he said. "And though I did not ask them to be here, we have representatives from the VCID. But they know this is a matter for our local jurisdiction. We'll get the credit." He gave the boys from Richmond a quick glance. And a smile.

Captain Larson checked his notebook, checking off names on an attendance roster much like a teacher at the start of the school day. "I also took the liberty to ask the judges back, even Mr. Grimsby. I believe they have decided on a winner. Oh, and MegaFood sent a representative to award the prize money."

That explains one of the nicest cars in the parking lot, I surmised. "Indeed, Captain, but I think solving the murder must be the first course served in this little culinary catastrophe."

"So you know who did it?" Larson asked.

"Well, I think so," I said. "Although it has been a struggle, since so many of the competitors have motives—almost honorable ones—to cause Pierre's early demise."

Captain Larson took out his pair of handcuffs and moved toward my grandmother. "I am very sorry, Velma, but—"

"Not so fast, Captain. You may *want* my grandmother out the picture, but she didn't kill Pierre. Far from it."

"Winnie, the man took all the apples. Your grandmother would lose. Not only would she lose the coveted Saucy Skillet trophy, she would lose the chance at being named the town's first Chef du Cuisine *Emeritus*. I almost don't blame her, as big an arrogant fool as Pierre had been acting."

"Ah," I retorted, "so you think the apples, or lack thereof, were the spark to this fire? Why, Captain, we can see that Velma did not even need apples for her picnic lunch."

I opened my photo gallery and produced several photos I had taken with my cell phone camera that first day.

"Since we are here, and the old food is still in place, albeit more odorous, we can compare the snapshots to what we see today. There has been no change."

The Captain's face flushed red from impatience rather than embarrassment. "That's obvious. Photos or not, what's your point?"

I walked over to Grandma's cooking station and opened the oven door. "Why, look! Here we find Velma's apple pie. Pierre could have had all the apples in the world and it did not seem to matter to my grandmother. Hmm. There goes that motive. Too bad. And it was a good one, too. But then again, how, just *how* did Velma make her pie if Pierre had the apples?"

Grandma walked over and joined me at her work station. She reached down to a low shelf under the stainless steel prep table, retrieving a box. "That's because I use plain old crackers for my pie, instead of apples. Always have. With enough sugar and spices, you can't tell the difference."

"A veritable apple pie alibi," I said, swishing my hand at the Captain to put away his handcuffs.

The judges, as surprised as the rest with the revelation about the apple-less apple pie, made comments about how they would *never* fall for an old kitchen bait-and-switch tactic. All said they had spotted the substitution right away, but were just being polite.

Grandma reminded everyone that the judges had fallen for the cracker bit last year, when she did the same thing. "And each of the ten years before that, too."

I was proud of my grandmother. I knew she was not one to be pushed around for her cooking.

"Ladies," I said, "I imagine Velma learned how to make apple pie from her own mother not long after the Great Depression. Fresh fruit was scarce, so people just made do with what they had."

"You knew about the switch, though, didn't you?" Grimsby asked.

"To be honest, I had eaten her apple pie for years without a second thought. Then I saw her make it one day. I assumed everyone made pie that way. Regardless, there goes the motive, right Captain?"

"Well," Larson said, not allowing himself to be so quickly dismissed, "there is the matter of her public threat. We have that on tape, and you cannot deny it."

"It's digital." I replied. "There isn't any tape; but that's not the important thing right now. Let's take a look at the video feed, shall we?"

I asked the technician to start the video playback. "Pay close attention to the date and time stamp in the bottom right corner of the screen." As the time elapsed, my grandmother could be seen working at her table. Drake Grimsby then walked into the frame. The producer could be seen whispering something into Grandma's ear, but it was too quiet for the microphones to pick up.

As he was turning away from my grandmother, Drake stopped and said one more thing, then lifted his handheld microphone up to record her reply. My grandmother's words were as clear as they could be. She said she wanted to kill Pierre St. Pierre.

"I guess this proves Velma Kepler can be charged with making a public threat," Larson said, reaching for his citation book. "Like you said, Winnie, the tape proves it."

"You weren't listening, were you? Like I said, first off, it's digital. There's no tape in the machine, anywhere. Second, the date and time stamp at the bottom of the video tells the true story."

Turning to the technician, I laughed. "Men. What can you do?"

She laughed for the first time since she took the job working for Drake Grimsby. We had a bond going. I asked her to play the feed again, but this time at half-speed.

"Now please, notice the time here," I said, pointing to the small white digits in the lower right corner of the screen. "And now, as my grandmother speaks, look what happens."

The Captain maneuvered to get the best view of the screen. As the moment went by, he pressed stop on the machine, and then reversed the feed to see the verbal exchange one more time.

"Now I see it, Winnie. There is an eighth-of-a-second jump, making this evidence corrupted. Grimsby, what do you have to say about that?"

The producer looked at the Captain. "I would say . . . I would say . . . that I won't say anything else until I get a lawyer. But I still didn't kill Pierre. This only proves I was trying to build the ratings of the show. And that's all."

"Mr. Grimsby, you need to rethink your concept of remaining silent," I said. "And while this proves you were not always the most ethical of show producers, you are correct. The mismatched time means nothing. All it proves is that my grandmother's so-called threat wasn't one. And since she did not leave the stage at all, she was not anywhere near the murder scene. In my book, she is innocent. Time to look elsewhere."

Parker, who had been silent up to this point, asked, "What about the other cooks? The video showed none of them left the stage area, either. Are you saying none of these people are suspects?"

Parker, Parker, Parker. Well, at least he stepped up. Good for him. It was about time. I was sure someone would call him out for using the pedantic term *cook* when these professionals were anything but. Even Bailey could be considered a chef, given her culinary vision.

"The competitor with the most to lose was George Harrison Windsor," I said. "He had revenge as a motive, plus a huge need for the prize money. All worthy reasons to consider perpetrating a crime and taking the risk he could end up spending a life behind bars. A fine plan, except for the fact that he would never get to see his kids again."

I gave George a quick wink. "Your ex-wife would just love that, wouldn't she?"

Before he could answer, I continued, "I am sure she would. In fact, she'd get the kids, but they wouldn't be too much a bother for long. They would both soon be in college, but the tax deductions in the meantime wouldn't hurt. And with George convicted, he would spend years behind bars. Just long enough for the ex's lawyer to convince the court to lower or eliminate the alimony payments."

Larson approached George, handcuffs open. He kept stopping and starting as he internalized what I had said.

"Captain, hold on another minute," I said. "I know it looks bad for George. Atrocious, in fact. You notice that if we let the video continue, he and Pierre even had words at one point. Judging by the body language, they were not asking about their last family vacations."

George banged his fist onto the table; his face red with anger. "He cheated to win *my* scholarship," George said. "We had just finished our final exam at the culinary school, a four-course meal suitable for any decent dining establishment, and the judges spat my food out of their mouths, it was so bad."

"Let me guess," I said. "Pierre had switched the sugar with the salt, making all of your food taste like a salt lick."

"Exactly," he said. "He ended up with the higher score and finished first in our class. With the high ranking came a full scholarship to the French culinary school and advanced training I could not afford. By the time he returned to Seaview, he had changed his name from Peter Babbitt to Pierre St. Pierre. Such a pompous—"

"George, tell us the real reason you had the feud. It wasn't all about the scholarship. Was it?"

"No, there was more. Plenty more. Pierre found a few investors willing to set him up with a nice restaurant that had come up for auction. He was dealing with millions of dollars. Me? I had to take the only decent cooking job in town, spooning out grits at the bed and breakfast for only fifteen dollars an hour. And to think, Pierre took advantage of his *own* family."

"So there's new information for some," I said. "What a shock to the entire family, having a relative purchase the family business out from under them. Bailey, how did you handle all of this?"

Young Bailey Babbitt stood up and crossed her arms in front of her torso, a last act of defiance. "We were not thrilled Uncle Peter changed his name, but angry was an understatement when we learned he took advantage of my parents. My father, Peter's own brother, asked him to buy into our business as a partner—a majority partner, in fact—but the high and mighty *Pierre* would have none of it."

I noticed she sidled up next to George. I had a quick thought that they might be in on the murder together. But the evidence didn't support collusion. Maybe it was coincidental; maybe I was just being paranoid.

"So back to you, George. Losing all the potential earnings gave you a motive," I said. "And I know many divorces are caused by money. And we know, as you have told us, you are no longer married. Your motive to kill Pierre is getting stronger now."

George stood like a defendant on trial. "You got that right, Winnie. I married the woman who I *thought* was the love of my life, thinking she would be happy with an up-and-coming chef destined to have his own restaurant. When I ended up being *just* an employee, the shiny glimmer of the food and beverage business wore thin."

"So your paycheck didn't cover the bills?"

"My wife wanted nice designer clothes and got her hair styled almost every week. That added up to money we didn't have and were not likely to get. No, the good life of being married to a celebrity chef was what she wanted. And we could have had it, if it weren't for Pete."

"So she left you for some big shot she met down in Florida, right?"

"Yeah, the guy worked for MegaFood, of all people." George looked at the industry giant's spokesman. "I doubt you know him. He transferred away from the Shore a while ago. It's all water under the bridge now, though. I don't see her at all; she hasn't expressed an interest in the kids except for claiming half the tax credit each year. I'll give her credit, though: she *is* funding their school costs. If it weren't for the monthly alimony check she sends *me* each month, I would not even know that she existed. And with her new stable of hairdressers and stylists, she's changed her look so often I wouldn't recognize her again if she walked right up."

"Maybe we'll get back to that sometime, George," I interrupted. "In the meantime, I don't think you killed Pierre."

Captain Larson spoke up. "Not so fast, Miss Kepler. Windsor here could have switched the sugar and salt himself, just to throw us all off his trail." The police captain reached back around his sport coat, again palming his set of handcuffs.

"No, I don't think the honorable Chef George Harrison Windsor would have switched anything in his own restaurant on the day judges would taste his food. He is too self-respecting a professional chef to do such a thing," I proclaimed.

"Cosmo Finnegan, then?" Larson asked. It was obvious Captain Larson would find his killer, even if it meant going down the line of people sitting in the room until he found him or her.

He continued his improvisatory accusation, saying, "The dishwasher had the motive to screw up his boss's chance at winning the big money. Maybe *he* killed Pierre to eliminate the main competition, and then, to make certain he would be declared the winner *and* get a little dig into his boss, he sabotages

George's contest entry by switching the salt and sugar."

Seeing the young lad's face turn ashen, Larson's smile spoke volumes of a self-inflated ego, confident in his own thought process. "Not a bad plan, trying to resurrect a little history to throw us off your trail. You, sir, are under —"

"Um, excuse me, Captain," I said. "I don't think Cosmo did it, either. Or Bailey. True, he was a competitor trying to win the ten thousand dollars. And that is more than enough money to make people consider murder, but not him. You see, Cosmo has two passions in life: one, cooking by way of steam-operated mechanical devices, and two, his girlfriend. And we'll want to reverse the order there, I am guessing." Cosmo and Bailey joined hands and gave each other the look of two young lovebirds ready for the world.

"And Captain," I continued, "I'm sure your investigation discovered that Cosmo and Bailey became engaged today. Right?" I pointed to the two cooks, now both sporting shiny new promise rings on their left hands.

Cosmo hugged his new fiancé. "We never liked Pete, either, after he took advantage of his own brother's misfortune. But we wanted to win the contest through our cooking, and by no other means. She entered first, and then talked me into entering because with two of us competing, it increased our chances of winning. And, just like Velma and George here, we never went to the break room after the opening toast. We couldn't have killed the man."

Captain Larson put down the handcuffs and reached for his ticket book. "Speaking of the toast, I'm glad you brought that up. Someone is getting charged with something today, or I'll eat my hat. And it may only be a misdemeanor case of underage drinking when she participated in the toast, but Miss Babbitt is getting a citation. That, I can assure you."

Larson scratched his pen on the back of the ticket book to get the ink flowing. "Winnie, you said you knew who killed Pierre St. Pierre. Please get on with it before I reach mandatory retirement age. In the meantime, I should present Miss Babbitt with a citation for the misdemeanor of underage drinking. However, without a blood test or a breathalyzer reading, I'm afraid my citation would not stand up in court. I *could* give one, however, to her fiancé for contributing to the delinquency of a minor."

"Captain," I replied, "Bailey isn't a minor. She just isn't old enough to legally drink. But don't let facts stand in the way of a well-written citation."

If looks could kill.

19

Both the Captain and now Parker held open pairs of handcuffs. I needed to regain control.

"Before you cite anyone, let us recreate the crime from the beginning," I said. "We know everyone was in the break room at the start, having their celebratory toast to begin the final round. This was recorded; no one disputes this part of the day."

I walked over to Pierre's work station, picking up a chef's knife in one hand, a sauce pan in the other.

"Now the contest has begun. The chefs have spent ten minutes looking through the pantry, deciding what they might cook to make for a great all-American picnic. The whistle blows and they can be seen scrambling back to the pantry and the walk-in cooler, grabbing the materials they need. Here is where Pierre snags all the apples."

I thrust the knife point into the cutting board so the blade's handle wobbled in mid-air. "Time to count the knives in the set."

I had everyone's attention, which was just as I had wanted it. By going through the sequence of events, I hoped to draw a clue or two out from the crowd, hoping to solidify my hunch. I couldn't let on that I wasn't positive about who done it. I picked up a wooden spoon, just in case things got sketchy.

"Everyone is cooking and the cameras are recording," I said. "Nothing out of the ordinary. Oh, and it appears, by my count at least, that everyone had their own knife set—make that their own *complete* knife set. And while no one is drunk, the chefs who were closest to Pierre have all had at least one glass of red wine, and now they are toiling like crazy under these horrendous stage lights. Everyone remember?"

Captain Larson scratched his head, trying to absorb all the information. "Winnie, there were five wine glasses, one for each competitor, including an underage cook." He gave Bailey a stern look of disapproval.

"Like I said, I wouldn't write out any tickets just yet, Captain," I said. "True, there was one glass with Bailey's lipstick on the rim, but had you run a breath test on everyone you would have found this lass innocent of imbibing. What she was guilty of, if you could call it a crime at all, was smooching with Cosmo behind the curtain leading to the break room. When I examined the security feed from the break room camera, I noticed about five minutes' worth of nothing. The camera filmed an empty room."

"But the cameras were motion sensitive," Parker said.

"Yes they were, Parker. But what we don't *see* because of the poor resolution, and the angle of the camera, is that the curtains are ruffling just enough to set off the motion sensor. If you zoom in, you can see four shoes at the bottom of the curtain. Judging by their alternating positions, it would appear that those two pairs of shoes were in very, ahem, *very* close to each other. Wouldn't you say so, Cosmo?"

Before the red blush could fade from Cosmo's cheeks, I continued.

"A few minutes later you see that Drake Grimsby brings in the lot, offering them a celebratory toast for surviving the first two rounds and making it to the finals. My grandmother, a teetotaler since the days of Prohibition, and Bailey were the only two who abstained from the alcoholic warm-up. As you would say, Captain, it's on the *tape*."

"But the lipstick?" Parker asked.

"Do I need to spell it out for you, Parker?" I asked. Poking the wooden spoon into his chest. "Maybe I'll show you later, if you are lucky." The crowd chuckled. Even J.B. gave his young officer an elbow in the ribs.

"The murder; you haven't explained the murder," everyone chanted.

"Okay, calm down, people," I said. "Continuing on, the toast is now over and everyone is at their station cooking or baking or, well, whatever." I gave Cosmo a wink. He smiled until Bailey popped him in the side, too, as if to tell him this was not the time.

"Pierre," I said, "being the rude, crude, and socially unacceptable jerk he was, boasted. Am I right?"

Even the judges nodded in agreement.

I moved forward with my analysis of the timeline. "He has secured all the apples in a vain attempt to stop Velma. And to add salt to the wound—no pun intended—Pierre even had, if you look at the video long enough, a toy panel van painted red with the initials *CF* hand-stenciled on the side. Cosmo, I think that little inside joke was for your benefit, so to speak. He knew everyone had a button to push, and like a kid in an elevator, he had tried to push them all."

Parker walked over to the playback monitor. His hand hovered over the play button, just like we planned. "Now, Winnie?"

"Yes, Parker. Now would be a good time."

As the video started, I became the *de facto* narrator, giving a play-by-play of the actions of each of the players in the small-town drama.

"Notice," I said, "that just before noon, the camera is sweeping back and forth, trying to get action shots of each chef. Very good camera work, ma'am." I knew the woman had skills and wanted to give her props, especially since her boss never seemed to do so.

"Then, we see Drake, off in the upper corner of the frame. Do you see him there? He is taking a phone call. By the looks of how he slammed his phone down, it must not have been good news. What was the phone call about, Mr. Grimsby?"

"It was my contact at MegaFood. They were considering canceling their sponsorship if Pierre didn't win. Worse, they disliked Pierre complaining online about the processed foods in the pantry. Mega directed Pierre to win *and* be nice about it. That was a tall order, considering the man's ill temperament."

I pressed pause on the video and walked over to the open-air wire shelves. Reading can label after can label, I said, "Pierre was all about using the best ingredients, right? Let's see what was stocked in the pantry." After a quick perusal of the ingredients in a can of peas, I confirmed my suspicions. "Not organic at all. I can't even pronounce some of this stuff."

Parker hoisted a can of green beans in the air for all to see. "This one has artificial ingredients *and* genetically modified substances."

I stacked more canned staples on a table. "So do this one, and this one. How about this one? Yes, it does, too. In fact, Mr. Grimsby, all of these cans have GMOs, don't they?"

The MegaFood representative, prize money in hand, stepped forward. "Now just a minute here. Yes, Miss Kepler, they do. But that's not a crime. The labels are on the cans. Anyone who can read could see it. What does this have to do with anything?"

Grimsby rushed to stand by his benefactor. "Let's not get out of control here. We all know MegaFood is a respected company, one that supplies food to almost every major restaurant in America. And we *are* glad they did not pull their sponsorship, instead opting to be here in person today, putting little Seaview on the map."

"Oh, let's calm down again," I said. "Taking it from the top, we know Pierre died in the break room, but no one was there with him when it happened. The video shows everyone on stage at the presumed time of death. Everyone except Cosmo and Bailey. Look at the video, right about here."

A quick flick of my eyes toward the camera operator signaled her to stop the playback a few minutes before the demise of Pierre St. Pierre. The two lovebirds could be seen leaving the stage, walking back to the break room.

"The camera work is rock-steady on this. We can see the entire stage from the wings; everyone is accounted for except those two." I gave a thumbs-up to the smiling technician. She knew her job well.

Captain Larson looked at me. "I suppose I shouldn't get my handcuffs out yet, should I, Miss Kepler?"

"Not yet, Captain." I went on with my explanation. "We can see Cosmo and Bailey walking back to the break room; in fact, it looks like they are walking apart to not arouse any suspicion of their intent. Now let's stop the main video and switch to the security feed in the break room; Parker, forward it to the same time."

Parker, with the help of the camerawoman, worked on the playback machine controls, synchronizing the two tape feeds. Being closer to the television monitor than the rest of us, he spotted what I had hoped to see.

"Hey, Winnie. We see these two leaving the stage, but they never made it into the break room. The monitor shows nothing!"

"Exactly," I said, flipping my spoon and holding it like a pointer. "But look down at the curtain. There is something, isn't there? It seems there are two pairs of shoes again. The motion of the curtains activated the camera, just like it did before the opening toast. Now, five minutes later, we should see Pierre come in for his last, and final, break. But first things first. Parker, when do we see Cosmo and Bailey return to the stage?"

Parker starts both feeds going again, now synced up in real time. "I see them coming back . . . now." He pointed to the couple walking back on stage and returning to their respective work stations.

"And Pierre?" I asked.

"Here. You can see Pierre walking into the break room. And that means Cosmo and Bailey were already back on stage, so it couldn't have been them. They're innocent."

"Thank you, Parker. My thoughts, exactly," I said. "So if Velma didn't have a motive, and George had too much to lose, and Cosmo and Bailey were more interested in lip-locking than pig-sticking, how did Pierre St. Pierre get a mortal knife wound in his back? Could it have been the now-proven-unethical show producer, Mr. Drake Grimsby?"

You could hear the judges gasp, many of them saying they never trusted the man from the start. The Captain gave me another look. This time, however, he did not even bother to touch his handcuffs.

It was time for me to make Grimsby squirm. I had decided on the spot that this was a necessary and fun part of concluding my investigation. He saw my stare and knew something bad was coming his way. Bad for him, hilarious for the rest of us.

"You know, Mr. Grimsby, I've said this before, but sir, your camera*woman* is awesome. You should have treated her better. Maybe you were trying to overcompensate for your lack of skill and talent? Hard to say, since I haven't seen you do anything worthy of being called *talent*."

I paused for a moment, realizing I now had my proof. "And *pictures* never lie. They will make great pieces of evidence in court."

I motioned toward the video, proving my point. "Here, for instance, we get a clear shot of the entire stage; all the competitors can be seen, and the camera never moves. This view shows everything we need to see, except one thing."

I pivoted toward the woman standing next to the camera tripod and finished my sentence. "Except one thing. One thing is missing, isn't that right, ma'am?"

Everyone turned to look at the camera operator, wondering what I had meant by my cryptic statement. I continued, "When I first arrived, I remember seeing the remote control units for the video equipment. There is a second set of buttons on the controller, down at the bottom. They're used to control the camera, aren't they?"

The woman had a quizzical look. She answered, saying yes, the controller had the ability to work the camera. I think she felt uneasy with the attention focused on her. She went into a defensive stance, positioning herself halfway behind the camera's tripod, and then finally spoke up in her own defense.

"Miss Kepler, I don't know where you are going with the innuendo, but this controller is essential. It allows one operator to control several cameras simultaneously. It's a must-have piece of gear when you are dealing with a cheapskate like Drake Grimsby."

"And why do you think he couldn't afford more people on the crew?"

"He told me he barely had the money to pay me, let alone enough to hire another operator. In fact, this jerk still owes me. He's lucky I'm still here with the right stuff. And forget about post-production work, Grimsby. You can find another company for that. After we're done shooting here, you'll need to pay up to get the hard drive; then I'm out of here." Grimsby simmered, climbing to a boil. "I should never have come here or taken this job in the first place."

I raised my free hand, palm down to calm the situation.

"Oh, I imagine you would have been here one way or another," I said. "You needed to convince your ex-husband to lower the amount of alimony, isn't that right—Mrs. Windsor?"

I slapped the wooden spoon down on the desk, cracking a sharp sound that caused most everyone to jump. "That's right. I noticed your green eyes were a dead-on match to the family photo George carries in his wallet. And there's no denying you are his daughter's mother."

George stepped up to get a better look at the disguised woman. I stopped him from getting too close, saying, "George, what do you think? Am I right?"

He looked the woman straight in the eye. "It *is* you. What are you doing here? Why didn't you tell me?"

The woman remained silent, although the stern look of silent contempt told everyone in the room that my guess was spot-on.

I put my arm around George like a big sister. "Oh, George. This is where it gets interesting. But it may not be too much fun for you to hear."

I faced the woman again. "Care to explain, Mrs. Windsor? You are clearly not here just to shoot video footage. That was a ploy to get close to your victim. Tell us why you killed Pierre St. Pierre."

People milled about, checking with each other to ensure they had heard me correctly. The woman, now stepping away from the camera tripod, walked up to George. Though facing him, she addressed me.

"It's *not* Mrs. Windsor anymore, you idiot. I'm now Mrs. H.G. Warren. My husband Harding and I live in Richmond." Her Southern accent was now more pronounced and manufactured.

"Where he works for MegaFood, I imagine?" I asked.

Before the woman could answer my somewhat rhetorical question, Grimsby flipped through the vast number of pages attached to his clipboard. He tapped his finger on one of the last pages. "Warren? Hey, that's the name of the guy I've been talking to. I thought it was his first name, not his last. Are you sure you have this straight, Winnie?"

"Dead sure. My guess is that it all came down to alimony, isn't that right, Mrs. Warren?"

I gave Captain Larson the high sign he had been waiting for. Unfortunately, after so many false starts, the law man did not believe me and stood motionless.

Mrs. Warren confessed. "Yeah, I killed Pierre. Had to. He didn't follow the plan to beat old George here and take the prize money. I knew George was trying to buy the bird's nest or whatever it's called, and needed the extra money. Without the prize money, I could have negotiated a better long-term alimony deal in trade for short-term investment money. But no, once the contest started, Pierre didn't want to play the game by our rules."

"So Pierre, he wanted more money?" I asked.

"No. In fact, after the contest started he told me he wanted none of the money. The pompous, high-and-mighty culinary genius had a change of heart about our line of food products. Genetically modified food, the same stuff he had been serving in his restaurant, successfully I might add, was no longer welcome in his kitchen. I almost killed him on the spot when he yelled about the pantry items."

"So it was more than just alimony. You couldn't let a celebrity chef like Pierre St. Pierre badmouth your husband's company. You had become accustomed to spending your husband's generous paycheck, and poor publicity might affect his future with MegaFood. Isn't that right?"

"Look, Kepler. I don't know what type of idealistic world you live in, but for the rest of us, everything works in dollars and cents. I've married a rich man who I intend to keep that way. No corpulent fry cook was going to ruin my meal ticket."

"So you had to come up with Plan B, isn't that right?"

"I *had* to come up with a Plan B. That's when I made the decision to kill him and blame George."

I nodded. "Why reduce the alimony, when you can eliminate it when George goes to prison. My, what an ingenious plan. But I suppose it is ingenious only if you don't get caught."

"That would have been the desired outcome, yes. But I hadn't planned on a private detective's daughter getting involved. When I heard that Velma was your grandmother, I then knew who your parents were. And it would have been my luck that they taught you a few tricks of the trade. I had to leverage your time and effort away from George. I had an associate in Richmond find some of your friends and force them to jump into your life at full speed, dangling an irresistible carrot in front of you. At least we got our money back on that waste of time."

"I figured as much. Too many coincidences. So when you found out that my ex-roommate, Francine, was in a relationship—a serious relationship—with her boss, Tricia, you knew you had something to work with. It was so simple. Use the threat of exposure to force the girls to drive to Seaview and organize a job fair at the Cat and Fiddle. You knew I would want to help them *and* my grandmother."

Needing to defend herself, Tricia said, "Hey, I'm sorry for my part in all of this, but I want you to know your grandmother being a suspect was not my doing."

"Apology accepted, and no, it wasn't," I said. "We can thank my grandfather for that one."

Grandma's complexion turned pink from embarrassment. "Winnie, what does he have to do with this case? He passed away over ten years ago."

"Oh, Grandma, I think you know. But it's not what everyone else is thinking, to be sure."

Turning to the others, I continued my explanation. "The reason Velma was the focus of Captain Larson's investigation was that he wanted no one else to look into her, and eventually *his*, private life. He knew if the VCID, for example, had done a complete investigation, they would have uncovered the relationship between my grandmother, her husband—meaning my grandfather—and the good Captain here. And what a sordid tale it would be."

"But I never had a relationship with J.B. He's an okay guy," Grandma said, looking at the police chief. "We never even went out. In fact, he never asked me."

"No, I suppose not," I said. "But once, a long time ago, he told someone he *wanted* to ask. When Grandpa was working up the courage to ask the prettiest girl in school to the senior prom, old J.B. here almost to beat him to the punch."

"That's ridiculous, Winnie. Where did you hear a tale like that?" Captain Larson said.

I ignored the question. "And judging by the large biceps you have, Captain, muscles gained through years of working out at the gym, you two young lads settled the argument by using one of the oldest tests of machismo there is—the arm wrestling contest. Winner got to ask Velma to the dance."

I looked for any sign of agreement from the Captain. "How am I doing, so far?"

"He was a field hand," Larson admitted. "I worked in town at the newspaper, setting up the tiny lead slugs for the next day's edition. Your grandfather, however, worked on the farm, lifting bales of hay and straw, shoveling slop for the pigs every day. He had no problem beating me. You're right, Winnie. Because of that one match, I lost the chance to date the first love of my life. I vowed never to let a lack of physical strength get the best of me again."

J.B. Larson took a deep breath, trying to calm down. In a softer, and slower voice, he said, "Velma, I didn't want to hurt you in all of this, but I couldn't let my secret out of the bag. My career would have been over. No one would want a weak police officer on the beat. And as a police captain? No way."

Grandma blushed. "Doc Jones was right. He stopped by yesterday and on the spur of the moment mentioned the arm wrestling contest. He took me so much by surprise, I almost passed out choking on my tea. When I came to, I was already in the ambulance, looking at my granddaughter."

The more-than-embarrassed police captain responded to all the suppositions being bantered about. "Well, I wanted to ask. I should have just asked."

"I'm available now, if you want to ask again. Who knows? I might even say yes. Or, is there someone here who would like to arm wrestle Captain Larson for their own opportunity?"

Hearing no takers to Velma's challenge, I finished the evening by closing the noose on the culprit. "Grandma, they were just boys being boys. Us girls, we have a certain ability to make them say and do stupid things. Don't we?"

I glared right at Parker.

"After the good captain secures a comfortable cell in the town jail for Mrs. Warren, perhaps Velma and J.B. would consider a date back *at my café* for a piece of chocolate chip cheesecake?"

Grandma smiled at the senior police officer. "You have led a life half-lived, J.B., harboring a secret like that. Why don't we see what we can do about that later? Wouldn't you agree that a slice of cheesecake sounds like a great way to end this culinary contest, too? What do you think, James?" This was the first time anyone had heard the police captain addressed by his given name.

"I'd be happy to join you, Velma. And I hope we can mend the fence between us."

"We need not fix any fence, James. We need to pull it up from the ground and get rid of it. Just come in and sit down with me."

20

I hated to interrupt the love fest, but there was still one bit of unfinished business. "This is just great. I think you two will make a lovely couple. But in the meantime, Parker, would you mind stopping the killer? She seems to be escaping."

Officer Parker Williams sprang into action, only to meet face-to-face with the culprit's two-shot Derringer, which she had been hiding inside a fake battery pack on her belt.

"I only wanted to kill one person and ended up sticking the wrong guy. No one make me add another notch to the old belt here." She turned to the crowd of judges, all standing motionless at the sight of a firearm. "And that includes updating your Facebook page. I better not see any cell phones at all."

No one had expected gunplay. The woman backed away, reverse baby-stepping her way to the door leading to lobby and the open hatch of her equipment van. Her small pistol never wavered, its barrel pointed at Parker.

Before she disappeared, she barked a few final orders. "Captain, disassemble your own weapon and take the kid's piece, too. Break them both down to the firing pins and toss those across the room. Guns are dangerous, you know."

The metal firing pins made a *ping-pang* sound as they hit the tile floor on the far side of the stage. A glint of brightness came and went as the two most essential parts of the handguns disappeared under a row of seats. The woman flicked the barrel of her pistol at the table.

"Cuffs next. Put them bracelets on the kid there."

Another judge was told to handcuff the Captain and then toss the key over to the killer. Though three people searched Parker, his key was nowhere to be found.

Feeling much more secure in maintaining her freedom, the woman backed herself through the door and into the lobby. The clip clop of her running feet grew distant as she made it to her getaway van, the back hatch closing with a slam. As I ran toward Parker, we could hear the woman cranking the engine.

"Don't worry, Parker. She won't get far without these." I opened my clutch and produced a set of spark plug wires. A timely Internet search earlier had told me how to disable the van—a preventative measure I thought might come in handy later. And now it was later.

A few of the judges combed the aisles, picking up pieces of the two semiautomatics. One lady even reassembled them. These judges were more than they appeared. I asked if any had a spare handcuff key in their purses, but alas, it was not to be.

The crashing sound coming from the pantry area caught everyone's attention. Someone, or something, had just upset a pile of sauté pans. As soon as I saw the calico flash zip by Drake and come to a stop between my legs, the mystery was solved.

"Tinkers! What are you doing here?" I asked, not expecting an answer from a stray cat. As I picked her up, I noticed something caught in her collar.

"Ladies and gentlemen," I announced, "it seems our good cat-about-town, Tinkers, has just saved the day."

Using two fingers, I removed the missing handcuff key from the cat's collar. "Parker, do you remember when Tinkers climbed up your one pant leg and then down the other, when you first came to the Cat and Fiddle? Intentional or not, Tinkers ended up with your handcuff key. Probably snagged by her collar and ripped right off your belt. Really, you should be more careful where you put that key. Anyway, here we are!"

Moments later, and thanks to the Seaview Police Department's handcuff keys being universal, the duo was free to apprehend the woman as she was trying to start the engine of another car in the parking lot. She had become so mad at the van engine's failure, she never noticed that she had left her gun on the passenger seat. Parker saw the unattended weapon and grabbed it before she knew what had happened. Captain Larson dragged her out of the car, most appropriately by the collar.

Parker led the woman back, this time with his cuffs on the proper set of wrists. Without the aid of a reference card, the beaming young officer read the Miranda rights to his suspect.

Captain Larson announced that his new protégé would take the lead working with the VCID in finding Warren. "This young man is a fine example of the quality police officers we have here in Seaview. Someday, he may even be the Captain."

* * *

The charged atmosphere of the moment was broken when Larson started a sneezing fit. Little beads of sweat formed on his forehead and cheeks. He caught a break between sneezes and said, "Man, for some reason I can't seem to stop tearing up in here. Must be the stage lights."

Seeing the Captain in minor distress, I asked, "Mr. Grimsby, could we borrow a tissue? I think you have some in your desk, as I recall."

As Grimsby went to unlock his desk and retrieve a handkerchief, I stopped Parker for a moment and pointed out a little piece of fluff on his prisoner's blouse.

"Parker, I think if you go to your suspect's home in Richmond, you will find the main accomplice taking care of their cat. By the way, Captain Larson, are you allergic to cats?"

"How did you know?"

"I can see the cat fur on her clothing from here. I thought it was a twittle, a spare thread or something, but your instant sniffling told me otherwise. I figured it had to be either cat fur or possibly her perfume. I saw *something* on her blouse and just took a guess. And now with Tinkers wandering about, it just made sense."

"But the husband," Tricia said. "How did you connect the guy in Miami, now her husband, with the contact in Richmond?"

"That was easy," I said. "George had mentioned his wife had left him for an executive she had met at the South Beach Food and Wine Festival in Miami. It's no secret that the biggest food service companies would be there, and that would include our beloved sponsor, MegaFood, Incorporated. Do you remember what was on the envelope of cash you gave to Francine?"

"I remember the envelope, but there wasn't anything written on it. It was blank."

"There may not have been any words printed on it, but the envelope did provide a few very visible clues. First off, it was a number 9-sized business envelope. Those are typically used as return envelopes, since they fit nicely into the even more standard number 10 envelope."I could see most everyone was still trying to figure out the importance of the envelope's size. Tricia, on the other hand, knew. It was time to press forward and put a few people on the spot.

"Once the job fair we were planning had gone off without a hitch, and my time supposedly taken up by the whole affair, you, Tricia, were probably directed to take the cash and, using the envelope, return a newspaper article proving you did as you were asked. Isn't that what Mr. Warren wanted you to do?"

Not waiting for an answer, I put down the spoon and opened my portfolio and pulled out the actual envelope. "Since there was no address on it, the man assumed you would be at the next major job fair. He could then put your envelope into a number 10 and mail it off to his superior. Why risk being seen together so close to a crime scene when you can use the good old postal service and a stamp to make the final payoff?"

"Tricia, why did you do all of this?" Francine was torn between her renewed friendship with me and her reclaimed relationship with Tricia. "I mean, I understand the blackmail part of it, but why did you give me the cash when you left?"

The guilt of hurting Francine was too much for Tricia. I could see she was struggling with words, trying to find the right ones. With the tension so thick you would need a chainsaw to cut your way through it, I came up with an answer that would hopefully defuse the situation.

"Tricia, that's why you gave Fran the cash, right? You decided it would be better if you left her rather than hurt anyone else. You thought the mobsters would follow you and leave Fran alone."

Tricia started nodding her head, letting me know I wasn't too far off-base with my assumption. She turned toward her partner, finally admitting, "Fran, I love you. I *never* wanted to leave you, but it was the only way I could guarantee you would be secure in your future. That man threatened to expose our relationship to all of our clients. We'd never work again."

"It's all right," Francine said, giving her woman a bear hug. "When it comes to love, it always works out. We will just have to play this out to the end and see where we end up. Maybe we aren't destined to have a business in D.C. Maybe we are just supposed to be *us*, living wherever *we* can be happy. And we could always open a pizza shop."

"Trust me," I said, "I know about changing plans and chasing happiness." I wiggled my ring finger, shining the glint of my college ring at the two women. "There remains, however, the matter of identifying the company that funded all of this deception. Check out the embossed watermark on that envelope. Two diamonds, offset laterally about 30 percent. Had we seen the full-color version of this logo, we would have easily seen that the logo is blue and red, with the blue lines forming a very angular version of the letter *M*."

"Ahem, could someone please take me to jail so I can call a lawyer instead of listening to little Miss Marple here?"

Someone was getting tired of being handcuffed.

Parker sat his prisoner down in a chair. Captain Larson took the envelope and examined it carefully. Finally, he searched for the image using his own phone. We could all tell by his expression when he had found the answer.

"I bet you already know the answer, Miss Kepler. And now I can see it right here." The Captain had picked up a can from one of the cooking stations. On the back of the label, in small print at the bottom, was the pointy M logo with the words *MegaFood— Bringing Health and Prosperity to the World* printed underneath.

He tossed the can in the air, flipping it so it landed with the label facing me. *A man with flair; Parker should take note.*

I could only agree with the officer. "So it was a leap in faith on my part, but I made the assumption that if a woman was *so intent* on ruining a man's life, she would go to the great lengths we have witnessed here. She would certainly not take a chance on having someone she didn't trust do her dirty work. Her husband was the only logical answer. If you ask me, the poor man will probably enjoy the separation prison life will bring to him."

The killer spoke in her own defense. "I may be going away for a while, but that man will soon realize how good he had it. I've got plans for him." I, for one, was glad she was still in handcuffs. Unpredictable, this one was.

"Winnie, you did a marvelous job solving the murder," Grimsby said in full suck-up mode. "With this woman on the way to jail, we can all rest comfortably and get on with the show. I don't know how to thank you enough. But, you know? I have an idea. I'll write a glowing account of today's events for the newspapers, and I'll give you a prominent role in the story. What do you think?"

I thought Grimsby needed to be more careful about what he asked for. "Oh, Mr. *Grigsby*, I mean *Grillsby*, or whatever, I think the statement this woman is about to write will tell more than any tale you could imagine. And I do mean *any*, sir."

"What?" Grimsby protested, "I had nothing to do with any crime. Your grandmother Velma can, and should, be charged with evading police and obstructing justice. After all, she gave them all the slip the other night."

Then something unexpected happened. Parker straightened his collar and pointed his finger into the middle of Grimsby's chest, pushing him back a bit.

"Not so fast, Grimsby," Parker said. "I never actually put her under arrest. I had no warrant. Until the warrant could be produced, she was free to go about her business. Thusly, no charges can be made now."

Parker gave his boss a sheepish look. "Except possibly against the Captain, for fibbing a little to push the warrant through in the first place."

It was time for me to save a little face on all sides. "But honesty is always the best policy, Parker. Thanks for bringing up the business about the warrant, but I think the VCID will decline to pursue those charges since there were such extenuating circumstances. I am sure the matter will be referred to the mayor for action, if any; and with enough support from his troops, I bet Captain Larson will come out with his badge still shining."

A relieved Parker Williams gave his boss a verbal boost of confidence. "No worries here, Winnie. The Captain will be just fine. I guarantee it."

Captain Larson was given the honor of leading the killer away to the squad car. Parker—or as I should call him in public at least, Officer Williams—was now the only local law enforcement on the scene. He needed to take over control of the scene like a champ.

But poor Parker was still a little unsure of himself, and clearly uncomfortable with a roomful of eyes staring at him as they waiting for his next command.

Like a new teacher trying to not look foolish in front of his students, he led the entire crowd out to the front steps of the building, so we could witness the killer being carted away. In a heartbeat, he handed the conversation's lead back to me.

"Miss Kepler, why don't you show us how Mrs. Warren managed to kill Pierre in front of everyone, including the cameras."

"Excellent thought, Officer Williams. You know, one of the concepts my parents love to think about when they are on a case, especially when it's a locked-room type of mystery, is to look for the invisible person."

"Invisible person, yes, of course," Parker said nonchalantly, as if he understood what I was talking about. "Remind me again, please. How do you see a person who is invisible?"

"It's not that they are truly invisible, Parker. It's a figure of speech. But there are all kinds of people we see every day, but we never notice them. The mail carriers, the plumbing repair guy, the taxi driver. Even the boy throwing newspapers each morning. They are always there. Of course, we do notice when they are *not* there, but while they are working? You probably couldn't say what color boat they were driving."

"Winnie, we haven't had a paper newspaper thrown in this town for over ten years, thanks to the Internet," Parker said.

"Analogy, Parker. Come now, keep up."

I pulled out my cell phone and opened the Internet browser,

checking the online version of the *Seaview Times Herald.* "To your point, though, so I see. Perhaps a poor example. Anyway, as the investigation went on, I stood back and asked myself, *Who are the invisible people here?*"

"And as it turns out, there were many. First, and most obvious, we had the judges. They were all very well-known and highly respected churchgoing, upstanding citizens. But, they were never on the stage, so they had no opportunity to murder Pierre."

"The chefs, and even Drake, they're not invisible," Parker said. "Not at all. So who is left?"

Finally, one of the judges started to raise her hand, asking to be called on for the answer. It wasn't like she was the obnoxious kid in school who always knew the answer. She was one of the few introverts in the bunch, sitting off to the side hoping not to be noticed.

"Yes, ma'am? Your thoughts?" I asked.

"The cameraman. She's the only one left?"

From the back seat of the Captain's sedan, a handcuffed woman yelled out a snarky: "That would be camera*woman*, thank you very much. Didn't we already have this conversation? Doesn't anyone listen to me? Idiots, all of you!"

Captain Larson pushed the window control, lifting the pane up as his prisoner kept trying to get the last word. As the car pulled away from the loading dock, we could all hear the woman's final, muffled clamor.

The woman's diatribe was still audible as she pressed her face against the inside of the window glass. "I don't know what you are talking about. I'm just a technician who made the mistake of hiring on for this stupid contest. I should have stayed in the mall, taking pictures of crying babies. And they don't whine as much as you people. You've got no proof. I want a lawyer! I should have killed you all!"

21

As the squad car sped off, Parker regained control of the scene. "Well, that's that, I guess. Winnie, you were saying?"

"Yes. Excellent work, Officer Williams. Anyhow, as I was saying, Mrs. Warren was indeed the only other person everyone tended to ignore. She moved about the crime scene with impunity. By setting the cameras to operate without the need for anyone to be at the controls, she was able to leave her post and kill Pierre."

"Winnie," my grandmother interjected, "how did she do it? No murder weapon was ever found. And all the knife sets were complete; and most were found to be clean. The only blood was on Cosmo's knife, and he had cut himself earlier. How do you explain it?"

"Mr. Grimsby, how many competitors were there in the contest?" I asked.

The producer looked at me with a furled brow, saying "Isn't it obvious? There were five. One is dead so now there are four."

"I mean in total. You had two previous rounds, yes?"

"Well, if you include the people *who were not even here* into your fantasy—I mean, explanation—there would be fifteen in total."

"And you had three rounds, correct? All fifteen competed in the first round, and then you eliminated five, which meant ten chefs cooked in the second round. Five more gone at the end of round two left you with our four here, plus the deceased. Is my math correct, Mr. Grimsby?"

"Yes, but I don't follow where you are going with all of this, Miss Kepler."

"Oh, but I think you do, sir. Let me ask another question. The chefs, they all received a gift set of knives to use on the stage, yes? And they could keep them once they left?"

"Of course, we don't want to appear stingy, no matter what that woman said. She may have been married to an unethical, high-up muckety-muck at MegaFood, but the company overall was great. They *gave* us all of our stuff. And, they wanted to open a regional headquarters here. Really, they needed all the public goodwill they could buy."

Grimsby was starting to look around, fidgeting to the point that Parker, normally the last person to pick up on what was really going on, surreptitiously moved behind him, sensing he may need to take the man down whenever I pronounced the promoter guilty of something.

"Interesting choice of words, Drake. And please, allow me to call you Drake, since no one knows how to pronounce your actual last name," I said. "Back to the knives. Each competitor, even the ones who were not chosen to move on to the next round, was able to keep their knife set. That *is* what you are saying, isn't it, Mr. Grimsby?"

"I've already said so, yes."

"So, fifteen chefs, and fifteen sets of knives?"

"Like I said, yes."

"And every chef has possession of their set? A gift set, I believe, if I understood your words correctly?"

"Naturally."

"What about the chef who cheated in the second round? Did he get to keep his knives?"

There was a pause in the conversation. You could hear everyone inhale as if they knew something big was about to break wide open in this case.

"Drake? I'll ask again, did he keep his knife set?" I knew

everyone had forgotten about the chef who had brought his own ingredients onto the stage. Velma chimed in to remind everyone the man had been simply awful at trying to hide the fact that he was cheating, saying the boy made no effort to hide the food. It was right there for all to see when you opened the carry bag.

Grimsby came to his own defense. "Well, no. We did have to confiscate *that* man's knife set. That was one of the rules. Cheat and you leave with nothing."

"I'm sure if we find the young man, he will tell all about how someone paid him to cheat so poorly he would get disqualified. That's how the murder weapon came in proximity to the victim. Grimsby here was hoping everyone would have forgotten about that lost set of knives. Care to tell us where they are, Drake?"

As we walked back onto the stage, Grimsby, with almost an involuntary reaction, gave a quick look at his desk in the wings, stage right. He tried to play it off. "I'm not sure where the knives ended up. They were first put on the production table and I haven't seen them since."

I looked at Parker. "Since this could be an active crime scene, do you need a warrant to search for the murder weapon?"

"It kind of depends. If I have a suspect, and probable cause, I could get a search warrant for his vehicle or his house. But this crime scene? That's sort of fair game. Depends really. I can look on top of the desk, but to look inside I would need *cause* for it to be admissible in court. What did you have in mind?"

"Suppose someone else, someone who was not an officer of the court—say, oh, I don't know, perhaps a café owner who has a hobby of being an amateur sleuth—suppose that person were to rummage through a desk looking for an aspirin."

"Winnie," my grandmother said, "do you have a headache? I think I have something in my purse if you need it."

"No thanks, Grandma. I think my headache remedy is in the desk here. Let me check."

I came upon the production desk, where several papers lay about, but no knife set was sitting out in the open. If it had been, Parker could have confiscated it as Exhibit A.

I started to pull on the desk drawers, hoping one would be unlocked. "If I had just taken a knife set from a cheating competitor, would I have to put it here, on top of the desk?

Anyone could have walked off with it. These knife sets are quite valuable. Aren't they?"

Grimsby sighed. "They cost several hundred dollars, yes."

"So, I would have wanted to secure the knife set. Put it somewhere out of sight; somewhere people would not have noticed it, especially if one of the knives went missing. Someplace like the bottom desk drawer."

The last drawer was still unlocked. Grimsby really needed to brush up on his bad-guy skills.

I opened the drawer a few inches, just enough to see inside. I purposely stopped short of opening it the full amount.

I faked a sneeze. "I am thinking I need a tissue, too. I could be allergic to cats, too, you know. Fortunately, I don't need a warrant to blow my nose, right? Parker, be a gentleman and see if there's a tissue in there, will you? Please and thank you."

Parker reached down to pull the drawer out further. Before he had actually touched to handle, he looked up, his smile bigger than a lopsided crescent moon. "Sorry, Winnie, there's no tissue. I guess the Captain still has it, but look what I see—in plain sight and admissible in court as evidence. There's the knife set, and the large chef knife is missing."

"No tissue? That's a shame. I guess I'll have to suffer. But wow, there's a knife set inside. I never would have guessed."

Parker then opened the lowest drawer all the way, where a bloody knife partially wrapped in a kitchen towel could be plainly seen. He immediately reached for his own set of handcuffs, and then realized that he had let the Captain drive away with them. He improvised, grabbing Drake Grimsby by the collar.

"You can't pin the murder on me. The woman already confessed."

"Oh, Mr. *Grimesbut*. I am sure she will tell us the whole story when she writes her statement, just like I said a while ago. You see, when we looked at the video a second time, we all saw the two pairs of shoes at the bottom of the curtain. Then we saw Cosmo and Bailey return to the stage. But—and this is what made me start to rethink my conclusion—I noticed the shoes were not the same. If you compare the shoes we see at the start, before the toasting, to the shoes we saw at the end, they are *not* the same. Those shoes belonged to you. And Mrs. Warren."

Grimsby, trying his best to distance himself from a possible stint in prison, started spilling his guts.

"She told me she wanted to put George out of business *and* have her own television show. Her husband's career had fizzled, and she thought we could make a go of it with my television production experience and her as the on-camera talent. We waited until the naïve little love birds left the curtain, and then we sneaked back for our own rendezvous. But *she* had the knife. She had cut a slit in the curtain so we could see if anyone was coming; we didn't want any interruptions, if you know what I mean."

Parker tried to get the rambling man back on subject. "I don't think we need the details. Just get to the part where you killed Pierre."

Regaining his composure, Drake continued. "Yes, well, when we saw Pierre walking back to finish off the second bottle of wine, she grabbed my hand. I thought she was going to pull us closer together so Pierre wouldn't notice. But as he walked by on the other side of the curtain, she lunged at me, and in the process, the knife went through the slit in the curtain."

Grimsby's eyes started to bulge out when he realized the obvious. "*That* must have been when she stabbed him. I could hear the man stagger down the hall; I thought he was just a bit tipsy. I had no idea she stabbed him."

"So, when did you panic and hide the knife?" I asked.

"Not until later. I mean, I didn't hide the . . . well, once she told me, I had to go along with it, or she'd blame me for the murder. At first, when I was still innocent, you know, having no idea a crime had been committed, we kissed one more time. I knew I had finally met my soul mate. I was floating on air, I was so happy. It didn't register with me that I had just helped kill a man. That fact didn't become clear to me until after the body had been found. I wasn't in my right mind. It could have been temporary insanity, I think. Somebody get a notary. I want my temporary insanity documented for the judge!"

Drake looked around, hoping to find someone, anyone, willing to give him a break. "And speaking of that, call a judge! I'm ready to make a deal. She's going down first!"

George Harrison Windsor laughed. "Hey, my divorce was

finalized a while ago. She's your problem now, sir. Enjoy." We all got a chuckle out of that one.

Seaview's best police officer, in my opinion at least, was now Parker Williams. Without prompting, he twisted Grimsby's arm behind his back and started to lead him to the door. "You may have met your soul mate today, but soon you will be meeting your cell mate. Drake Grimsby, you have the right to remain silent and I surely hope you do so. I'm tired of hearing all of this crap."

As Parker and Drake were driving off, Velma stood and asked, "Hey, what about the contest winner? We need to have a winner, don't we?" She looked at the judges, who were busy conferring.

A little old woman, probably Doc Jones's first patient, slowly stood, her cane at the ready in case she started to lean too far in one direction. "Yes. We have decided on a winner for this year's Saucy Skillet."

The room hushed. The only sound was the low hum of the air conditioning unit in a window at the other end of the building. The tension and excitement increased by the second.

The woman shuffled her papers, trying to make sure she had the correct name to announce. My grandmother ran her fingers through her hair, wanting to look as good as possible when she was called up to accept her award.

The foreman of the culinary jury continued. "The judges were very appreciative of all the entries. We enjoyed every dish we tasted, even those with a little too much salt." With those words, George sat up a bit straighter, knowing he had just won the contest.

"And while we did enjoy every single dish, we had to take into consideration the theme which for this year was the traditional picnic." Both George and Grandma slumped a bit in their chairs.

Cosmo, anxious to hear his name as well, said, "We know that, ma'am. Could you please just announce the winner?" He took Bailey's hand and pulled her to his side.

"Patience, sir. You young people are always in such a hurry. You all need to learn to have patience." The woman found it necessary to reexamine her papers, thinking somehow they were no longer in the correct order.

"Like I was saying, the fried chicken on a stick was a good

one, as was the sweet potato biscuit. And the waffle train? The cat's meow."

Cosmo tried to correct the judge. "Actually, it was supposed to be Mexican flan on top, not syrup, but—"

"Now you are trying *my* patience, young man. Call it what you want, we liked it. But none of those entries had the true essence of the traditional picnic. Remember, we are a town built by poor farmers and fishermen. For us, a picnic is more about love and not so much about the food. Simple is better, and the faster we girls could throw together some food for our picnic basket, the sooner we could be out at the beach with our boys."

"So, you are saying *no one* won?" I asked.

"Far from it, my dear. In fact, Miss Babbitt takes the prize this year. Her peanut butter crunchy pickle sandwiches were the best. They brought back so many good memories, we sat around for hours reminiscing about old boyfriends. Her meal was sublime, and the brownies were beyond description!" The other judges started to giggle like young schoolgirls when the spokesperson mentioned the all-night gossip session.

I took the liberty of presenting the Saucy Skillet trophy to Bailey, who graciously accepted it. Taped to the bottom of the trophy was a check for ten thousand dollars. I carefully penned in Bailey's name and presented the prize money to the stunned girl.

"Congratulations, Bailey. Great job! And the prize money will make for a great wedding and honeymoon."

Bailey took her fiancé's arm. "No, Winnie. I'm sorry, but no need to shop for a wedding dress. At least, not yet. This money will go to rebuilding our new rolling restaurant train, the *Southern Comfort*."

Cosmo's eyes widened. "What are you talking about, Bailey?"

"I mean, we could use your talent to finish the redesign of the dining car and the kitchen, and my talent to decorate the caboose's living quarters. Once we're done, we'll have a dining car with a show kitchen operated by all of your amazing steam-powered gadgets. It will be like going back in time, but with a bit of modern mechanics thrown in. We can have a rolling steampunk fine dining experience, maybe once a day for either lunch or dinner. Then, once we are done cleaning up, we can retire to the caboose and ah, you know, *stoke* our own furnaces, as it were."

With the winner declared and the trophy and prize money awarded, everyone left the fairgrounds to return to their respective abodes. As Velma and I started to walk off the stage, I picked up my wooden spoon and holstered it through one of my belt loops. It wasn't a deadly weapon, but I had a feeling more than one bad guy would avoid a knuckle-rap if at all possible.

* * *

As Velma and I walked back to the Cat and Fiddle, the winning lovebirds waltzed across the fairgrounds to the side track where Bailey's train cars were sitting. Even Fran and Tricia had renewed their relationship, walking with linked arms back to the Seagull's Nest. It would take them longer to get there than George, who was quick-stepping alone and whistling a cheerful tune.

As we reached the café, a man was standing on the front stoop. He was wearing a dark blue suit, the pinstripes extremely thin but there. His red tie made him look almost like a politician; all he needed was the American flag lapel pin.

"Can I help you?" Velma said.

"I hope so. Am I guessing correctly in that you are Winnipeg Kepler?"

"I am she," I said. "Would you like to come in?"

The three of us walked inside, where Velma started a pot of coffee. The visitor and I sat down at the four-top table by the bay window.

The man introduced himself. "I am from MegaFood, Incorporated, Miss Kepler. You interviewed with one of our subsidiaries, Mint Street Bankers, a while back, and I must say, everyone there was very impressed. Unfortunately, that position has been filled."

"And so, you are here why?" It seemed like I had just finished doing battle with the corporate giant, and here I sat, face-to-face with another one of their representatives, possibly sent on a peace mission—with no job offer. That made no sense.

"Excellent question. Well, we have a similar opening at MegaFood. And based on the recommendations from the human resource manager at Mint Street, we decided you would be a perfect fit in our marketing department. Normally, we just email the person being offered a job, but my VP insisted I come out to see you in person. I had called several times, but you were never in."

My instinct told me the man sitting in front of me was serious, and had nothing to do with the recent quasi-criminal activity. To be sure, I probed.

"Your boss. The VP. By any chance would that be a Mr. Warren?"

"Harding is the vice president of my division. He must have spoken with the VP in Mint Street's HR department, though, since he was very familiar with your interview. He insisted I come out here today to meet you in person. I hope it's not too late. Are you still on the market, looking for a position?"

"Oh, now that is an interesting question," I said. I peered through the window at Seaview's old buildings being revitalized one red brick at a time. Then I imagined the modern steel and glass surrounding the window of a high-rise office. I'd have maintenance brush down the dust on the plastic green plant in the corner. My phone would buzz; it would be my assistant reminding me of the next meeting. Stale, bitter coffee would be waiting. Maybe Grandma's dream for me wasn't actually my dream? Bitter coffee? I could do better.

I offered a question to my inquisitor. "You know, I have a thought. What if, and please don't read anything into this, but what if Mr. Warren were to step aside? Who would take his place?"

The man shrugged his shoulders, not expecting to have a new hire ask *him* a question. "I suppose the company would open the position for anyone to apply. I've been there for a while; I guess I would have the best shot at it. Why do you ask?"

"Never mind. Thank you very much for the offer, but I have to decline." I looked up as my grandmother was placing two cups of coffee on the table. "You see, I am currently in negotiations to become the owner of this fine establishment, and if successful, I'll need to stick around a while to make sure the spicy crab poppers are cooked just right. What do you think, Grandma?"

"I think someone down at the police station will be very interested in hearing *that* news, Winnie. But it's your choice. Not much of an office here, compared to working in a skyscraper somewhere. But I can't just give the place away, you'll have to buy it. This deal must be legal if it's anything."

What kind of cash are we talking about, Grandma? All I have is a twenty in my pocket; any more, and I'll have to go to the bank and get a loan."

Grandma pushed her way in front of the food executive, holding her hand out. "By strange coincidence, ownership is on sale today. Twenty dollars it is."

A few seconds later, I was a sole proprietor and financially anchored to Seaview, Virginia for the foreseeable future.

I thanked the man for his time and sent him on his way with a few cinnamon rolls to go. I also suggested he update his résumé.

As the door closed, Grandma gave me a hug. "Why don't you go down to the station and tell Parker the news. And, by the way, did you really expect Bailey and Cosmo to go off and get hitched right away?"

I laughed. "Yes, but I also asked her about her award-winning brownies. It was the one thing I did not see her make back in the caboose's kitchen."

"The brownies? They *were* delicious, I agree. How did she make them?"

"Grandma, you have your apple pie; Bailey has her brownies. If you promise not to tell, I'll give you a hint."

She crossed her fingers and motioned an *X* across her heart.

I leaned in, looking left and right as if to prevent the nonexistent customers from hearing my reply. "They're from a box."

Grandma gasped. "No! Really?"

"As real as the apples in your apple pie, Grandma. Claimed her mother taught her it was the only way to bake them right each time."

"I guess we all have an alibi or two. And speaking of secrets, I think it is about time you and Parker figured things out, especially since it looks like you will be staying around town for a while, Miss I-Own-a-Café-Now."

"I suppose so," I said. "Plus, as I recall, I still need to explain to the man how lipstick works." I picked up my purse, checking to make sure a tube of the reddest red lipstick was inside.

"One more thing, Grandma. Are you available to open up tomorrow? I may be coming home a bit late tonight."

SECRET RECIPES

My grandmother tried very hard to turn me into a good cook. Sometimes it worked—many times, not so much. I still keep a few packages of dried noodles in my room, just in case I get hungry when she isn't around.

Once the case was solved, Parker asked me if I could cook up some of the dishes we had seen in the contest. After a little flattery—and yes, at least one outright bribe of jalapeño poppers—I managed to get the recipes. Making the food, however, would be another matter entirely.

French Toast Casserole

Courtesy of me, Winnie Kepler. Who else?

Prepare the night before; bake and serve the next morning.

Dry Ingredients

> 1 loaf plain white bread
> 4 tablespoons cinnamon
> 1 tablespoon nutmeg

Wet Ingredients

> 8 eggs
> 2 cups milk
> 3/4 cup white sugar
> 2 teaspoons vanilla
> 2 tablespoons cinnamon

For the Topping

> 1/2 cup flour
> 1/2 cup brown sugar
> 1 tablespoon cinnamon
> 1 stick (1/2 cup) butter, room temperature
> (later) maple syrup

Directions

- Tear the bread into pieces, about the same size you would feed to a duck. But don't feed any ducks. Unless your duck is hungry. Then give them freshly shucked corn instead. But use bread for this recipe. Not corn. Nor ducks.
- Place torn bread pieces into a greased 9x13-inch baking pan or casserole dish.
- Sprinkle 2 tablespoons of cinnamon evenly across the bread. Save the other tablespoons.
- Sprinkle the nutmeg on top of the cinnamon.
- Toss the bread pieces a bit to mix up the cinnamon and nutmeg.
- Even the bread out again and sprinkle the last 2 tablespoons of cinnamon on top.
- In a large bowl, lightly whisk the eggs.

- In a separate bowl, mix the milk, sugar, vanilla, and cinnamon.
- Add the milk mixture to the eggs and lightly whisk until mixed.
- Pour the liquid onto the bread. If you miss a piece or two of bread, it'll be okay.
- Cover the casserole dish and refrigerate overnight.
- Before you pour that wine and go watch television, mix the dry ingredients for the topping, and then cut the butter in until crumbly. *Crumbly* is a technical culinary term, I think. Keep separate from the casserole, but refrigerate overnight, as well.

The Next Morning

- Preheat the oven to 350°F.
- Sprinkle the crumbly topping evenly across the top of the bread. See? There's that word *crumbly* again.
- Bake at 350° for 45 minutes.
- When the casserole is nearly done baking, warm up the maple syrup. And make coffee. Strong coffee, if you drank that wine last night. You better add another scoop of grounds.
- When the timer dings, remove the casserole from the oven, and using a spatula or knife, slice into 18 to 24 pieces, but do not remove from casserole dish yet.
- Drizzle the warm maple syrup over the casserole, tracing the slice marks.
- Turn off your oven and pour yourself a cup of coffee. It's time to eat!

Faux Apple Pie

Courtesy of my grandma, Velma Kepler

Ingredients

2 premade pie crusts, unbaked

25 plain round crackers (plain and lightly salted variety works best, nothing with added flavorings)

1 1/2 cups cold water

1/4 cup white sugar

2 teaspoons cream of tartar

1 tablespoon cinnamon

1 teaspoon nutmeg

1/2 teaspoon cayenne pepper (can you believe it?)

6 tablespoons cold butter, sliced into pats

Directions

- Preheat the oven to 450°F.
- Treat a pie plate with cooking spray, and then carefully place the pie crust in it, leaving the edges flapping over the side. Set aside to rest. The crust, not you!
- Combine the water, sugar, and cream of tartar in a medium saucepan. Set the stove to medium heat and stir the mixture with a wooden spoon until the sugar has dissolved.
- Add the crackers; turn up the heat and bring the mixture to a boil for 2 minutes. DO NOT STIR.
- Remove the saucepan from the heat.
- Sprinkle in the cinnamon, nutmeg, and allspice. Again, DO NOT STIR.
- Pour the contents of your saucepan into the crust that has been resting in the pie plate. This will mix the spices without causing undue damage to the "apples."
- Put the pats of butter on top, evenly dispersing them around the top of the pie as best you can. It is not an exact science; it's just butter. It'll melt.
- Place the second crust on top; fold the edges of both crusts together to form a decorative seam around the perimeter of the pie plate. Sprinkle some leftover sugar on top if you want. Some people also brush the top crust with a wash of egg whites. Your choice.

- Using a fork, poke a few holes in the top crust to allow steam to escape during the baking process. You can be as creative as you want—make designs, spell out words. Or just poke it four or five times.
- Bake for 10 minutes in your preheated, 450° oven. Reduce the temperature to 350° and bake for 20 more minutes.
- Once the crust has turned a nice tan color, you are done!

Breakfast Sammich

Another favorite of my grandma!

My grandma always said that this will "put the zippity back into your doo-dah." Not in the normal recipe format; it isn't that hard to read, and it does make sense.

Reprinted verbatim from our conversation: "The breakfast sammich is really quite simple, dear. First, set your toaster's temperature control to low. Then, insert a plain sliced bagel and push the lever down. Watch the toaster; you want the bagel warmed, not toasted. If there's smoke, you'll just have to start over. When done, drizzle the top of each bagel half with honey, not too much now, and finally top it with a single swirl of your favorite salsa."

I tried this one, using black bean and corn salsa for my topping. For a *deluxe sammich*, I added a cheese omelet on top of the salsa. I prefer this version, actually, since—in one bite mind you—the soft bread texture is followed by the sweetness of the honey. The bite of the salsa and the creaminess of the cheese omelet? Pure heaven!

Oh, and by the way, don't even think of using a microwave oven to heat your bagel. Turns them into hockey pucks before your second sip of coffee. And no one would want to eat a hockey puck. I mean, really. Have you seen the front teeth on those hockey players? Me neither.

Brand X Seasoning

I have discovered that one of Grandma's "go-to" spices is a little jar of cayenne pepper. In fact, she has two versions. One is just straight cayenne, but a second version contains a one-to-four ratio of cayenne pepper to cinnamon. You'd never know it by looking at the label, though. Stenciled on the side using a black laundry marker are the words *Brand X Seasoning*. Probably what adds more "zippity in the doo-dah."

And what does Grandma use the spices for? Almost everything she cooks, but to set her breakfast muffins apart from the store-bought, she adds a pinch or two of Brand X seasoning. The customers love it, and now so do I. Give it a try once and see what you think. Have a cold glass of milk on hand, just in case.

Mini Cinnamon Roll Muffins
One of the most popular items at the café.

For the Dough
>　1 package dry yeast
>　1 cup milk
>　1/2 cup white sugar
>　1/3 cup butter
>　1 teaspoon salt
>　2 eggs
>　4 cups flour

For the Filling
>　1 cup light brown sugar
>　4 tablespoons Brand X seasoning (see notes above)
>　1/3 cup butter, melted

For the Topping
>　1/3 cup confectioner's sugar

Directions
- Make the dough first. In a large bowl, warm the milk to a temperature no greater than 110°F. Add the yeast and stir gently to dissolve.
- Add the sugar, butter, salt, eggs, and flour. Using a large wooden spoon, mix well until a large dough ball has formed. You may want to use your hands after a point, to help knead the dough into that ball. Do yourself a favor and dust your hands with a little flour first.
- Clean your hands, and then preheat the oven to 400°F.
- Cover the bowl with a clean kitchen towel and let the dough rise for 1 hour. I place the bowl on the stove top (note from lawyers: not on the stovetop burners) and crack the oven door slightly to let the heat warm the air just enough to help the yeast rise.
- Once the dough has risen, transfer it to a lightly floured surface. Roll it out into a large rectangular shape, fairly thin—no less than a quarter-inch thick, certainly not a half-inch thick. These are "mini" muffin rolls, after all.
- In another bowl, combine the brown sugar and the Brand X seasoning.

- Now, take a pastry brush and spread the melted butter over the rectangular dough.
- Sprinkle the brown sugar mixture over the butter.
- From the long edge of the dough, tightly roll the dough into a long log.
- Cut the log into sections just large enough to fill your muffin tin spaces swirl-side down. A typical mini muffin pan would require sections about 1 inch in height.
- Place your dough sections swirl-side down into a greased mini muffin pan.
- Bake at 400°F for about 8 minutes. Start checking them around 6 minutes. Time will vary depending on the thickness and height of your muffins.
- Once the muffins are lightly browned on top, remove from the oven.
- Put the confectioner's sugar into a wire mesh strainer. Holding the strainer a foot or more above the muffins, tap the strainer. This will cause a light snowfall of confectioner's sugar.
- Eat two for yourself—otherwise you'll miss out once you serve the guests!

Velma's Fried Chicken on a Stick

Courtesy of—well, who else?

Ingredients

4 boneless chicken breasts, split lengthwise to give you 8 strips

2 cups milk

4 cups flour, divided equally in gallon-sized ziplock plastic bags

8 tablespoons chili powder (divided equally in each bag of flour)

4 tablespoons smoked paprika (again, split between the two bags)

2 tablespoons white pepper (yes, you got it—1 tablespoon per bag)

2 tablespoons salt (Do I need to say it? Yes, 1 per bag. Come on, now. Keep up.)

peanut oil (vegetable oil, if there are allergy concerns)

8 bamboo skewers

Directions

- Preheat the oven to 350°F.
- Pour the milk in a bowl and soak the chicken in it while you get the rest of the ingredients together.
- In a gallon-sized ziplock plastic bag, combine half of the flour, chili powder, smoked paprika, white pepper, and salt. You can adjust the seasonings up or down, depending on your own tastes. Repeat with the second half of the ingredients in a second gallon-sized bag.
- Now that the chicken has soaked for a while, take one piece and place it in the seasoning bag. Close the bag and shake it up until the chicken is thoroughly coated.
- Remove the coated chicken and set aside for the moment.
- Continue the same process with the rest of the chicken. Since the wet chicken will tend to cause clumps of flour to form in the bag, after the first four pieces, switch to the second bag. Grandma once told me, "The last piece must taste just as good as the first piece, right?" Hence, the two-bag system. Don't worry about waste; it's just flour and spices. You have more.

- With the chicken seasoned and sitting off to the side of your workstation, get a large, heavy-bottomed stock pot. Add to the pot a few cups of peanut oil (use or vegetable oil, if you or a guest have a peanut allergy) and turn the heat up to medium high.
- Use a cooking (candy) thermometer to check the oil's temperature to see if it is around 350° - or you can carefully drop a little ball of damp flour into the pot. If it starts to sizzle up, the oil is ready.
- Get some tongs for safety's sake and carefully put a few pieces of chicken into the hot oil. (Grandma puts a wire mesh grease screen on top of the pot when she does this. Claims it helps later when it is time to clean up. I think it is a more preventative measure against a grease fire. Take your pick, but I vote for fire prevention every time.)
- Turn the chicken over a necessary, allowing all sides to brown up. We aren't cooking the chicken all the way through here, just browning.
- Once the chicken has a nice crust forming, remove from the oil (use the tongs, remember?) and place on a paper towel or two to drain the excess grease.
- Repeat the process with the rest of the chicken. The oil temperature will decrease as chicken cooks, so you may have to wait until it heats back up before you put more chicken into the pot.
- Now that your chicken has been browned, place them on a baking sheet and put into your preheated oven.
- Bake at 350° for 30 minutes or until the juices run clear when you poke the largest piece with a toothpick.
- When the chicken has finished baking, remove from the oven. Like a pirate in a sword fight, run each piece through with a bamboo skewer, leaving enough out to act as a handle.
- Serve with your favorite barbecue or honey mustard sauce!

Chocolate Pecan Pie in a Jar
Courtesy of Chef George Harrison Windsor

George Harrison Windsor, as you may recall, had to come up with one recipe on the spur of the moment. I think he did rather well. The nice thing about this recipe is that it is served cold, meaning you can prepare each of the three parts a few days in advance, and then assemble them just before serving. Anything that can reduce the stress in the kitchen during the day of a social event is a winner in my book. This is my personal favorite of all the recipes. And no matter how you pronounce the word *pecan*, your friends will long remember the time you served this awesome dessert!

For the Crust
2 cups graham cracker crumbs
1/2 cup sugar
1 stick (1/2 cup) butter, melted

- Mix the graham cracker crumbs, sugar, and melted butter in a bowl.
- Spread evenly on a baking sheet.
- Bake at 350° for 8 to 10 minutes, or until the crust starts to become noticeably more brown. It needs to be thoroughly baked, but not burnt.
- Once baked, set aside to cool.
- Once cool, cover with wrap and save for later.

For the Chocolate Filling
1 cup brown sugar
1/2 cup white sugar
2 eggs
6 ounces chocolate chips, either semi-sweet or dark (your choice)
1 stick (1/2 cup) butter, melted
2 tablespoons milk
2 teaspoons vanilla
1 tablespoon flour

- Mix the brown sugar, white sugar, eggs, and chocolate chips in a large bowl; stir until it starts to look like an off-color creamy peanut butter.
- In a separate bowl, mix the melted butter, milk, vanilla, and flour. Fold into the dry ingredients, then pour into an oven-safe casserole dish or something similar. You could even use a pie plate.
- Bake at 350°F for 30 minutes, then check to see if it has "set." The top will look less shiny, and if you shake the dish slightly, the mousse will jiggle just a bit. The baking time will vary depending on what baking vessel you decided to use. But, this should be baked for at least 30 minutes.
- Once done, set aside to cool. Once cool, cover and refrigerate for at least four hours. I wait until the next day.

For the Topping

2 cups pecans, shelled (of course)
1/2 stick (1/4 cup) butter, melted
4 tablespoons brown sugar
1/3 cup of your favorite bourbon

- In a skillet (cast-iron, if you have one) over medium high heat, stir the melted butter and pecan bits until the nuts are thoroughly coated.
- Add the sugar and stir; again, you want the pecans coated.
- Keep stirring until the sugar starts to caramelize on the pecans.
- Add the bourbon. Stir until the candied pecans are floating in a sea of thick sauce.
- Once done, remove from heat and pour onto a cookie sheet covered in either parchment or wax paper. Allow to cool.
- Once completely cool, cover with wrap and set aside until it is time to assemble the dessert.
- When ready, break the sheet of bourbon-glazed pecans into chunks that will fit into your serving glass.

The Mash-Up

- Once the filling has had a chance to chill, you are ready to assemble the dessert. You will need four parfait glasses for this one. If you don't have a parfait glass, any sturdy glass will do—even a regular bowl will work if that is all that you have on hand. Mason jars? Why not!
- Break the graham cracker crust into chunks. Evenly distribute the chunks into the parfait glasses. This is the bottom layer. You only want to fill the glass up about a third of the way. If you have more crust, get more parfait glasses. Your guests won't complain if there is more dessert. If they do, you need to get different guests.
- Spoon the chilled chocolate filling on top of the crust bits. You can almost fill the glass here, but save room for the guest of honor, the pecans.
- Heat the candied pecans in your microwave oven until they become soft and gooey again. It should not take more than 30 seconds—maybe 1 minute at the most.
- Spoon the bourbon-flavored, sticky pecan mixture on top of the chocolate filling.

Serve immediately so your guests will find a bit of warmth from the pecans, enjoy the aroma of the infused bourbon, and savor the richness of the chocolate mousse (that is what this really is) as it mingles with the texture of the graham cracker crust.

Southern Corn Pudding
Courtesy of Chef George Harrison Windsor

Aside from tobacco, cotton, peanuts, tomatoes, soybean, winter wheat, potatoes of all types, and even collard greens, one of the most prolific crops grown in the Southeastern United States is corn. Every summer, Eastern Shore farmers will open their roadside food stands (or pull their pickup truck alongside the highway) to sell baskets of the stuff to anyone with an out-of-state license plate on their car. And there are a ton of those. Especially on Friday and Sunday.

For those who live in the area? They just go to church. Those same farmers will bring in a few bushels on Sunday morning, and everyone can take what they need. At least, that is what I have found since moving to Seaview. No wonder the Methodists are never hungry. I think they carry a spoon in their pocket, just in case they come across an unexpected "pot luck."

Anyway, George Harrison Windsor shared this recipe from his three-times-great-grandmother's stash of papers found behind the abandoned whiskey still in back of his house. No worries" he told me; they hadn't cooked up moonshine in generations, although he wondered about his friend Cosmo, since the lad had taken a good part of the old equipment for some unknown reason.

For your culinary enjoyment, here is George's old family recipe. It has been (very much) modernized for those of us without a nearby corn field.

Ingredients
   1 cup sour cream
   1/2 stick (1/4 cup) butter
   1 can cream corn
   1 can whole kernel corn, drained
   1 habañero pepper, finely chopped (optional—for those who like to tempt fate)
   2 tablespoons white sugar
   1 package cornbread mix

Directions

- Preheat the oven to 350°F.
- Mix all the ingredients in a large bowl.
- Transfer to a greased 8x8-inch pan, at least 2 inches tall.
- Bake at 325° for approximately 45 minutes or until the top starts to set. This should not turn brown on top, just slightly tan.
- Once you think it is done, let it bake 5 more minutes.
- Now it is probably done all the way through. Remove from the oven and let stand for 5 minutes. If you try to eat a spoonful now, it would be like putting a glob of molten lava into your mouth. Don't do it. Just wait. In fact, use this time to find the white wine in the cooler. You'll need it later, especially if you chose the habañero option.

Buena suerte, mi amiga. That's all George said to me when he let me have a taste.

Spicy Crab Poppers
Probably the most requested item at our tea service!

This bite-sized morsel is a conglomeration of shredded fresh crab meat mixed with finely chopped celery, onion, and bell pepper, plus the requisite "secret" spices. It's a winner! And even as a vegetarian, I sometimes slip into pescatarian mode just to try one!

Ingredients
    1/4 cup olive oil
    1 stalk celery, of decent size, trimmed of the white end and devoid of leaves
    1 white onion
    1 green bell pepper
    1/2 cup sun-dried tomatoes
    2 cloves garlic, minced
    1 tablespoon fresh-cracked black pepper
    1 pound lump crab meat (If shellfish allergies are a concern, use a flaky white fish.)
    3 tablespoons Old Bay seasoning ("It's a law," my grandma once told me.)
    10 shakes of your favorite hot sauce (This translates to about 2 tablespoons. I think. Live dangerously. Add a few more shakes, if you are unsure.)
    1/2 cup real mayonnaise (not the fake stuff)
    1 box puff pastry
    enough flour to dust a cutting board
    1 egg
    1 cup water

Directions
- Preheat the oven to 375°F.
- Chop the celery, onion, and bell peppers finely.
- In a large saucepan, heat the olive oil over medium high heat.
- To determine when the oil is hot enough, drop a piece of chopped vegetable in the pan. If it sizzles, it is ready. CAREFULLY add the chopped vegetables.

- Stir occasionally to allow all the veggie bits to sauté until soft.
- Chop up the sun-dried tomatoes as best you can and add to the pan of vegetables. Add the minced garlic and black pepper, too. Stir a few more times.
- Now add the crab meat! Continue to sauté for 5 minutes. While everything is dancing in the pan, find another bowl.
- In this new bowl, combine the mayonnaise, Old Bay, and hot sauce.
- Remove the pan of crab and vegetables from heat.
- Combine the crab and vegetables with the spicy mayonnaise.
- Dust your cutting board with flour.
- Take some puff pastry, put it on the floured cutting board, and shape it into a large rectangle.
- Spread the crab mixture over the entire surface of the puff pastry.
- Roll the pastry up lengthwise into a long "log" and place on a baking sheet, seam-side down. Depending on how thick you made the layer of crab meat, you may need another sheet of puff pastry. That's okay. The more, the better!
- In a small bowl, mix the egg and water.
- Using a pastry brush, paint the puff pastry log with the egg wash.
- Bake at 375° for 35 minutes or until golden brown.
- Remove from the oven and cut into bite-sized pieces.
- Enjoy!

Peanut Butter Pickle Banana Crunch Sandwich

Winning recipe from Bailey Babbitt

This treat, also the judges' favorite, is made from a savory homemade peanut butter. I think you could use any decent peanut butter on regular bread. Just spice up the peanut butter with a teaspoon or two of chili powder and a dash of crushed red pepper and top with a few long slices of sweet, fresh banana. Drizzle some honey on top of the bananas and add a thin layer of bread and butter pickles. Cap it all off with a single layer of salty potato chips. "A winner!" according to Bailey. I think she is right.

As she described it: "Your palette will taste the earthy flavor of the chili powder intermingled within the creaminess of the peanut butter. A not-so-subtle zing from the red pepper will soon take over, only subsiding as the tongue relishes the cool sweetness of the banana slices. The tartness from the pickles will elevate your senses again, and the salty chips give you that satisfying crunch."

When I tried this, I realized it was simple to make, yet complex in flavor. I could feel the crunch of the potato chips and enjoyed the natural taste of the salt. You get everything - sweet, sour, salt, savory, and heat—all between two pieces of soft bread. The judges said it: "It's the best picnic food, ever!"

The Seagull's Nest Sweet Potato Roll

George told me that these rolls are good with just a little butter on them, but if you want to be *official*, you need to slice the rolls horizontally and make a mini sweet potato roll "sammich" using a thin slice of Virginia ham. Yum!

And, from George himself, "Lawd have mercy, child, for goodness sake, use Virginia ham. If you use that pressed and steam-baked pig in a can, you might as well be from Norfolk." I used the Virginia ham, after soaking it in water for a few days, and it was perfection.

Ingredients

> 2 large sweet potatoes
> 2 tablespoons butter
> 1 teaspoon cinnamon
> 2 cups flour
> 1/2 cup sugar
> 2 tablespoons baking powder
> 1 teaspoon salt
> 1/2 cup lard or vegetable shortening
> 1/2 cup milk
> extra flour for dusting

Directions

- Preheat your oven to 400°F.
- Wash your sweet potatoes; try to scrub the dirt off with your hand. Do not use any type of cleaner. The dirt, what's left of it, won't kill you. Hopefully. No guarantees.
- "Poke them 'taters with a fork," George said. He did several times. This helped the steam escape and prevented the very messy exploding potato syndrome from occurring.
- Once the oven is preheated, carefully place the sweet potatoes in the oven. I put them on a baking sheet. Sweet potatoes are notorious for leaking sticky resin-like sugars all over the inside of your oven when they are cooking. Sounds cool, right? Yeah, but smells terrible. Use a pan under those potatoes.
- Bake the potatoes for at least 1 hour. Once the potatoes are squishy and squeezable, they are done. Remove from the oven and let sit for a few minutes. George took this

opportunity to have a mint julep. Normally, I do not recommend drinking while cooking. But for George, what could I do? It was his kitchen.

- Remove the potato skin. There are a number of ways to do this. I put the potato in a large glass bowl and smash it with a potato masher. The pulp escapes, leaving the skin flattened upon itself, making it easy to remove from the bowl. Plus, your sweet potato meat is now in the correct vessel for the next step!
- Sans skin, continue to mash up the potato until it is relatively smooth in texture.
- Separate 2 cups of sweet potato for use with the rolls.
- The rest of the sweet potato? Ah, here's the lagniappe:
  ◦ Put the remaining sweet potato in a bowl.
  ◦ Add the butter and cinnamon.
  ◦ Eat as a snack in progress while you finish making the rolls.
- Back to the rolls: add the flour, sugar, baking powder, and salt to your bowl containing the 2 cups of sweet potato mash.
- Mash some more until the dry ingredients have been incorporated into the sweet potato.
- Add the lard/shortening. Knead it into the dough using a wooden spoon (or your hands if you are a devil-may-care cook and don't mind orange-ish dough all over your hands).
- Add the milk. Fold the sweet potato into itself until you have something approaching cake batter. It won't be as creamy as that, but you get the idea.
- Dust your cutting board with some extra flour.
- Roll the dough out onto the cutting board evenly. Try to get an even thickness, about a half-inch all around.
- You can use a biscuit or cookie cutter, a glass, or, again, your hands to form the individual rolls. Cut away and reshape the scrap to make more rolls.
- Place the rolls on an ungreased cookie sheet and bake at 400° for 15 to 20 minutes.
- Once completely baked through and lightly brown on top, remove the rolls from the oven and let cool.

Tex-Mex Sushi
Courtesy of dishwasher-chef-inventor Cosmo Finnegan

The most unusual cooking came from Cosmo Finnegan. The food tasted great, which was to be expected in a culinary competition, but the amazing thing was the experience of watching him combine colonial technology with a modern culinary fusion of ethnic cuisine. Just by looking at the plate in front of you, you didn't know if you were going to be tasting Tex-Mex, Japanese, or chuck wagon food. Sometimes, though, you just have to put fear aside and go for it.

I could never get the straight recipe, but here is the gist. Read it through first, and then get your *mis en plas* on.

For the Brisket
> 1 large hunk beef brisket (a couple of pounds will do)
> 2 cups water
> 2 cups soy sauce
> 4 tablespoons lemon juice
> 4 tablespoons cumin
> 4 tablespoons chili powder
> 2 tablespoons cracked black pepper
> 1 tablespoon smoked paprika

Directions
- Place the brisket fat side up in a large roasting pan.
- In a bowl, mix the remaining ingredients to create the marinade.
- Pour the marinade over the brisket, cover, and refrigerate until the next day.
- Assuming you want to serve the brisket for dinner, six hours before serving, uncover the brisket and let it sit on the counter to start to lose its chill.
- Preheat the oven to 350°F.
- Using a sharp, long-bladed knife, slice the layer of fat off the brisket.
- Spoon some of the marinade over the top of the brisket, to refresh its memory.
- Roast the brisket in the oven.

- How long, you ask? Try 30 minutes per pound, and then add 10 more minutes at the end. Brisket, cooked well, takes a long time. That's why we started at noon, remember?
- Once the internal temperature is . . . well, once the meat is so tender you can shred it with a fork, the brisket is done.
- Spoon some more marinade over the top again, cover with foil, and let sit in the oven (set on "warm") until you are either ready to slice—or just make it easy on yourself and shred the whole thing. Every once in awhile, baste with the juices collecting in the roasting pan. When you are ready to serve, either shred with a fork or slice on a bias (against "the grain").

For the Rice

2 cups white rice, or your favorite variety (they will all work well)

3 cups water

1 cup water infused with a little saffron

Directions

- If you use a rice cooker, follow the directions for your particular machine. If you prefer the old-school way to cook rice, put the rice and 4 cups of water into a large pot and bring to a boil. Then reduce heat and allow to simmer, covered slightly, until the water has been absorbed. You are looking at about 40 minutes or so.

For the Stir-Fried Vegetables

2 tablespoons olive oil

1 red bell pepper, seeds removed, finely chopped

1 celery stalk, no leaves, finely chopped

1 small yellow onion, skin removed, finely chopped

1 cup diced tomatoes

1 small can chopped green chilies

1 can (8 ounces) of cooked black beans

optional side garnish: goat cheese

Directions
- Heat the oil in a large saucepan.
- Add the remaining ingredients. Sauté until the onions seem translucent.
- Once done, remove from heat and set aside until the rice is done.

Putting It All Together
- Mix the stir-fried vegetables in with the rice.
- Using an ice cream scoop, form the rice into a ball and place on the plate.
- Using a spoon, create a well in the top of the rice ball. It's almost like a rice volcano!
- Take some of your shredded brisket and fill the volcano's hole.
- Drizzle a little marinade on top.
- Optional: Serve with a smattering of crumbled goat cheese on the side.

And what about Cosmo's Dr Pepper-flavored barbecue sauce? *That's one secret yet to be revealed!*

Acknowledgments

I would like to thank the writers who encouraged me at every step along this journey, especially Lucy Silag and Janice Peacock. For quite a few years, we lurked about the online writers' haven known as *Book Country*. A mention must also go to the cohort of writers from the mystery anthology *50 Shades of Cabernet*. You know who you are!

I must also acknowledge the kind words from my publisher, John Köehler. He gives life to his company and verve to his writers; I am blessed to have met him. And I cannot go another sentence without thanking my editor, Joe Coccaro. A fellow Virginia Beach expat now living in Cape Charles, Virginia, Joe can be seen about town walking his dog. Rumor has it he plays banjo. I have yet to see it, though. Behind the scenes? Heather Floyd gets the kudos for dotting the *T*s and crossing the *I*s. Maybe it was the other way around? Whatever is correct, Heather will know—and tell me to fix it. And of course, the cover artists and designers at Köehler Books. What a team!

Finally, though the crews change often, a hearty thanks to all of the baristas at the Northampton Starbucks in Norfolk. They start making my grande decaf Americano precisely at 5:30 every morning. By 5:35, I am typing away. You all are rock stars! You get a double-shot of *Thanks*!